REMEDY FOR A BROKEN ANGEL

A NOVEL

TONI ANN JOHNSON

REMEDY FOR A BROKEN ANGEL

NORTIA PRESS, ORANGE COUNTY, CALIFORNIA

www.nortiapress.com

2321 E 4th Street, C-219
Santa Ana, CA 92705
contact @ nortiapress.com

ISBN: 978-1-940503-02-8

Printed in the United States of America

For Mandy, Mabel, and Maisie.

One

Artie, 2004

Two months ago, Artie drove home late one night when her husband Kendall wasn't expecting her. She pulled into their driveway behind his road-hogging Escalade and heard his band's CD cranked up on the car stereo. She called his name. He didn't answer. She climbed out of her car, zipped her cardigan as her heels clicked up the stone pavers to his open window, and on tiptoes she looked in. He wasn't in the driver's seat. A spicy fragrance wafted out the window into her face. Opium. Her mother's scent. Sweet notes of jasmine and mandarin tempered with amber threatened to take her someplace she didn't want to go. Artie hadn't seen the monster in years, so she was shocked to find her reclining in the passenger seat with her dress hiked up above her waist. Kendall was upside down; the six to her mother's nine, his face buried between her thighs.

Artie is a patient now at a swank acute care psychiatric facility in Malibu. For weeks she's been dazed from the drugs they gave her, but the dosage has been reduced; she's beginning to think more clearly now. She hasn't felt like talking. The only other patient she's spoken with is a girl who hears voices and then only because their rooms adjoin via the bathroom they share and the girl is chatty. It's mostly gossip. Artie doesn't bother to listen closely. Despite being one of about twenty-five residents in this mansion in the Malibu hills, she's enjoying an odd sort of solitude. It's not so bad being alone, inside her head, and being able to tune everyone out; even Kendall, to some degree. *Pendejo.*

He's here again. Outside. She won't see him, speak to him, or read his letters or emails. So he appears in the courtyard below the day room window and serenades her with his saxophone. *Bicho.* His Gucci-loafer-wearing big feet trample the yellow gazanias and his white shirt bears sweaty underarms. Notes trill out in cascading wails. Kendall is a jazz musician, a tenor player. Twenty-seven years old and he's the recent recipient of a MacArthur Foundation Genius Grant for composition. *Genius? Please.* His band has recorded three CDs with Verve Records and he composed and produced most of the songs. He thinks he's the shit. Artie used to think so, too, but now she hates the sight of his sweaty ass down there blowing his damn horn. *Pinche perro motherfucker. Might as well be whacking off.*

Yet she can't keep her eyes off of him for more than a few seconds. Still drawn to this idiot she used to love like crazy, but doesn't want to anymore. When she does let her eyes wander she can tell by the light that it's late afternoon. The sun bounces off the Spanish style building and dances onto Kendall's sax. It kisses his face and lights him up like a celestial being.

Why is it, she wonders, that no matter where he goes, or what foul shit he does, there's always light around him? It's as if he has an invisible gaffer shining him up like a movie star. So unfair. *If I had my camera*, she thinks, *I'd shoot his ass right now and catch that glow. The long lens would throw the Jacarandas out of focus in the background. The flare would shine around his face like a halo. Cool beans!* She's giddy, imagining it. Then she realizes: *he planned this. He knew damn well I wouldn't be able to resist the composition, the light, the contrast and... Ugh!*

He thinks he can engage her, as he always has, and he almost did. Makes her feel too easy, like a trite piece of music he can read with his eyes closed and play with no effort. *Why hasn't he moved on to a more challenging piece? That's what he wanted, right? He went out and found himself a new piece of complicated ass. So why the fuck does he keep coming around here messing with me?*

The denizens of the day room are curious. Roxy, the petite, teenaged blonde who shares Artie's bathroom moves to the window and tugs at the yoga pants riding up her narrow butt. A buff male nurse in blue scrubs leaves an elderly patient and crosses the parquet floor to stand at the window beside her. Artie doesn't budge from the cowhide leather sofa. She's comfortable and she refuses to give Kendall any more attention. This place is costing him a grip, which is likely why he's out there huffing and puffing, but he's not blowing her out of here until she's ready to go.

The music stops abruptly. The bodies at the window occlude Artie's view.

"Ouch," Roxy says, watching. She glances back at Artie. "Jacques just grabbed him around the neck." She looks out again. "He's pulling him off the lawn, like last time."

Buff Nurse looks at Roxy. "You know the guard's name?"

She turns. "So?" She eyes him from head to pelvis, her focus like a laser on his crotch. He hurries away. Roxy presses her nose to the window. "Don't think he can see up here," she says. "But they're telling me he's praying his ass off that you're watching." She laughs.

"Thanks," Artie says. "And I bet he's looking up with pitiful eyes, like I'm the one doing something messed up to him."

"They want *me* to describe it," Roxy snaps, turning to her.

"Sorry," Artie says. "But it doesn't take any special powers to read that fool."

Roxy marches away. "She doesn't wanna hear it," she mutters to an unseen someone. "Fine." She looks back at Artie. "There's a difference between *thinking* you know, and knowing."

Artie watches her disappear through the French doors with the unbreakable glass.

These past couple of months she's thought of her mother but she hasn't said much. What Artie has shared is that she never had a single picture of the woman holding or hugging her. No memory of being hugged or held by the puta either. Not one.

Years before the night that triggered Artie's unraveling, her mother left her. She also left a photo album that archived a life with the husband and child she abandoned.

Twelve-year-old Artie clutched the album as she sat at the kitchen table and watched her father Rico chopping garlic for the black beans he was preparing.

"But Papi," Artie said, "My friend's dad left when she was little, and she told me that moms don't leave their kids, only dads do."

Papi bit his lip and looked out the barred window that faced the fire escape.

"Well, mija, sometimes that's not true. Sometimes mamis have problems."

Artie stared at the floor, squeezed the photo album to her chest, and banged the heel of her sneaker into the worn linoleum. "I never heard of any mamis who left except mine."

Papi squatted in front of her. His knees cracked as he placed his garlic-stinking hands on her thighs. She focused on the floor until he leaned in close to her cheek and brushed it with his eyelashes. A butterfly kiss.

"Sometimes problems make mamis do things that don't make sense," he said. "But that's not the kids' fault."

The album was one of the only things Artie had left after papi got rid of almost everything that would remind them of Serena. Purple velvet on the outside, it had a lock like a diary, but there was no key and the lock was broken anyway. It was purchased in a junky antiques shop on 10th Street in the East Village in New York, and it had been made in the 1940s. Artie was with her mother the day she bought it. She was in the fifth grade at P.S. 41. It was just days after she completed a school project wherein she took pictures of her parents at work.

Serena met her outside of school on West 11th Street. She was holding the envelope of newly developed prints. She looked like a movie star in a white dress, short black jacket and red lipstick. As Artie padded up to her lugging her backpack, Serena's gleaming grin was a surprise.

"You 'ave de eye of an ah-tist," she exclaimed. "These ah brilliant." As they walked to the East Side, Serena thumbed through the photos of herself singing.

"I as-pacially like how you framed me be-tveen de microphone and de cuh-tain. And heah, where I'm blowin' de audience a kiss, I quite like how de mowement in my face draws de eye in."

After Serena bought Artie the album she gave her a shoebox full of old snapshots to include with the new ones, and she encouraged her to keep shooting.

Artie enjoyed poring through the images of her parents when they were young and of herself when she was little. It was her history; it belonged to her and she belonged to it, and she liked that.

She told herself, *there're no pictures of me in my mother's arms 'cause she was always the one taking the photos. Papi probably never offered.*

But, wouldn't Serena *want* a picture of herself with her baby? Wouldn't she ask *someone* to take one? Artie's been able to avoid the subject for fourteen years. No one demanded that she say how she felt. They only tried to comfort her, because she was a child. She's twenty-six now, and seated across from her psychiatrist in the facility, Dr. Phoebe Ligon.

"I want you to tell me something else about the album," Dr. Ligon says.

Artie looks up at the wicker ceiling fan. The spinning helps her think. She wrinkles her nose. The odor was like the junky antiques shop it came from.

"It smelled musty," she says.

The doctor exhales. Her foot shakes impatiently.

"And? What else? Tell me something about it that you wouldn't tell just anyone. What is it about the album that makes you uncomfortable?"

An abstract pencil drawing hangs on the wall behind Ligon. Its shapes of dark and light gray look like a Madonna and child. But maybe that's just Artie's imagination.

What makes me uncomfortable about it? A dull ache throbs in her chest. There's a twinge in the bridge of her nose. Her eyes water.

"Every childhood picture of me is in it," she whispers.

"Every picture," Dr. Ligon says, nodding. Her lips disappear inward as she tucks a lock of gleaming black hair behind one ear. "And what does that mean?"

Artie forces a smile.

"What comes up when you think about that?" Ligon's voice gets louder. "Your mother left, and *every* childhood picture of you is in that album."

Artie leans forward in the overstuffed chair. Elbows on her thighs, she rests her cheekbones on her knuckles. She doesn't want to say it. She has to. It's part of the work.

"She didn't keep any of them for herself."

"Yes," Ligon says. Her eyes fill with tears.

Jesus, Artie thinks. Must be the hormones. Ligon is pregnant.

Quietly beautiful and Filipina, she'd be lovely to photograph. Her skin is so smooth it looks airbrushed. But why is she staring at me like I'm some indigent child in a stop-the-hunger ad? Her baby will be wanted when it gets here. Her kid'll never have to speak to some shrink about being abandoned by its mother.

"You know what?" Artie says, sitting back. "I like the album the way it is. Every picture has a place. If she'd taken one it would have left a gap."

Dr. Ligon's eyes are warm. "How did you feel about it when you were twelve?" she asks. "Do you think those pictures meant anything to your mother?"

Artie's cheeks are hot. Is she *trying* to make me cry? She looks back at the drawing; a woman holding a baby. Or is it a man embracing a woman? The shapes morph into each other, some sort of Rorschach test.

She knows things about Ligon. She knows them because she's read them. Roxy pilfered a key to Ligon's office when she let the security guard feel her breast implants. She found computer files on herself and on Artie, and she printed them out. Dr. Ligon keeps notes, like a journal, on each patient. Artie saved an entry and taped it into her own journal. The doctor said that she appeared younger than her age. "Baby-like, butterscotch skin," she wrote, "with big brown eyes and long dark braids."

Artie doesn't think she looks that young, but Dr. Ligon said she'd remained the girl she was when her mother left. And the oddest thing she said was that she could see Artie's "aura," and that it had specks of red in it when she was angry. Then she contradicted herself. "Auras don't exist," she wrote. "The image is generated by one's own eyes." *Visual perseveration,* she called it. Yet Ligon insisted that she did, indeed, see a shimmer of light around this patient and it puzzled her. She said that Artimeza Reyes *glowed.*

Artie can't bring any of this up, of course, but she wishes she could ask about the aura, because she sees light around people, too. She likes to photograph it. When she's told others about this light they've said she was crazy. Maybe Dr. Ligon is crazy, too?

"Please don't pity me," Artie says. "And stop trying to make me feel sorry for myself."

"Is that what I'm doing?"

Artie answers with a glare.

The doctor shifts her weight and tries unsuccessfully to cross her legs. "I have compassion for your experience, Artie. Is there something wrong with that?"

"You don't know what anything meant to my mother and neither do I. You feel sorry for the sad little girl and you're trying to make me feel sorry for her, too. It's insulting."

"I don't pity you, Artie. That *would* be condescending. What happened to you was hurtful. I'm acknowledging that. Why can't *you* acknowledge it?"

Artie doesn't answer. She won't be manipulated.

"It *is* appropriate to say that it hurt," Ligon says. "It's not going to help you to pretend that it didn't. Pretending is a defense mechanism that's not useful to you now." The doctor edges her big belly forward in her chair and leans forward. "I know it's frightening to deal with these feelings, but our goal is to access them so you can let them go. That's the work you have to be willing to do, or there's no progress. Think of it like this: It's as if we're cleaning a greasy roasting pan that's been in the oven. When we soak it, at first, it looks worse than when we took it out. The dross is grimy and disgusting. But soaking is just part of the process we go through in order to clean it and make it like new again. That's why we want the old, ugly feelings to bubble up. So we can clean them away and they won't keep you stuck anymore."

Artie climbs the terracotta tile staircase back to her room in flip-flops. Her repulsively long toenails have remnants of polish clinging in spots. She's fascinated by the unsightly things the body does without maintenance. Nail clippers and metal files are forbidden. Razors, too. A service comes bi-monthly for manicures, pedicures, hair removal and such, but Artie's never used it. Why should she care about grooming in here? If Kendall were to see her disgusting feet, hairy armpits, and overgrown bush he'd run away shrieking.

A woman's plaintive moans echo from the floor above. The sharp smell of Pine-Sol cleaning solution masks the odor of a pile of human excrement Artie saw on the stairs earlier. These distractions remain in the background. Her focus is on the work.

Why have I been reluctant to acknowledge how I felt when my mother left? There was a reason when she was a kid. She didn't want anyone to know. This became a habit. A defense mechanism. Of course. She just hadn't seen it.

The door to her room is unlocked when she enters, but she can latch it from the inside.

She relishes the privacy. The walls are sea green and the bed-sheets are 1000-thread-count Egyptian cotton. It's not that she *wants* to be in a place like this. She couldn't function. She figured expensive meant good. There's an oak desk with a bookcase and matching chair. It's more like a guest room in a bed & breakfast than a psychiatric hospital. But the sounds of screaming, nurses in and out pushing pills, random piles of shit, and her own unkempt appearance reminds her: this is no vacation.

She pulls off her sweats and T-shirt, her uniform here, and slides into the smooth sheets.

What am I defending myself against now?

Dr. Ligon has encouraged her to write things between sessions; things she remembers, or wants to organize in her mind. She'd been too out of it with the drugs. But things aren't as hazy now.

"When my mother left, I knew it was because of me. I thought it was God's punishment for my flaws. There was a litany of things wrong with me. I was stupid in math. Sucked at most sports. Talked too much in class. I picked my nose at night and wiped it under the bed. Bit my nails and sometimes my toenails, too. I broke shit without admitting it. Cheated on spelling tests. I was nosy and a snoop. I talked back to Papi. Used profanity. Told lies. Sometimes, when Mami hit me, I told her I hated her. I stole change off of Papi's dresser. Didn't say my prayers. The list went on and on. I believed that because of my imperfections I didn't deserve to have a mom. And I knew I couldn't handle the teasing if kids at school found out. So I kept it to myself, withdrew from my friendships. That way no one would see and know the truth. I was worthless, like she said I was."

Crying feels self-indulgent. Weak. But Artie lets it flow to "get the feelings up and out." She doesn't want to be stuck anymore.

After hours of releasing, bubbling up and flowing into the next day, and the day after that, she does not feel *clean and new*, like Dr. Ligon said she would. That was some bullshit. All she's done is realize that she's still, even after all these years, ashamed that her mother didn't love her.

Admitting it is so overwhelming she's unable to move. And so she doesn't. For days, Artie sits with the shame and lets it be. She sits with it, and sits, until finally it occurs to her that this is an irreparable wound. It's not going away. Ever.

How does one survive this? If your own mother doesn't love you, who will?

Artie holds that thought. And as she does she feels something stir inside her. Something light...

What is that? Is she imagining it?

Ideas begin flooding her mind. Where are they coming from? *Wise* ideas, so evolved they seem whispered from another dimension. Something tells her that the wound is part of *her* soul's very own journey. She can't erase it, because she *is* the wound. She's grown and developed in response to its pain and she's so entwined, she wouldn't exist without it. She's been embarrassed by it, because she thought it was ugly, and it *is*, but it's beautiful too.

Artie decides to embrace this scar on her soul, because it belongs to her, and she belongs to it, and because if no remedy exists that can fade it away, it's probably meant to be.

Two

When she finally leaves her room Artie takes a walk on the gated grounds. Her feet mush through purple snow fallen from Jacaranda trees. Jasmine perfumes the air. The ocean sings from below the cliff. She's not that easily seduced. This place is far from paradise. She wants to function again, to get back to her life.

"But *what* life?" she asks Dr. Ligon during their session. "Not one that includes Kendall." Artie twirls a braid between two fingers and notices her split ends in the sunlight coming through the shutter slats.

"What *does* it include?" The doctor asks.

"I can't picture it. Never imagined a life without him."

"Have you tried?" Ligon grabs her belly. "Oo. Excuse me. She's kicking."

"Does it hurt a lot?" Artie asks.

The smell of rotten eggs pervades the room. Artie holds her breath. She'd cross her eyes, but she doesn't want to embarrass the doctor.

"I'm okay." Ligon says, rubbing her stomach. "What do you see when you think about life beyond your marriage?"

Artie looks up at the fan. She breathes through her mouth. "I end up thinking back, not forward," she says. "Couple of months ago, there

I am shooting stills on a film. I'm walking the aisles of Trader Joe's, picking up stuff to make his dinner. Folding his socks and T-shirts the way he liked. Boiling brown rice, roasting organic chicken. I go to the gym after dinner, and I do my best to look good when I come home and climb into bed with him. Was he thinking of her while I was doing all that? My childhood wasn't enough; she had to ruin the rest of my life, too? Why? Why did they do this to me?" She looks at the abstract pencil drawing behind Ligon and her recliner. Today it's a man embracing a woman.

"What they did and why they did it isn't the work we have to do," Ligon says. "We need to unpack the past to see what's stuffed back there. Things happen when we're young and we feel emotions we may be forced to suppress. So we hold onto feelings about ourselves that we'd be better off letting go of."

Artie pictures an old chest where things have been locked away in storage. She imagines herself stepping toward it and flipping the latches open.

Artie, 1990

The last photo Artie put in the album is the only one that was developed after Serena left. She took it shortly before her twelfth birthday. She and Papi drove to Coney Island Beach in their boxy BMW 2002 like they did many Saturdays with Mingus, their black Lab. Those beach days gave Artie and Mingus a chance to run free and play. Their two-bedroom apartment on East 13th Street was cramped and she wasn't even allowed to walk Mingus by herself outside; too many junkies, hookers, and other hustlers parading between First and Second Avenues.

That day, Papi forgot that Serena was expecting him back no later than

5:30pm. They were going to a cocktail party at B. Smith's Restaurant for the release of Lionel Hampton's biography.

When Artie and Rico came home two and a half hours after the party was supposed to have begun, her mother was wearing too much perfume, a spaghetti strap black dress, and a frown. She stood up at the kitchen table.

"You promise me, den ya don't show?"

"Huh?" Rico crossed to the refrigerator.

"Hamp. Tonight vas *my* night," Serena said. "I needa be out meetin' de right people, Rico."

"Oh." He turned, popping open a beer. "Sorry, I'll get ready."

Serena crossed her arms. She was always scowling about something, but Artie thought her mother was a spectacular beauty. She was special, because she was from someplace exotic. Artie assumed Bermuda was exotic, though she'd never actually been there. Her father was black and Puerto Rican, which didn't count as special, 'cause he was born right uptown in Harlem Hospital.

Serena was the color of gold and luminous like it, too. She had almond-shaped eyes and high cheekbones. Her long hair was usually pulled back in a braid or bun. Her body was lean like a dancer's.

She glowered at Rico standing across the room sipping his beer. Artie snapped a photo of her with the camera she'd received early for her birthday.

"Gat outta my face, Artimeza," Serena shouted. Get was "gat," because Serena sometimes pronounced e's like a's. Sometimes she pronounced her w's like v's, and her v's like w's, too.

Mingus scooted under the kitchen table. Artie had to pee, so "gattin'" out of her mother's face was no problem.

As Serena chewed Rico out in the kitchen, Artie discovered the first sight of her menstrual blood. She'd been waiting for this forever. Her two best friends at school already had theirs, and she'd worried something was wrong with her because it was taking so long.

She sat on the toilet and waited for her mother to stop yelling.

"I know you'd like to think your some kinda super deddy, but it's tired, Rico. And ya bess catch yourself, 'cause it's obvious you're usin' her to avoid somethin'."

"Ay dios mio," Papi groaned. "I said I was sorry, mami. It's not that late. We can still go."

"I sent the sittah home arready."

"Artie can stay by herself for a couple of hours," Rico said.

"She's a lit'l garrl."

"She's a young lady."

"Oh. Is she?" Serena said. "I see. Dat vhy you been treatin' her like de wife lately? Goin' on dates."

"Woman, what the hell you talking about, now?"

"I set here for days like a fool waitin' for you!"

"You should have gone ahead," Rico said.

"By myself? Since when? When'd you start wantin' me to go places wifout you, Rico?"

It was silent. Then Artie heard a thud. Someone threw something against the wall. Probably Serena. A door slammed. Their bedroom. But Serena was still in the kitchen. Artie could hear her crying. She was afraid to open the bathroom door. It opened into the kitchen. But she was bleeding.

"Mami?"

Serena was sitting at the table now, with her head down. She'd taken her thick hair out and both her hands were hidden in it, scratching her scalp. She did that when she was stressed. "Please don't badger me now," she said, without looking up. "Please."

"But mami, I—"

"Ya gattin' on my last drop a nerve, garrl."

"Yes, but—"

Serena's head sprang up. "Did you hear me? YOU WOFFLESS PAIN-IN-DE-ASS."

Woffless. Worthless. Artie wanted to ask her mother to please not call her that, but the last time she did, Serena slapped her. She took a step back and bit her bottom lip. Her heart pounded. Mingus cowered under the table. Rico flew into the room.

"Don't talk to my kid like that," he shouted.

"Fuck you! She's my kid too!"

"You better calm down if you want her to *stay* your kid."

"*What?*" Serena stood up.

Rico looked at Artie. "Mija, why don't you go take a bath?"

"*What-do-you-mean-by-dat?*"

"Just—stop it, woman! Chill the hell out, would you please?"

He disappeared back into the bedroom. Artie stood there staring at her mother. Serena turned away.

Artie whispered, "Mami, sorry to bother you, but—"

"Artie, please."

"I'm sorry. But Flo's here. She finally came to visit me," Artie smiled. "About time, huh?" She called it "Flo" because that's what Serena called it. *Damnit, Flo's bek arready,* she'd say.

Serena turned to face Artie. "*Whaat?*"

Artie got quieter still, "Please don't tell Papi."

Serena sucked her teeth. "Lemme see your knickers," she said. Artie started to walk back to the bathroom.

"Right here. Right *nahw.*"

Artie stopped. She looked at her mother. "What if Papi comes in?"

Serena drew back an open palm. Artie unbuttoned her shorts. She stepped out of them, pulled down her pink cotton panties, and handed them over. There was a reddish-brown stain. Serena's eyes darkened.

"Splendid. Nahw I gotta make a run for some flippin' peds." She dropped the panties on the floor, put on the high-heeled shoe she'd flung at the wall earlier, and walked out. The metal security door clanged behind her.

Artie was left standing half naked in the kitchen. She bent down to pick up her underwear from the dingy linoleum, but Mingus beat her to it. He was play growling and the panties were in his mouth. She wanted to hurry and dress before her father came back into the room. Mingus teased her with the underwear. He tried to fake her out, ready to run if she made a move. She knew how it worked, and though Mingy was adept at this game, she went for it.

Then her father re-entered. Shit. Half naked, she could feel a trickle of blood oozing down her thigh as Mingus trotted off to his spot in the living room with his nasty new treat. She and Papi froze for a moment looking at each other. He closed his eyes, ran both hands through his dark curls, then turned and bumped his elbow into the doorframe rushing back out of the room.

He'd seen her naked before when she was little. It was different now. *She* was different. Papis weren't supposed to know. Only mamis were supposed to know.

Three

Serena, 2004

Serena stares at the water as she power walks along the beach. She imagines herself swimming, riding the waves, joyful, and carefree. She's neither. Just over two months ago, at the end of March, she met a young saxophonist at Hal's Bar and Grill in Venice, got hammered and needed a lift home. Every day since, she's wished she rung a flippin' taxi.

Her sneakers pound the wet sand. Eyes toward the ocean, she meditates on peace. Her daily routine. After the walk, she stretches and then heads past the shops, restaurants, and dogs on their leads tied to parking meters, for a Grande Soy Latte before going back to the flat to work on music.

Today, as Serena crosses Washington Boulevard, she sees Rico sitting in the window of the Starbucks on the corner. Her stomach plummets. *Rico!* Since that night with Artie's boy, she's been ringing his cell to explain. Countless messages. She's wanted to see him, hoped he'd come, but he's never rung back.

His hair is mostly gray now, still full, past his ears, and curly. He's wearing his usual white guayabera and sitting at the first table to the right of the door. He doesn't look up when she enters. His face is partly obscured by the *LA Times*, which he holds close, squinting into, making his crows feet more pronounced. She sits across from him. His dark eyes, framed by thick brows, finally meet hers above the paper.

"Please, Rico, lemme axplain—"

Whack!

His hand knocks against her face with such force she nearly tumbles from the chair.

The din of chatter goes silent. Patrons turn. Stare. There's usually music playing, but the only sounds are of coffee brewing and the gurgle of milk steaming. Serena holds her cheek. Rico returns his attention to the newspaper as if she were never there.

The barista, wide-eyed behind the counter says, "Um, you okay, ma'am? Should I call the police?"

Serena stands and walks out. She wants that bloody Grande Soy Latte, but not from there after that. She tries not to cry as she crosses the street and heads back past the shops, toward the beach and her condo.

How she wishes she'd never come to this city. Flippin' Los Angeles. *The Angels? Ha.* Wasn't her idea to leave New York, it was it was her partner Jamie's. She's had nothing but pissy luck since they arrived.

The left side of her face stings as she moves against the breeze, cheek in one hand, the other scratching her scalp. The wind pushes her back. Forces are against her.

She did not know who that boy was. She's still not sure how it happened. Some cosmic joke? Artimeza thought I was a horror *before* the disaster. Why *wouldn't* she believe I did it on purpose? Apparently Rico thinks so, too.

Serena's grieved these past months. She can't call Artie, or visit her. They weren't in touch *before* the imbroglio. How could they possibly connect now?

She's thought of writing a letter. But when she wrote Artie in the past, several times, there was no response. She's been trying to say the things in her heart through the songs she's composing. If she can accomplish that, even if Artie doesn't listen to them, at least they'll exist in the world. Maybe the Universe will be kind; let the music find her. Right now the bloody Universe doesn't appear to be on her side. But the tides could turn, couldn't they?

She'd planned to write today. Too shaken. Instead, she'll imbibe. Despite the day's calamitous beginning, Serena knows she's fortunate. *'Least I cen sit on my bumpy, look out de glass walls, drink red wine, and watch de waves.* Proximity to the ocean is one decent thing about this city.

Her face tingles as she passes Jamie's window on the way up the concrete steps to her flat. That blasted portrait of his great-great whatever she is stares through the glass, dark eyes following her like a stalker. Bitch.

She rubs her cheek. She's hurt more than vexed with Rico. After all they've been to each other couldn't he at least let her explain? Still so protective of his *"niña."* Not the first time he's slapped her because of Artie.

👀

Serena, 1990

He wasn't speaking to her. They'd had a huge row couple of nights earlier, when he stood her up. She washed the dinner dishes while he practiced in the living room.

I should be practicing instead of doin' blasted chores, she thought.

Rico practiced every night if he wasn't out playing a gig. She quite liked it, but they had to pay the neighbors next door and the family above a monthly fee for the racket. He played trumpet, mostly Latin jazz, and he had a bit of a following. He hustled to support them, playing gigs with different bands, teaching trumpet lessons, working as a studio musician, but Serena admired his career. 'Least he *had* a bloody career.

She fell in love with the sound of his horn years earlier, in the mid-70s, when they both played a salsa meets jazz evening at the Village Gate. She was performing, though she was still a student uptown at City College. He embraced her backstage in the dark one night. His big hands slid up her back, down her hips. "Te quiero," he whispered in her ear and pressed against her. He called her his angel. Told her he knew from the moment he saw her that he'd always adore her. She was young enough to be impressed.

Serena still loved him like crazy fourteen years later. She *craved* him; wanted him to want her with the same passion. But he'd been aloof of late and it was driving her mad.

The way he played, and his gift for composition continued to fascinate her. As did the rasp in his voice, the mystery in his black eyes, his muscular arms, and tight bum. The things he whispered and sometimes yelled when he made love still stirred her. When he was away she slept with one of his guayaberas—one he'd played in, unlaundered and musky. She couldn't live without his scent. But what she most adored about Rico was the way he made her feel loved. She missed that. For weeks, he turned away in bed and wouldn't embrace her. When she asked what was wrong, he refused to say.

She finished drying the dishes whilst listening to him play. Earlier, she made codfish cakes and fish chowder with rum and sherry pepper, but Rico didn't compliment her island cooking as he typically did. He barely spoke and when he did it was to Artimeza.

He began to practice a different song. One he'd written for her when things were good. Was this his way of reconnecting with her? She hoped so. She put away the dishes, poured a glass of pinot noir, and then lit a candle. She sat at the Formica table. Perspiration ran down her back. She pulled her T-shirt over her head. The cut-off shorts and black lace bra were for surviving the heat, but if Rico was tempted, she certainly wouldn't mind. She sipped her wine and hoped they'd have a talk when he finished. With any luck, talking would lead to something more satisfying… He was playing something different now. Unfamiliar. What happened to her song? This sounded vexed… It grew frantic. Rico wailed on the trumpet as if he were fighting to escape something. Loud and discordant notes banged about like a caged bear. Serena pressed her hands to her ears.

The ankle biter skipped out of her bedroom toward the living room. Serena raised her voice above the music. "Don't badger him, Artie."

"He told me to tell him when it was nine o'clock," she yelled back.

"You gotta go ta bed."

Artie shouted over her shoulder, "He wants us to watch Spanish TV for half an hour." She kept going. The strange music stopped.

"There's my angel," Serena heard him say. Sounded like he scooped her up and kissed her. The television came on. Spanish voices. Serena's jaw clenched. Her chest tightened. She inhaled deeply, and exhaled to blow it off. Begrudging her husband and child their time together seemed petty, even to her. But he was purposely shutting her out. She didn't bloody speak Spanish. *And why didn't he mention dat he-n-Artie were havin' another date tonight?* There was salsa music on the TV.

Serena got up and peeked into the living room. Rico stood with Artie, holding her hands. They were dancing along with the people on the show. Mingus was curled up in the corner. Rico glanced at her and then looked away without so much as a smile.

Serena gulped down the rest of her wine. She blew out the candle, went into the bedroom, and closed the door. Though she felt like breaking something, instead, she climbed into bed and reached inside the nightstand for her journal. She needed to vent. *Why's he callin' her his angel? That's my bloody pet name.* She took another deep breath. Then she picked up her glasses and noticed something that silenced the chatter in her head. It was a vintage, granny-style pair of magnifying glasses she'd bought in an antiques shop. They reminded her of the ones her mother wore back in Bermuda. The temple of the frame, the part that hung onto the ears, was curved into a "C." One of the Cs was broken completely off. Artie had done it.

Tsssk. Sometimes dat garrl cen be woffless. Awweys peezin', arawhn, snoopin' in my god damned stuff.

Serena leapt out of bed with the glasses and into the living room. Mingus's head popped up. Rico was leading Artie through a turn.

"Lookit these," Serena said, shoving the frames in the girl's face. "I know you did this. Admit it."

Rico frowned and lurched his head back. "Stop yelling."

Artie cowered under his arm.

"The garrl broke mah flippin' glasses, Rico." Serena grabbed Artie's arm and plucked her from Rico like fruit from a tree. She smacked her across the face. "Stay outta my things."

Rico's eyes were crazed. His cheeks flamed red as he stepped in front of his daughter.

"Don't you touch her," he yelled into Serena's face. "Want me to hit *you?*"

She stepped back. *What'd he jus' say?* Before she could respond, *he slapped her.* She staggered for a moment. Her left cheek throbbed. She couldn't believe it. He'd never hit her before.

Artie ran from the room. Mingus whimpered.

"How do *you* like it?" Rico barked. "Huh?" The hostility pouring from his eyes was unfamiliar. "I know you been beating her again, Serena. How many times I gotta tell you, I'm not cool with that? Tryin' a make me leave you? That whatchu want, Mami? 'Cause, I will. I swear, I'll fuckin' leave you, you put your hands on her again. "

All she could do was stare at him. Her eyes blurred with tears. What was there to say? After fourteen years, she was having a hard time making sense of how the marriage had come to this. One thing she *did* understand quite clearly: she was not his angel anymore.

Four

Artie, 2004

Artie sees that Dr. Ligon looks tired. Bags under her eyes dull their sparkle. Her skin lacks its usual luster. The office is gloomy; the shutters closed tightly against the sun like a small child's mouth refusing peas.

"You feeling okay?" Artie asks.

"Yes," Ligon says. "I do have something to discuss with you, though."

Artie blinks. Okay.

The doctor covers her mouth and yawns. "Excuse me. I'm going to be here until my delivery, but then I'll need to take a few weeks off. In my absence, Dr. Schwartz will be with you. He's familiar with what we've been working on." Her eyebrows rise, creasing her forehead. "Do you have any questions?" Her voice goes up in pitch.

Artie shakes her head.

"You may be uncomfortable or even angry about my leaving, and if so, we can talk about it."

"I'm not angry."

Ligon's lips turn inward, making her mouth a straight line. Brows still lifted, she looks skeptical. Her eyes drift up from Artie's face and hover above her head.

She's checking out my aura, Artie thinks. Looking for specks of red.

"Sometimes patients can feel upset or abandoned," Ligon says, focusing on Artie's eyes again. She leans forward, hugging the round blob in her lap. "It's okay to express anything you're feeling."

"I'm not gonna take it personally that you're having a baby."

"Emotional responses to events that occur during the therapeutic process aren't always logical. I'm leaving, disrupting our work, and causing a change in your world. That can bring up feelings from previous times when your world changed without your control."

Artie sighs and looks up at the fan. It's motionless today.

Artie, 1990

When her eyes opened the morning after Papi slapped Mami, Artie was supine, focused on the ceiling, and listening to the sounds in the apartment. Papi was breathing heavily in the living room. The refrigerator buzzed. Mingus snored like a drunk. Her mother had finally stopped crying, thank goodness. Artie got up to go to the bathroom and saw that the bedroom door was ajar. Serena was gone. Artie knew she was gone, because the dog was sprawled across the unmade bed with his paws in the air.

Artie began to tremble. She pulled open Serena's dresser drawers and found that what she feared was true.

Papi was still asleep. She'd have to wake him so he could take her to school since her mother wasn't there to do it. But if she woke him, they'd have to talk about what was happening. She sat at the kitchen table and ate a bowl of Cheerios. When she was done she placed the dish into the sink without a sound.

Artie knew how to get to school. It was straight across town. She was old enough to go alone. Especially now. She was twelve years old. Today. As she left the apartment, she closed the security door gently so it wouldn't make that loud clang. Outside, the super's wife was sweeping the stoop. Artie said hello, and whooshed past her, down the steps. She didn't want to answer any questions.

She passed a junkie, ragged and smelling like pee-pee, nodding at Second Avenue. She walked west on 13th Street, the same route she usually took with her mother. She stopped on red, walked on green and smiled so hard her cheekbones hurt. She'd heard that smiling, all by itself, could make a person feel better.

While standing at the light at Fifth Avenue where the buildings were prouder and the street cleaner, an older kid, high school she figured, stood nearby in a green private school jacket. He stared at her and tilted his head. Artie knew she looked weird. She didn't care. She would smile all day at school, too. That way no one would know she was scared because her parents were fighting. It was her birthday. She was supposed to be happy.

Five

Serena, 1990

Rico would be sorry for what he did. Serena knew that. It was still dark out when she took a suitcase full of clothes, her journal, sheet music, some jewelry and toiletries and she rode the train to her Auntie's house on East 230th Street in the Bronx. Not the loveliest neighborhood, but not the worst either. As she walked down the hill from the elevated subway, the pine and maple trees were taller and fuller than she remembered. Small birds chirped. Faces passing on their way to work were vaguely familiar. She began to breathe more deeply.

Annie's narrow, three-story house sparkled in the rising sun with its white aluminum siding. The lilac tree they'd planted together was blooming in the front yard. She breathed it in, sweet and robust. On a better morning, it would've made her smile. She punched in the code on the wrought iron gate. To her surprise, the front door opened just as she was bumping her small suitcase up the porch steps.

"Oh, goodness!" Annie's hands flew to her mouth. Buddy looked surprised, too. They were wearing matching white T-Shirts and black athletic pants. Annie wore a house key on a shoestring around her neck. Her short, brown hair had a touch more gray at the temples than the last time Serena saw her.

"I just dreamed about you last night, love. Didn't I?" Annie held her niece's face and kissed her cheek. "You were singing; in front of a giant audience. It was brilliant. And I was in a fancy dress…"

"Sorry I didn't call, Auntie." Serena hugged her, and didn't want to let go. Annie patted her back.

"Planning on makin' yourself at home, I see," Buddy said, noting the suitcase.

His Jamaican accent made everything he said seem musical, even when he sounded less than delighted. "How long are we to have the pleasure of your company?"

"Oh, stop with that tone," Annie said, eyeing him sharply. "Ree can stay as long as she likes."

Serena released her. "Not too long, I hope." She knew Buddy well enough to know that he loved company. He enjoyed giving people a hard time, too, and she was a bit raw for that.

"You're always welcome, love," Annie said. "I don't have to tell you that."

Buddy sighed. "Well, what brings you here, lookin' like the world's comin' to an end?"

Annie swatted Buddy's arm.

Serena sniffled. "Bit'v trouble at home, I'm afraid." She tried to smile, but couldn't manage it.

"Sorry to hear that," Buddy said. "Happens, though." He picked up her suitcase and stuck it inside the door.

"Of course it does. All couples quarrel, don't they?" Annie's eyes grew moist. "Don't worry yourself, darling. It'll be all right. You'll see."

"G'wan in. Make yourself a pot of tea," Buddy said. "We're off for our mornin' walk. Got to keep da gal healt-y."

"Buddy, you go." Annie tapped him on the chest. "I'm feeling a bit sluggish today."

Buddy sucked his teeth and poked his lip out like a toddler.

Annie pushed him playfully. "Oh stop the dramatics, love. I'll go with you tomorrow."

"Fine, fine." He took the key from around her neck and kissed her forehead. "Don't miss me too much," he said with a laugh, and jogged down the steps.

Serena watched her Aunt's eyes linger with him a moment. "Fit for his age, inn't he?" Annie said. "The big baby." She winked.

Inside, the house was tidy and formal as it had been when Serena lived there. There was a stillness to it that felt monastic. Quiet, however, it was not. Every fifteen minutes the English mantel clock chimed in the front parlor. That blasted nuisance had been in Aunt Annie's house back in Bermuda before they came to the States. The awful thing disturbed Serena's sleep and made bad days by worse by calling attention to how long they were.

The kitchen, which felt lived in, unlike the front parlor, was in the back of the house. It overlooked a small yard with rose bushes. Annie stirred three sugar cubes into her tea.

"What about Artie? Aren't you worried that she might need you, love?"

"Not worried." Serena shook her head. "Rico's better with her anyvay."

"But a girl needs her mother, Serena. She's welcome here, too."

Serena looked at Annie for a moment before she spoke.

"Truth is, Auntie, I'm not good with Artie."

"Oh, Serena, every mother makes mistakes."

"No. I've never been good at motherhood."

"Don't put yourself down, love," Annie said, setting her cup on its saucer and touching Serena's hand.

"You don't understand. I'm... unkind to her. I've always been." Serena took her hand away and examined her nails. The red varnish was chipping. Untidy.

"Oh, I don't believe that. I've seen you with her." Annie's elbow was on the table and she rested her chin in her hand.

"Not in fron' a you... I never told you, but she annoyed me from de start. Didn't appreciate the near hundred pahwnds I gained. And Rico fawned over her. About how pretty she was-- her light caramel coloring, her sweet little smile. But when she cried or mussed her diaper, who took care of it? I vas de one wifout sleep, up all bloody night wif a stinkin', screamin' baby," she yelled. "Sorry. I don't mean to shout. "

"Serena," Annie said, "newborns are always overwhelming for a mother."

"Remember when she vas a toddler and he went to Palermo for dat jezz festival? He wouldn't let me go, 'cause she was on a schedule. I was so vexed, Auntie. Ignored her fa days. Couldn't stand to look at de garrl." Serena began to pick at the chipped nail polish. She glanced at Annie before removing a paper napkin from its holder in the center of the table.

Annie's eyes were hot pieces of coal searing into Serena's face. "How could you ignore a toddler? I don't see how that's even possible."

"I fed 'er. Bathed her. But I wouldn't read to her or play wif her, and when she came to me I pushed her away, or put her back in her room." Serena scratched at the polish on her thumbnail and let it fall onto the white napkin.

"You were depressed. Some mothers go through that."

Serena shook her head. Her eyes met Annie's briefly. "I wasn't depressed. I just never--" she scraped at the nail again. "Never took to 'er. When she was five she asked me, 'Mami, who do you love most in the world?' I knew what she wanted to hear, but the neediness grated on me. Told her de truth: 'I love your Papi and my Auntie most.'"

Annie winced. She covered her mouth with her hand. Serena looked at her nail. It was clean now and there was a pile of red flakes on the napkin. She started on the other thumb before glancing up to see her aunt with a clenched jaw, her eyes cast down at the table, as she adjusted the lace doily underneath the sugar jar and creamer.

"Artie stared at me, seemed like for days, when I said dat. As if she was tryin' to make sense of it. When she walked avay, she looked puzzled. More confused than hurt." Serena continued picking at the polish, chipping it away, revealing the bare nail underneath.

Annie shook her head, her eyes bewildered. "She was a beautiful, sweet little girl."

Serena nodded. "She was. What mum wouldn't want a sweet little garrl, so beautiful that people stopped on de street to admire her? But she rankled me so. I'd look at 'er sometimes, sleepin', and wonder, why was I so mean to my lil' garrl today?" Serena swallowed. She continued picking at her thumbnail without looking at it. She focused on Annie. "I'm not normally a mean person, Auntie. She brought it out in me."

Annie sniffled. Dabbed the corners of her eyes with a napkin. "And now? How've you been with her lately?"

The second thumb was clean now. Serena looked at Annie and then shook her head. You don't want to know. She started on her index finger.

"I knew you were stern with her. But I never-- Why did you wait this long? You're a smart girl, Ree, you might have gotten help sooner."

"Right. Kinda help I had in secondary school? Vaste-a-money."

Serena saw that one of her aunt's eyes was twitching.

"Well, I love her," Annie said, raising her voice. "I love that little girl. If you need some time alone with your mate, send her here. I'll take her." She shifted in her seat and turned sideways, away from Serena. "Poor thing," she said. "And on her birthday, no less."

"Rico doesn't want time alone with me." She peeled the varnish off her middle finger in one whole piece. "He's more vexed than he's ever been."

"For now, maybe. You both need time to cool off."

Neither of them spoke while the clock chimed in the other room.

"Must be awful for him," Annie finally said, "if he knows how you feel about his daughter. I can't even imagine." She shook her head.

"Thanks, Auntie. That really helps."

"I'm sorry." Annie put her hand on Serena's hand and squeezed it. "You're still my little Ree. And I love you, no matter what."

Three weeks later, with no word from her family, Serena carried Annie and Buddy's mail in along with the groceries she picked up for them. She was placing the letters and bills on the parlor table when she noticed her own name on one of the envelopes, and then on another, and another. She set the grocery bag down. There was an alumni announcement from City College, a royalty check from a jingle she'd recorded, and a letter from her credit card company. Rico had closed the account.

Serena let out a moan and collapsed on the stairs. The mantle clock chimed the second quarter: bling, blang, blang, blong, bling blang, blong, blong. She wanted to tell it to shut up. Annie ran in from the kitchen.

"What is it, love?"

"Oh, Auntie, I should've gone back. I thought leavin' would make 'im want me again. But he doesn't," she wept. "He's moved on."

Aunt Annie sat beside Serena on the stairs and hugged her. "Oh, my poor baby. My poor sweet baby."

Serena eased out of her embrace and leaned against the staircase railing. "I know you mean vell when you say that, but it doesn't help. Brings back de past."

Annie was quiet. Her eyes dulled. She looked past Serena and nodded.

"Today is so much like dat day," Serena said.

Annie's eyes returned to her. "Shhh, darling. Shh." She caressed her face.

"Always unwanted," Serena said.

"Oh, Ree, that's not true."

"Tell me again. The way dey dumped me off like rubbish."

"Stop," Annie said. "Why think of such things? What does it matter now?"

"It's always mattered. It always will."

Annie touched Serena's forehead and smoothed back her hair. "You ought to call Rico. He's not a mind reader. Maybe if you talk to him."

"Auntie. He-doesn't-want-me-anymore."

Later, sitting on her bed, Serena wrote in her journal, "Why do the most awful things repeat themselves? Why, God? Let me understand." She stared at the page as if waiting for an answer.

She put the notebook and pen aside and curled into a ball. She wanted to be cuddled like a baby. Like she had never been as a small child. She was in her early teens, and living with Aunt Annie when she first heard Charles Mingus play the bass and saw his picture on an album cover. He began appearing in her dreams. When she was lonely, she'd curl up on her bed and pretend to be nestled in his arms. She talked to him as she fell asleep. He was husky and smelled of cherry-cocoa pipe tobacco and coconut hair oil. He was a good listener. She needed him now. Facing the wall with her eyes closed, she tried to be completely still; to smell him, hear him—a process of conjuring. Soon she felt his chest against her back. The intervals of his breath. She sensed his arm was on her waist and they began communicating mind to mind.

I vas only a lit'le garrl, she told him. This time, it might be my fault, but what happened in Bermy wasn't fair.

Fair? Baby, don't expect schitt to be fair. Sure way to find yourself sick at heart.

She felt him shake his head.

My mum and Annie's father, died when they were in their teens. He was white, from England. Granny Clara was copper-colored. And accordin' to Auntie, she was pleased dat my mother, Artimeza was fairer and more beautiful than granny was herself. Annie, bein' honey colored, was too brown to win favor in de family.

Hmphf. Now, that's not fair, is it? Mingus asked.

Auntie said that my mum did just as she and granny always planned. Married white, and her first two children were as white as any truly white children. Only thing that gave away their secret was me-- de golden-brown baby.

Bet you were the prettiest one, too.

Phyllis and Brian went to a white school wiffout a problem. 'Ccording to Auntie, mother feared that when it was time for me to go it would threaten the family's status. She told me my deddy didn't like the idea of sendin' his baby daughter away. Think it was because he loved me?

How could he not love his girl?

Why'd he have to be so weak?

She waited for an answer. Mingus only shrugged.

He vas from an Irish family, whose ancestors were bondservants. Yet they had de audacity to be bigots. Never met my father's parents. When Phyllis and Brian visited them, I wasn't even invited.

Mingus scatted his umbrage: Ooo waa ba di jib a di jib a doojaba da O ba ba ta bibbity bibity boobata waay basama luuuumaamaa wa dooey oooOO MA ma.

Serena sighed. Annie worked at a dress shop on Front Street. Her godmother had bequeathed her a small, house in Paget. Wif no prospects of a husband, she was happy to inherit a small child, too.

Of course, she was.

I hadn't a clue of the real reason I was bein' sent avay. Watched my mum take arry article of clothing from de chest of drawers and closet, and each of my toys and books, and put them in an antique trunk that belonged to my father's great-grandmother who'd brought it from Ireland. My parents put me in de car. I set by myself in the back and they drove me to Aunt Annie's. When we arrived and I climbed out, de air was thick and smelled like seaweed. The limestone roof gleamed in de sun. Mother said, "You'll be stayin' here with your Auntie. You'll go to school nearby."

"But why can't I stay home and go to school?" I asked. "Phyllis-n-Brian don't go avay." She didn't answer. "How long will I be stayin', Mummy?"

My father's face flushed. He turned and walked avay. Mother kissed my cheek and followed my deddy back to de car.

I thought they were leavin' me because I'd misbehaved. I spilled some preserves on my Sunday clothes de day before. And a few days before that I'd eaten some baker's chocolate I wasn't supposed to and mother gave me a lashing. Yes, I was naughty sometimes, but no worse than other children.

"I'll behave, Mother. I promise," I shouted. She got in de car and deddy started de engine. "Please! Don't leave me!" My hands balled into fists and beat my own thighs.

The car backed outta de dirt road as I ran toward it. Deddy's face looked wet like he was cryin'. They were gone so fast I couldn't be sure. I set down in de dusty driveway like rubbish cast aside and stayed there 'til Auntie picked me up.

"My poor baby," she said. "My poor sweet baby." She carried me inside.

Serena felt Mingus's arms hold her tighter. And she heard his song. "All The Things You Could Be By Now If Sigmund Freud's Wife Was Your Mother." Hmphf. If that was supposed to be a joke it wasn't funny.

The song squeaked and squealed, fast, kooky. Crazy-making.

She sat up and grabbed her journal as Cholly's composition screeched in her mind. Rico has cast me aside, too, she wrote. And I know I'm not perfect, but I'm a person. I'm not just a thing with no feelings. I don't understand. If there's a lesson here, please show me what it is.

She stared at the page as if an explanation might appear.

Downstairs, the clock chimed the first quarter: Bling, blang, blong, blong, thankfully drowning out the wild riffing in her head. She dropped the pen and looked out the porthole window beside the bed. It overlooked the neighbors' drab garage with its peeling paint. Serena knew she had to stop feeling sorry for herself. She had to fight. Was that what God had in mind? To make her fight?

As a teenager, she'd look out this porthole, and imagine she was on a ship, sailing to someplace new, where she'd be adored. And she found her way to Rico. Would there be a new voyage in her life?

Serena wished she hadn't left her other journals at the flat. They were boxed in her trunk in the closet. The same trunk her mother had boxed her things in when she was a child. It contained at least thirty notebooks dating back to age thirteen, the year of her first kiss. Had she known better, she would have taken them with her. She wanted to re-read the fourteen years with Rico; to experience the sweetness of it once more before she let it go. She'd have to call him after all.

Six

Artie, 1990

The apartment was full of sundry boxes, and most of their furniture had been sold or given away. Artie took a peek through a pile of papers Rico left on the floor beside the bed where his nightstand used to be. She found a receipt for a bank check made out to Serena for seven thousand dollars.

"What's this?"

Rico was sorting white laundry on the bed. "Everything is not your business, mija." He snatched the receipt from her hand. "Do I go through your things?"

She stood, crossed her arms, and stomped away. He followed her into her room, where she flopped herself down on the bed like a dead duck in a cartoon.

"I'm sorry I yelled. Please don't go through Papi's papers. That was money I sent your mami. Half our savings."

Artie lifted her head and looked at him. "You knew where she was?"

He didn't answer.

"You said you didn't know," she shouted. "You said we couldn't call her. You said she'd contact us when she was ready."

"I thought she would." He dropped his head and left the room.

A week later they were in a motel near Kennedy Airport. When Artie went to bed, Rico took the phone into the bathroom. She could see the shadow of his feet pacing in the crack of light under the door.

"Everyday I was packin' up the apartment, I worried she might show up and I wouldn't be able to turn her away," he said. "I *wanted* her to leave me, Ray."

Artie sat up.

"Didn't have it in me to leave *her* and I couldn't let her keep puttin' her hands on Artie. Crazy as she is, she's still my heart. Probably always will be."

Artie rubbed her chest. It was thumping and it hurt. She didn't want to be the cause of their split, even if it meant continued beatings. The break-up would make her mother hate her even more. That was worse than a beating.

"Papi?" she called.

He opened the door. Sighed. "What is it, mija?"

She swallowed. "Who you talking to?"

"Go to sleep. I'm talking to Rayana. You'll meet when we get to L.A."

He closed the door again. Mingus yawned and changed position in the plastic crate that would house him the next day in the belly of the airplane. She could still hear Rico.

"She was the love of my life, Ray, but she wanted things to stay the way they were before we had a kid."

"Papi!"

Rico was quiet a moment. The door opened. "Stop it, Artie."

"Is she nice?" she whispered.

Rico frowned at her and closed the door. She lay back down and listened.

"Yeah," he sighed, "Mami suggested counseling, too, but Serena wouldn't have gone. She didn't believe in that stuff. Called it rubbish."

Artie thought back to a conversation she had with her father a couple of weeks earlier while she'd watched him make arroz con pollo. *"Your mother loves you, mija,"* he told her. *"She just doesn't know how much she loves you 'cause she isn't well. She has issues. Things that make her sad. And sad, scared people just can't love very well."* Poor Papi. He had such a hard time with the truth. Artie didn't challenge him. If it made him feel better to think he was protecting her she'd give him that.

He looked through Serena's trunk full of journals the night he told that lie. Artie had read some of them during snooping sprees. Serena never wanted a kid. She only had one because she loved Rico and *he* wanted one. She felt trapped by motherhood. Burdened.

While it hurt to read these things, Artie knew she wasn't supposed to have snooped, so she had no right to feel sorry for herself. But listening to Rico weep while he read the journals that night, that was too much to bear.

She jumped out of bed, ran in, and hugged him. He was cross-legged on the floor with several of the notebooks open around him, and one in his lap. Japanese beer cans littered the floor. She squeezed tighter and rested her face against his neck.

"It's okay, baby," he said. "I'm okay, go back to bed." His breath smelled of liquor. He lifted her up and carried her back to her room.

She heard him in the kitchen. She peeked and saw him grabbing the brown bags from Gristedes that they used for garbage. He went back into the bedroom and she heard him dropping the journals into the bags. He carried the bags from the room, and set them by the front door. She saw him in the kitchen again. He opened the window to the fire escape, reached out and grabbed the container of lighter fluid he kept out there with the grill. Then she heard the front door open.

Across the street from their apartment building was a vacant lot filled with motley weeds and garbage. There were two trashcans in the center. Sometimes when it was cold homeless people made fires in them.

Artie's bedroom faced the street. From her window, she watched

Rico drop the bags full of journals into one of the cans. He poured the lighter fluid over them, lit a match and dropped it in. Flames lashed out of the can almost immediately. Papi jumped back. Those journals were as angry about being destroyed as Serena would be if she knew. Rico stood and watched until the raging began to die down. He wiped his face with his sleeve.

Artie was scared. If her mother saw or even heard about her journals being burned she'd probably go crazy and kill someone. She loved Rico too much to kill *him*, which made Artie uneasy.

What Papi did was wrong. If he knew where her mother was, why didn't he send the journals to her, or save them? It was an act of meanness she didn't understand.

The same night Papi burned them, Artie woke to the sound of him moaning, "Ay-ay-ay mami." She heard a woman's high-pitched sighs, too. They were in the living room. The sighs weren't her mother's, but Artie hoped they were. And though she knew she shouldn't, she peeked. Papi saw her. He looked right at her. The woman was face down on the sofa. Rico closed his eyes and kept thrusting.

"Okay, let's stop here." Dr. Ligon's voice snaps Artie back to the present. "I want to talk about the lack of boundaries. How did it feel to be in that apartment?"

"Boundaries?" Artie says. "I was twelve. What'd I know about boundaries?"

Ligon's hand rests on her swollen belly. "He was with a woman, who wasn't your mother, in the living room, a common space you could easily walk into, not the bedroom with the door closed. He was exposing you to his sex life. On one hand, he was protective—intolerant of your mother's abuse, yet his *own* behavior was completely inappropriate."

Artie stares down at her feet.

"But when you're dependant upon a parent who's inappropriate, what can you do?" Ligon asks.

Artie shrugs.

"Exactly. Not much. But your feelings go *somewhere*. What I'm hearing you say is that *you* snooped. *You* peeked. You make yourself the focus of the inappropriate behavior. Consequently, your feelings about what happened are invalidated. Can you give your twelve-year-old self the right to the feelings that came with the experience?"

Leaning back, Artie places a forefinger on her lips. Her eyes drift up. "If I could remember what they were. I know it bothered me, but I think I was in survival mode. Honesty, I was more stressed out in that motel room, worrying that Serena might find out Papi burned her journals before we got on the plane." She looks at Ligon.

"Why were you so worried?"

Artie scoffs with a rueful nip of a smile. "'Cause I thought she'd kill me."

"Even though you weren't the one who burned the journals? She'd take that out on you?"

"I thought so."

Ligon nods. "And if she tried, would your father have protected you?"

Artie exhales. "I didn't think I could count on that. No."

Seven

Serena, 1990

By the time Serena finally worked up the nerve to call the flat, the number had been disconnected. *Is Rico gone?*

She paced barefooted on the hardwood floor. Where was he? How would she find him? His mother couldn't stand her. She'd never tell, if he didn't want to be found. Serena knew a few of Rico's mates, but when she thought of ringing them, and the explaining she'd have to do... She rang the building's super. His wife, Mrs. Aponte answered. She'd always been polite, but when Serena announced herself the woman's tone grew terse.

"They moved out. No forwarding address."

Serena suspected this was untrue. As a composer and musician, Rico wouldn't leave his royalty checks without a way to find him. She didn't argue.

"Did they leave anything in de flat?"

"Nada."

"Are you sure? Have you looked?"

"Si, I'm sure. Luis is over there now painting. There's a new tenant moving in, an NYU student. Her parents must have deep pockets. Dios mio, you won't believe what the owner is charging to rent your apartment."

"Mrs. Aponte," her voice was stern, "I left some important things—"

"—Already told you, niña. He didn't leave nothing." And with that Mrs. Aponte hung up.

Serena slipped on her kicks, grabbed her wallet and keys, and left the house without a word to Annie or Buddy. She ran up the hill to White Plains Road. She was inside the subway station before realizing she hadn't pulled back her hair, or put on lipstick, or even a jacket. It was summer, but it was drizzling and cool that day, and she was in a tank top. None of that mattered. Who cared if she looked rank, or caught a cold? More than twenty years of her life were recorded in those notebooks.

Her heart was racing. Her chest ached. She tried to breathe deeply whilst sitting on the rattling train. It was a long ride down to 14th Street. She pictured precisely how she'd walk from the subway, east to Second Avenue, then over to 13th. She'd use her key to get in the front door and she would walk right into the flat which should be open because Luis was there painting. She would go to the bedroom closet and find the trunk still in its spot. Rico wouldn't have taken that. She'd open it and they'd all be there. She visualized this and it calmed her. Everything would be fine.

The train got stuck. There was a track fire up ahead. The conductor said they'd be delayed for several minutes. Fuck. She heard a screech that reminded her of Rico's angry playing that last night with him. Violent notes, bursting from his trumpet like punches. She began rocking, banging her back against the seat. A ratty looking young man with piercing sea-green eyes seated beside her asked if she needed a fix. Good God, do I look like a junkie? She snapped at him to *bugger off.*

"Bugger off?" He laughed. "If you weren't such a bitch," he said, "you might be happier."

She didn't know him. Yet the comment roused tears. She resisted the urge to tell this demon on her path that *he* was the one who deserved a tongue-lashing, not her. *He* was wrong for assuming *she* needed a fix. It'd been just that way with Artie. The garrl had so often done things to provoke me and then *I* was de bad guy.

At 14th Street she ran up the east side stairs just as she'd visualized, and she ran all the way. She climbed the steps short of breath, praying this would all work out. She'd find her journals right where she'd left them.

Her key to the building worked. The door to the flat was unlocked as Mr. Aponte always left the doors when he was working, and she walked right in. The smell of wet paint was stifling.

"Hello?" she called out, trying not to startle him.

"Si?" he answered from the living room. He sounded annoyed.

"Mr. Aponte, it's Serena. Just wanna check somethin' in de bedroom."

She walked into the room and there it was sitting in the middle of the floor. The antique box that housed the history of her life was still there! Aponte appeared in the doorway, glowering.

"You move out and you're out, mami. Possession is nine-tenths of the law."

Serena knelt down and ran her hand gingerly across the curve of the trunk's top. She undid its latches and opened it. She couldn't breathe. She felt nauseated.

"Where are de notebooks that were in here?"

"I don't know nothin' 'bout no notebooks," Aponte said.

"My fuckin' journals were in dere," her voice quavered. "What'd you do wif 'em?"

Aponte leaned back. "Ay mami, first of all you trespassin', okay? And did you kiss your husband wit that ugly mouth? Maybe that's why you not togetha no more."

Serena glared at him.

"Get outta here right now before I call la policia," he yelled.

"Rico wouldn't've taken my journals," she said through clenched teeth. "Vhere are they?"

"Ahora, loca," he barked. "I'm calling 911." His eyes darted between her and the door.

"Call Jesús fuckin' Cristo if you want to. I don't give a bloody shit. I'm not leavin' 'til you gimme my god-damned journals." She hugged herself and rubbed the gooseflesh on her arms.

Mr. Aponte marched out and across the hall to his own apartment. Shivering, Serena stared at the open trunk, memorizing it. She ran her hand along the top and sides and stroked the thing like it had a soul. It had been in her life since she was born and it was part of her father's family's history before that. It was well over one hundred fifty years old and had traveled with her great—great grandmother who'd been brought from Ireland to Bermuda to work as a bondservant. It had accompanied Serena from her father's house in St. Georges, to Aunt Annie's house in Paget, then to the Bronx where they settled, and finally here with Rico. Despite being dusty, it was in pristine condition. She'd never displayed it, always kept it tucked away in a closet. Now she noticed it was beautiful. *These old trunks are coveted antiques now'days. Aponte must want it to sell it,* she thought.

She didn't want to part with it, but how would she get it uptown? It wouldn't fit in a cab. She could ring Aunt Annie and Buddy, but she didn't want to inconvenience them more than she already had. And truthfully, despite the family history, the trunk didn't mean as much to her as the journals it had housed. It was nothing more than a box, really, while the journals had her very essence inside them. Her parents had discarded that trunk and just as easily discarded her. Perhaps it *was* time to shed this relic of her past. But it grieved her to part with the life history she'd documented. She ached for it, and she was angry with herself for having left the notebooks behind. If they were indeed lost to her now, she could shout at Aponte or whomever else all she wanted, but there was no one to blame but herself.

She didn't realize she was crying until tears hit the bottom of the trunk with a tapping sound that startled her. She smiled as it occurred to her that she was marking the trunk the way Mingus marked hydrants, as if to say: *I was here.*

She was still kneeling on the floor when Mrs. Aponte trotted into the room, followed by Mr. Aponte. The wife crossed her arms over her bosom. Her poufy, blonde hair was neatly coiffed, and her face fully made up, but it wasn't pretty the way Serena was accustomed to seeing it. It was gnarled in irritation.

"Did you yell at my husband?" Her y's sounded like j's. Did ju jell at my husband?

"Sorry. I thought he took my journals," Serena said.

"You crazy woman. No one wants your journals. Who you think you are? You can't come in here and yell at people, comprende?" Her voice got lower. She clenched her teeth. "I used to hear you scream at Rico and beat that little girl. You sounded so diabólico. I said to myself, 'if she *ever* try to yell at me that way—' Ay! Get out before I slap you!" She pointed toward the door.

Serena was stunned by the venom the woman had toward her.

"I said go," Mrs. Aponte screamed again. She flicked her arm to reemphasize her point to the door.

Serena looked at the trunk one last time before climbing up from the floor. She left the flat, and the building, and headed uptown.

It was raining, but she didn't avoid the water. She no longer felt cold. She could've stopped and bought a five dollar umbrella. She could have caught the train. Instead, she let herself get soaked. Her hair hung in dripping clumps that stuck to her neck and cheeks. Her jeans became sodden, heavy. Her feet sloshed inside her sneakers.

And at the same time, something inside her was changing, astonishingly, for the better. Her skin tingled, but it began to feel good— energized. Her head started to clear. She sensed that the rain was cleansing her, inside and out.

Serena did feel sad about everything, of course, but inexplicably, she was exhilarated as well. Her life with Rico was completely over and she didn't even have a record to remember its lovely details. It was the worst thing imaginable. So why was she relieved?

As her heart cracked open, the knot of anger and resentment tied around it began to loosen. She felt the newly released cord being pulled up and out of her. It was like shedding a layer and turning into something, *someone* new. She was suddenly lighter. Possibilities that hadn't existed before swirled in her mind. She imagined death must feel like this when the spirit sheds the body and moves toward the next dimension.

Serena realized she could look back, feel pained and depressed, and be swallowed by loss. Or she could look forward and feel giddy about what the next incarnation would be. She laughed, even as she began to cry. She was a barking lunatic, but it was brilliant—raw and out of control. She knew that even though she'd made mistakes and things hadn't turned out as she would've liked, she was lucky, because she was still alive. She was headed toward new chances. Maybe she'd do better next time, maybe she wouldn't. One thing she was certain of. This was her life now; she owned it completely. And she was glad.

Eight

Artie, 1990

When Artie, her papi and Mingus made it to Los Angeles, she met Rayana, who was a distant cousin on Papi's mother's side of the family. "Ray" owned a white stucco and red-tile Spanish bungalow on a street lined with Magnolia trees in North Inglewood. She was in her early thirties, divorced, no kids, a high school English teacher by day, and a sometime singer/songwriter by night. Artie wondered why she had no man. She seemed nice enough. And she was pretty—slim with smooth skin the color of Nutella, light brown eyes and copper colored dreadlocks. She dressed in floor-length skirts and sleeveless tops. The perfumed oils she used smelled like incense. She smiled a lot, but Artie could tell that she was lonely, and that where Rico was concerned, cousins or not, she had a plan. Artie wasn't sure, however, of Rayana's plans for *her*.

Ray told her to feel at home. She didn't. At home, she'd sneak through stuff. Not doing that took more restraint than Artie realized she had. She kept her room neat. Pitched in with household chores. She didn't complain about school, or anything else, and she always did as she was told.

One day, she accidentally dropped a Fiestaware pitcher full of grape juice on Rayana's kitchen floor. It broke and a purple river ran across the saltillo tile. Ray was busy on the other side of the room. As she whipped around, Artie curled into a ball on the floor and covered her head with her arms. When no beating came, Artie looked up and saw that Ray was standing above her with tears in her eyes.

"What are you doing, Artie?"

"I'm sorry. I'll clean it up if you'll just give me a chance. I'm really, really sorry."

Rayana moved toward the floor slowly.

"It's okay, baby." Her voice was tender. " I know it was an accident."

Rayana sat there and hugged Artie for a long time.

"Mija, maybe you should speak to someone," Papi said, a few days later.

"Who?" Artie asked.

"Someone who talks with kids about things they don't want to tell their parents."

"Why?"

They were riding in his beat-up BMW. She could smell smoked meat coming from a barbecue place in a strip mall on Centinella Avenue. Mingus stuck his head out the window.

Rico stared at the red light. "I saw you stick your camera under the bed. You used to love taking pictures. You don't laugh lately, mija. You barely speak to me. Maybe you have things you need to talk about?"

Artie shook her head. "I'm fine. I'm just trying to behave, so Rayana won't have a reason not to want me here."

Rico turned to her. He reached over and squeezed her shoulder.

"Angel, I wouldn't bring you someplace where you weren't welcome."

Artie nodded. Yeah okay, she thought. She looked out the window. What made him think he could control how another person was going to treat her? She had to do what she had to do to survive.

For weeks, Artie waited for Rayana to go off on her about something. Luckily, Ray turned out to be someone who apologized if she said or did anything unkind, which was rare. She ate tofu, meditated in her back yard, practiced yoga, and went to an integrated church full of performing artists who were vegetarians and wore dreadlocks. Some of the white people even had dreadlocks. Ray dragged Artie and Papi there on Sundays. He respected the musicians who played there.

One Sunday, Rayana got up during service. Artie thought she went to the bathroom, but the lady doing the announcements said Rayana's name and she appeared up on the platform in front of the whole church. She played her guitar and sang a song that she wrote. It was about letting go of despair and embracing joy.

Artie watched Papi staring up at Ray. His eyes were shiny with tears. When she was finished everyone clapped. Papi stood up and kept clapping. Artie got up, too, because he did.

"She's amazing, huh?" Papi said.

Ray was just okay in her opinion. Her mother was a more talented singer/songwriter, but Artie kept that to herself.

Rayana's tactics weren't lost on her. When she and Papi arrived, Artie cracked her bedroom door and spied on them at night. Rayana sat up late with Papi, sipping red wine from elegant glasses, and talking in the living room where he slept with Mingus. She wore skimpy tank tops and sexy smelling oils. She let Rico tell her how broken up he was over his split with Serena. She'd hike up her skirt, stretch out her long legs, and her pretty painted toenails while telling him how painful her divorce had been.

Artie saw Rico staring at Ray's legs while she told her story. Ray ran her locks through her fingers while Rico told his. They weren't listening to each other. Not really. It was like they were talking to themselves. It seemed to Artie that they were each trying to fill a hole that disappointment had dug into their lives.

Sure enough, she heard them in the living room that Sunday night after Ray sang at church. She had to cover her head with a pillow to drown out their sighs and moans. Ew.

"Again?" Ligon's voice pulls Artie back to the present. "You're hearing your father have sex in the living room, *again*?"

Artie nods. She looks up at the spinning fan.

Dr. Ligon exhales. "What was that like for you?"

"Repugnante," Artie says, chuckling. "I remember saying that word to myself. And thinking, man they should have the good sense to keep it quiet. Elch."

"Yes." Ligon nods. "Did you ever say that to them?"

"Of course not."

"Your father's behavior—repeatedly exposing you to his sex life—is disrespectful, and it's a form of sexual abuse."

Artie's eyes widen. "Really? He didn't do anything to me, like, touch me or anything."

"He didn't have to. Exposing a child to adult sexual behavior, the way he did, is considered abuse. It can lead to stress and depression. And if you never processed it, it can still be affecting you."

Artie looks down at the floor. "Well, it definitely made me uncomfortable."

"Like your mother, your father put his needs before yours. That narcissistic behavior results in negative feelings. But you didn't learn that you had a right to express those feelings. They weren't acknowledged or respected. It's not that your father was wrong to have sex. But he should have respected your boundaries. He should have gone into the bedroom and closed the door. Can you acknowledge that girl? Tell her she had a right to her feelings?"

"I guess."

"Good. Let her tell you what it was like for her."

"...I feel silly."

"You can write in your journal if you'd rather do that."

Artie nods. Her eyes drift to the fan.

Artie, 1990

The next night Papi and his stuff moved into the bedroom with Rayana, which was, thankfully, more sound proof than the living room. Artie worried that her side of the triangle had shifted to her disadvantage. "Please don't let Rayana get mean," she prayed. "I won't snoop. Or break things. I'll study hard. I won't talk back..."

The next morning, and the mornings after, Ray woke Artie for school with a kiss on her forehead. She made breakfast, tofu scramble, and a fruit smoothie, and she sang and danced around the kitchen. She played with Mingus and chatted with Artie in the mornings before driving to her Catholic middle school. There was always kiss and a hug before dropping her off.

This kind of affection was new to Artie. She accepted it, but reciprocating didn't come right away.

One day they were dropping Rico off at the airport. He had a gig in San Francisco and when he walked off through the gate at Southwest, Artie saw that Ray was biting her lip and her eyes were moist. She took Artie's hand. They began walking toward the exit. Artie slipped her arm around Ray's waist and squeezed her.

"You still have me and Mingus."

It was the first time she initiated a hug. Ray squeezed back, and kissed the top of Artie's head. They rode the down escalator with their arms around each other.

"You're my sweet angel, you know that?"

Artie smiled inside. "Papi calls me that."

"Well now you're *my* little angel, too."

Artie began to worry about *why* Ray felt this way. Was it because she'd been such a good girl since she'd moved there? She was only being good 'cause she was afraid not to be. Would Ray still adore her if she knew about all her flaws? Artie wondered if she could keep up this good act forever.

Nine

Artie 2004

Artie hangs out in the day room with a *Sunset* magazine looking at recipes she might try when she gets out. Roxy's mother is there. Roxy wears mascara and lip-gloss. Artie's never seen her in makeup before. She's got on her black yoga pants, but instead of the loose T-shirt she usually wears, she's in a tight tank top that shows off her toned arms and tiny waist.

Roxy's mother is blonde like her daughter. She's probably forty, but she looks younger. Her body is svelte and sculpted in a black T-shirt and jeans. She's been on her cell phone for most of the visit, though there's a sign stating that cell phones aren't allowed in the day room. Roxy sits beside her, staring out the window. "No, I'm not putting up with that shit from some unknown prick," her mother yells and steps into the hallway.

"They're telling me she should make the deal," Roxy says. "Movie business."

Artie knows that the woman is a producer notorious for hurling stuff at underlings. She moves from a chair in the corner and sits beside Roxy on the cowhide sofa while the mother carries on her call near the door.

"How're you doing?"

Roxy shrugs. "She gave me a candle."

Artie sees it sitting on the end table beside the sofa. They aren't allowed to have candles or matches in their rooms.

"You look nice, Rox," Artie says.

"Look, I'm used to it," Roxy says. She fluffs her hair. "Don't worry about me."

Dr. Ligon's office smells like lavender. Roxy has given the candle to Artie to give to her.

"If I dreamed that I killed my mother, do you think that's a bad sign?" Artie asks.

Dr. Ligon is perspiring profusely in her black maternity dress. She sits in the large recliner, leaning neither forward nor back, balancing like Humpty Dumpty before his fall.

"I think that's your subconscious working out your rage," she says. The dress sticks to her chest. She pulls the fabric away and shakes it. She breathes deeply. Her swollen feet, in flats, hover above the Persian rug.

Artie looks up. The fan spins slowly. Its remote control is on the coffee table next to the tissue box. Artie clicks it up to high.

"Thanks." Dr. Ligon smiles at her. "What do you remember about the dream?"

"I was washing my car in my driveway and I saw Serena walking toward my house. I took the bucket of water and threw it on her. Then I hit her in the head with the orange bucket—doink— again and again. But the she started melting, dissolving in front of me. So as I hit her, it wasn't satisfying, 'cause there was nothing solid to hit. She turned into liquid gold and flowed into the street, and down the storm drain."

Artie, 1990

"My biological mother is dead."

Artie told a girl in her Catholic middle school this lie in the outdoor lunch area after being asked if her mother had a job. The girl wore micro-braids with pink beads at the ends. She gasped, and put a hand to her twelve-year-old budding chest. Artie added, "Oh, but it's okay. My stepmother's awesome. And, yeah, she has a job. She teaches English at Santa Monica High."

"How'd your mom die?" The girl had tears in her voice.

Artie looked up at a plane passing through blue-sky. She took a breath. She thought of saying, *in a plane crash,* but that would lead to more questions. "Suicide."

The girl cringed. Her eyes filled with tears. She leapt up and hugged Artie.

It was wrong to make up this stuff. Artie knew that. She hoped Ray never found out, but the shitty truth was really no one's business, was it?

Rico had begun working in San Francisco a lot. An older buddy of his had retired from touring, moved out there from New York and found a weekend gig playing piano in a restaurant at the Four Seasons Hotel. He'd put together a quintet with a bassist, a drummer, saxophonist and a trumpet player, but the trumpeter also played with another group and wasn't available every weekend, so Rico started filling in. Soon he took over. While he was doing that, other musicians heard he was in town and he was getting asked to gig all around the city.

Rayana didn't seem to mind that Rico was away on the weekends. She focused her attention on Artie. After she worked on lesson plans for school on Saturday mornings the rest of the weekend was all about her *little angel.* She'd help Artie with homework and then they would do stuff around the house together. Ray grew red begonias and roses in her front and back yards. Somehow she made it fun to weed, water, fertilize, and prune them. She told Artie, "Our amazing Universe can start with a tiny seed and make it flourish into something spectacular." Ray also taught Artie a bit of yoga, and how to make vegetarian collard greens and corn bread in a skillet from scratch. Delicioso. And they'd go to church on Sunday mornings. Sometimes they went out to lunch afterwards, and then shopping, and to the movies.

They were leaving the mall one Sunday afternoon and Artie asked, "Do you wish my dad would stay home more?"

Rayana glanced at the shop windows as they headed toward the elevator.

"I miss him, but he's contributing to our home together. And I love having you and Mingus with me. You're my family now."

Rayana threw dinner parties to which she invited friends from church. She seasoned by instinct—pinch of this, a shake of that. Watching Ray dance around the kitchen as she cooked was soothing to Artie. It was a relief to be in a happy home. They made party favors for the guests the first time Kendall and his mom came. Small paper bags were stuffed with tiny toys picked out at the craft store: cool stickers, maple sugar candies, tea candles, crystals and small tubes of scented oils. The favors made it like a kids' party, but the only kids were Kendall and Artie. Artie watched the grown ups' faces light up as they opened their gifts. "There's a kid in everyone," Ray said with a wink. She stacked the stereo with albums. The first was Jessye Norman, the opera singer, performing arias. They listened via an outdoor speaker while sitting around a table in the backyard. The mélange of candles in the center made everyone's face glow. Mingus crouched underneath waiting for crumbs.

Kendall and Artie didn't talk much that first night. But they checked each other out. She looked up to see him gazing right at her a couple of times. She expected him to look away. He smiled and kept staring until *she* looked away. Later, she wished she hadn't been so shy.

At the second party in the backyard Kendall sat beside her. He was so cute in his white polo shirt and jeans. His skin was smooth and reddish-brown, no zits, and he smelled clean, like Dial soap. She couldn't stop smiling. It was still early. The sun hadn't set. A Santana album from the 70s was playing on Ray's stereo. The adults, about ten of them, drank red wine out of fancy glasses, and Artie and Kendall drank grape juice out of plastic cups.

He asked her about her mother. Where was she? Artie sensed he wanted her to explain. Ugh. She couldn't lie to him, because he knew Ray. "Serena's back in New York. She's a jazz singer," she said.

He nodded. "My mom's on a soap opera," he told her. "She's been on it since I was born. But she's a really good actress," he said. "She graduated from Yale Drama School. Only the best people go there. She could've done bigger parts, like movies and stuff, but she wanted a steady job, 'cause of me."

Artie looked at Kendall's mother, Vanessa, across the table chatting with Ray. She was light brown, with long hair and delicate features, similar to her own. They could have been related. Artie once heard that boys liked girls who looked like their mothers. She smiled to herself. Vanessa's diamond studs glittered in the sun as she leaned close to Rayana and spoke in her ear. They both laughed. Vanessa's laugh was loud. She had a big, confident presence, like Kendall. He'd just sat right down and started talking to her. She wouldn't have had the nerve to do that.

"Uh, so listen," Kendall said, "there's something I wanna show you in my mom's car."

He took Artie's hand, stood up and tugged on her gently. She couldn't imagine what he wanted to show her, but she didn't care. This *cute* boy wanted to hang out with *her. Ohmygod.*

His hand was soft and a little sweaty. It was the first time a boy had held her hand in *this* way. She was twelve. He was thirteen. He seemed comfortable, like he held girls' hands all the time. They walked out of the backyard and past Ray's Volvo. Artie had left her sandals under the table. The driveway burned her feet as they moved along the side of the house. He held onto her hand as he led her past the front lawn to the street, and to his mom's Mercedes. The Santana album was still playing in the back, and she could hear it all the way in the street. She let the high-pitched, passionate guitar seep inside her. The music felt like waves; it began to lull her nervousness into something else. Something better.

Kendall opened the passenger side for her, and then walked around to the driver's side. The hot leather hurt the backs of Artie's bare thighs, but she didn't complain, because when Kendall got in, he took her face in both hands and he kissed her on the mouth. His lips were plump and soft, like pillows, and his breath smelled sweet, like grape juice. He slipped his tongue into her mouth and swirled it around in a circle over and over for what seemed like an awfully long time. Her first real kiss. *Am I doing this right?* She listened to the music and felt his tongue gliding around hers. She wanted to enjoy it, though it was hard to stop worrying. Maybe he didn't like how she tasted. Someone might come looking for them. She thought she should open her eyes, but she didn't. She couldn't admit that she'd never kissed anyone before. She'd sound like a loser. So she pretended and followed his lead. She liked it. The music and the kissing made her feel sexy—a new feeling for her. Okay, maybe not *new*, exactly, but it was the first time she'd felt that way while actually making out with a real live boy.

He finally stopped and when he did he looked at her for a long time. She smiled, wondering what the hell he was thinking. Am I supposed to say something? Is he waiting for a compliment? A thank you? She peered out the window to see if anyone had come outside. A neighbor was walking his little dog, but didn't look in their direction. The song ended and another started right away. Artie could not think of one cool thing to say. Kendall wasn't speaking, either, just staring at her. Good god. She was sure his silence was a bad sign. *He thinks I'm stupid. He thinks I sucked. He can't wait to get out of this car.*

He sighed and scratched his chin. "You're really pretty," he said.

Artie exhaled. She felt like she might cry.

"Thanks," was all she could think to say. Artie wasn't sure what this whole thing meant. Was he her boyfriend now? She couldn't ask him that, but she had to say *something.*

"I'm kinda thirsty, how 'bout you?" She wiped some sweat from her forehead.

"I could go for some juice."

Back in Ray's kitchen they drank more grape juice. They mixed it with red wine that had been left in glasses on the counter. The adults were having dessert in the back yard.

They went into the den and watched hip-hop videos on *Yo MTV Raps.* Slick Rick. Dana Dane. Kendall didn't kiss her again, but he did take her hand in his and he massaged it gently. It felt somehow familiar even though she'd only met him once before and they hadn't held hands that time. She liked the way he touched her. She wanted to grin, but she thought she'd look ridiculous, so she tried not to smile. She *tried.*

When Kendall and Vanessa left, Artie was so excited she told Rayana *everything.*

Ray smiled. "That's really great, angel," she said. "But, just so you know, kissing is all you're allowed to do. You're twelve. If he does it again and tries to do anything more, you're to tell him not to, okay?"

"Yeah, okay." Artie had no intention of telling him any such thing. "Does this mean he's my boyfriend?"

"Well, I don't know." Rayana's lips were pinched in a tight smile. "Did he say he wanted you to be his girlfriend?"

"No. But he said I was pretty. And he gave me his phone number and said to call him anytime."

"Do you *want* to be his girlfriend, Artie?"

Artie hadn't considered what *she* wanted. She assumed this was totally Kendall's call.

"I don't know. Kind of, I guess... Yes!"

Rayana laughed. "Wait and see what happens. I think you should see him at least a few more times before you make that kind of commitment."

Artie thought that was a smart idea. "Yeah, you're right," she said. "See how it goes. When's the next dinner party?"

"We'll see," Ray said.

Artie went to bed grinning, imagining future kisses.

"No, I'm not okay with it, Rico. You were supposed to be on your way home by now."

She woke to Ray yelling on the phone in the next room. Her father had driven up to San Francisco. He'd said he'd be home sometime that night.

"Because I miss you." Ray's voice was shrill. "What the hell? Am I in this relationship by myself? ...Then try harder to find work down here!"

Artie knew that Rayana's suggestion hadn't gone over well. Rico didn't tolerate being told what to do.

"So we can be a family. *That's* what you promised... Then at least bring your ass home when you say you're going to. I hate this, Rico. ... Hello?!"

Ray slammed the phone down and started to cry. Artie jumped out of bed, ran into the other room and hugged her.

"Please don't cry. It'll be okay."

She had a sinking feeling that it would *not*, in fact, be okay. She hoped her father wasn't going to mess this up.

Ten

Serena, 1990

Serena spent a lot of time gazing out porthole window, dreaming of what the next wave of her life would be. She expected Rico to send divorce papers. Despite the pain, the closure would be good. But weeks went by and none arrived. She had to create closure in her own way.

She could *feel* Rico when she needed to. There was an energy between them, a frequency she could tap into. One day she closed her eyes, and met him in her mind. She sat perfectly still, breathed, and saw herself in a room face to face with him. "I release you and I vish you vell," she said. She imagined his eyes glistening as he looked at her.

"Grief knows to transform itself," he said. "Sit with it long enough, and eventually the pain becomes appreciation for having had the person in your life while you did."

He'd said those words to her years earlier. He lost his father and through his own grief, made this discovery. She needed to believe that he remembered his own wise words.

Since the split, she'd been craving a closer connection with God. Her journals had always been her way to connect, but after losing them, she stopped. Instead she began hanging out at East West Books on Fifth Avenue and reading spiritual self-help guides. Through meditation, she came to believe that her lesson was to forgive her mother for giving her away. But she couldn't. Her resistance, she concluded, was what drew to her a child she couldn't love. God wanted Serena to find compassion for herself, which would ultimately help her find it for her own mother. She did have compassion for herself. The inability to bond with her daughter wasn't something she had control over. But choosing to pass for white rather than keep her, as her mother did, that was something that could have been different. Serena would never forgive the woman. She did hope Artie would forgive her one day, even if she knew it wasn't likely.

Being out of Rico's shadow turned out to be a good thing. He was the "star," in the relationship, the brilliant composer and player. She'd believed in her own talent, but he was more successful. He was also comfortable with things revolving around him, and that, she realized, made her feel small. Now she was expanding, spreading her wings.

First thing she did was audition all over the city at piano bars. She got a gig playing at the Gramercy Park Hotel four nights a week. She had to do jazz standards; that was their mandate, but what she really wanted to do was her own material. While she had that income and her expenses were low at Aunt Annie's, she used her time off to sit at her old piano in the living room and re-work several songs she'd written. She also composed a few new ones and she soon had what she felt were ten first-rate compositions of her own. She was in a creative flow and it took just a few weeks. The songs were contemporary jazz and she was satisfied that they were sexy and had a distinct style. She got a kid in her neighborhood with a mini studio to help her record them. Then she began ringing up contacts in the music business who'd slipped her their cards during the past weeks at the piano bar.

Jamie L'Heureux was the first to ring her back.

A white boy about a decade younger than Serena, he was a jazz pianist and singer whose music video she'd recorded and watched over and over when no one was looking. Filmed in black and white, he was lit like a screen star from the 40s. His face had the symmetry of a classical Greek sculpture. His dark eyes flirted with the camera, and he sang with gravel in his voice like an old black man who'd lived a lot of life.

The song was about a passion that endured even death. Critics gushed about the wisdom and sophistication of his compositions. One opined that L'Heureux embodied the reincarnated soul of an artist who'd never received recognition and came back in a marketable package.

Serena liked his music, but in her estimation Jamie L'Heureux was no better than many less successful people of color doing similar work. What brought his success, she believed, was what made her rewind that video over and over. Shag appeal. With his thick black hair, dark eyes, and fit body, he looked something like John Kennedy, Jr. Once the video aired, women went mad. Women who didn't give a flip about jazz bought his CDs. He appealed to all ethnicities, age groups, and socioeconomic classes—old, young, rich, poor, smart, dumb and everyone in between loved this shagalicious white boy. Serena read an interview where he lamented, "Had so much ass shoved in my face, kinda made me nervous. Ma baby back home in Louisiana wished me well, and dumped me."

He was a guest at the hotel when he saw Serena perform. After her set, he followed her to a table where she took her break. He sat down and said, "Dawlin' you can really *sing*." His eyes gleamed and scanned her body, lingering a moment on her bare calves. "And may I jus' say, ya ain't hard to look at neither." He arched an eyebrow.

"Thanks." She yawned, sipped her pinot noir and looked past him. Hard as she found it not to stare, she didn't. She knew better than to mess with him.

He scratched the side of his face. "Why'ont chu come on up to my room, dawlin'. And I'll buy ya a bottle a the best wine dey got in this dump."

Serena snorted. "Very generous of you, but dis'll do fine." She took another sip.

"Seriously?"

"Sorry, Ace."

"Bless your heart," he laughed. "Am I losin' my mojo, or whut?"

"Look, I've only just un-tied de knot. Fourteen years. Not in de place to be on de skank."

"On the skank?"

"No interest in a one night stand," she said.

"A'ight," he nodded. "Damn, girl. You's married that long? Don't look near old enough."

"Vell, I am," she said, winking.

"Know whut? Honestly, I ain't fittin' to get laid no way. Been wit so many chicks this past year, almost feel like a ho."

"Almost?" Serena laughed. "You're notorious for it."

He shrugged. "Don' matter. I'm a healthy twenty-five-year-old man, dawlin'. Ain't no different from most dudes. Just get more offers. But I 'preciate companionship, too, y'know?"

Dubious, Serena lowered her chin and offered a heavy-lidded look.

He laughed. "I ain't lyin'. Wouldn't mind just hangin', talking witchu. If tha's a'ight."

So they did. It always took Serena a few hours to come down after playing and Aunt Annie and Buddy were usually asleep by the time she got home. It'd be nice to have someone to unwind with.

He let her pick a bottle of wine from the bar and they went out, crunched across the gravel, and sat on a bench in Gramercy Park. It's a private park, but hotel guests have access to the key. It was fragrant that night, flowerbeds blooming nearby. Serena was surprised to find that he wasn't a mere pretty face or a dilettante. He knew his stuff and had great taste for someone so young. They both loved Charles Migus's work as a composer and they talked about getting together next time he was in the city and going down to see the Mingus Big Band.

"Aw, man," he said. "You got no idea how much I'd be up for that. A'int met no one pretty's you who really gets it 'bout Mingus's composing." He sighed and looked off sadly.

Serena studied him a moment. "Read about you and ya garrl. You *like* bein' in a relationship, don't you?"

He met her eyes for a moment, before looking away again. He shrugged.

"I can tell. Why don't you try and get her back?" Serena stared at his profile. Goodness. She licked her lips.

"Ondine couldn't handle all de women, y'know? I mean, some a these chicks are crazy aggressive. And, much as I love her," he hung his head, "was hard to turn some of it down." He put his palm inside his shirt and rested it over his heart.

Serena nodded. "Guess I can understand dat. Despite the *wisdom and sophistication* in your songwriting," she teased, "y'are tvenny-five."

"Girl, you mockin' me?"

"A bit. Not judging, though. What tvenny-five-year-old bye *wouldn't* have a hard time stayin' faithful under de circumstances?"

"Know'm'sayin'? Took Ondine to see The Mingus Big Band when she was here with me few months back," he said.

"And? Did she like it?"

"Bless her heart, she was expecting to see Charles Mingus."

Serena chuckled. "That's brilliant. She'd no idea who he was, had she?"

"That's my girl, but she's a Kenny G. fan." He shook his head.

Serena laughed again. "Oh, stop. Kenny G.'s great at what he does."

"May be true, dawlin' but whut he does ain't *jazz.*"

She shrugged. "I don't completely disagree, but I won't be part of de Kenny G. bashin' crowd. People seem to be buying it. And your Ondine has a right to her own taste. Don't know if you've noticed, but there aren't too many girls your age buying jezz records."

"Shiiit, baby, dey buy *mine*," he laughed and tapped her on the back.

His arrogance was stunning. Entertaining.

"It's a'ight," he continued, grinning. "That ain't everything. Ondine's a good woman." He put his palm back on his chest.

Didn't take much to see through his flimsy mask. Lonely boy. She was about to offer another piece of advice when they saw a flash go off. Repeatedly. Someone outside the gate was shooting pictures of them. Jamie stood up.

"Sorry 'bout that. I'm jus' a minor celebrity, but guess my picture's worth sumptin' to somebody."

"How do'ya know it's not *me* they're photographin', Ace?"

He answered with no more than a smile and they left the park. He handed her cab fare and his card and said he hoped she'd stay in touch.

They *didn't* stay in touch, at least not immediately. However, two days later their picture made Page Six in *The Post*. This brought a barrage of people in to see her at the bar. And she got a raise. Jamie L'Heureux had been lucky for Serena and she appreciated him immensely, though they hadn't spoken since that night.

When he returned Serena's call, he sounded genuinely delighted to hear her voice. Said he was in town, staying at The Plaza.

"I've recorded some stuff I'd really like to get your opinion on," she said. "If you'd have time to listen to it." She held her breath and hoped he wouldn't blow her off.

"I'm playin' the Blue Note this evenin' dawlin'," he said. "I'mma put chu on the list."

"I haveta work at de hotel tonight. Could we meet after?"

He hesitated. "My baby's here. We got back together, and a late night thing ain't gon' work, but we could meet tomorrow at The Plaza. Dey got this high tea thing in the afternoon. Wanna meet 'round one?"

"...Could we do it at three?" She wasn't checking for Jamie that way, but if meeting in the daytime made his girlfriend feel more secure, fine. *High* tea at one in the afternoon, though? Blasphemy. Why do Americans do things like that?

"You can't meet no earlier?" he asked.

Serena exhaled. She knew she seemed unreasonable. "Look, how 'bout I drop de tape off, Ace, and you call me if you like it. Ya don't call, I'll understand, okay?"

"I'd like to see ya dawlin', it's just, y'know how it is. Yeah, leave it at the desk today if ya can."

Serena dropped the tape off an hour later. By the time she arrived back at Aunt Annie's he'd already left a message on the answering machine.

"Girl, where y'at?! Call in sick and get to the Blue Note by ten pm."

She reached him at the hotel. "I can't call in sick. It's too late. I'd need someone to cover for me."

"If you get yo' behind to da Blue Note by ten you gon' be able to quit that job, Serena. Be prepared to play three a your tunes and look your finest, girl, y'hear?"

She was stunned. "Really?"

"See ya later."

She got the girl who played on different nights, to take her shift at the piano bar. She wasn't trying to get fired if Jamie was just toying with her. His first set was at nine pm. When she walked in at five to ten he was still at the piano. When he finished his last song, he introduced her and she took over as an impromptu fill-in between sets. People were paying their tabs and leaving, but once they heard her and got a look at her, most sat right back down. Three songs later, her life had changed.

Jamie had already given the tape to the A & R guy at his label. His name was Benny Buchanan and he was there at the Blue Note for her performance too. He trembled, ebullient, as he told Serena she was the "real frickin' deal." He was practically dancing a jig and said he wanted to sign her, and that Jamie wanted to produce the album. "Are you interested?" he asked.

She laughed. Of course she was.

After Jamie's second set they hung around until past one in the morning chatting about the future. Even the girlfriend was excited. Serena liked Ondine. It was her suggestion that since they were going to do an album together, Serena should open for Jamie on tour. He had an upcoming appearance at The San Francisco Jazz Festival at the Masonic Auditorium on Nob Hill. Serena had once been there as a spectator watching Rico. The idea of being on the stage herself lit her up inside.

Eleven

Serena, 1990

Jamie's schedule was too busy to get him and Serena into the studio before the San Francisco Jazz Festival came up, but the label had signed her and he began introducing her to musicians he wanted to accompany her on the album. She received a small advance and another sum for her publishing, but she wasn't ready to quit singing at the Gramercy Park Hotel just yet. Impressed by her record deal, her boss decided to let her perform original material even though they usually stuck to standards. Her fan base began to grow. Ben Buchanan created such a buzz about Serena it sent New Yorkers flocking to the humble piano bar to see her.

By the time Serena opened for Jamie at the Masonic Auditorium, word of mouth had spread in the jazz world. She knew the audience was sizing her up—who's this newcomer? But her rich voice, with its alto to soprano range went to work immediately, soothing the skepticism. She took her crowd on a journey. As they traveled step by step with her, she felt the alchemy at work. Reservation was becoming appreciation. When she left the piano to stand in the spotlight, dazzling in her sparkly red dress, there was such anticipation that the applause came before she began her next song. Ah—it was *on* now. She batted long lashes and milked each morsel of humor, irony and breathless desire in her compositions. Perfect pitch, *and* she could deliver a song from the heart.

She saw silhouettes of heads bobbing, fingers snapping with her swing. They were hers. Bringing her closing ballad to an end, she sang a note in a powerful whisper that lasted several measures, fading slowly, until there was silence; not a cough, rustle, nor breath from the audience. Several seconds elapsed and then… a collective sigh, followed by bodies rising from seats, feet hitting the floor, culminating in a thunderous ovation lasting several minutes. Serena's joy could not have been more satisfying.

The house lights rose as she continued to bow. Looking out, she thought she saw Rico in the crowd. She dismissed it. What were the chances? Then, to her great surprise, she saw her Aunt Annie and Buddy in the front row. Both hated to fly, but there they were, brimming with pride.

Backstage, she hugged Annie. She'd wanted to give this very experience to her Aunt since she was a little girl.

"So proud of you, my baby." Annie squeezed her.

"Best night of my life, Auntie. They'll hear about me in Bermy when my album comes out, won't they? They'll be sorry."

"Oh, Ree, darling, why think of such things?" Annie touched Serena's cheek. "Be happy, love. Enjoy your night."

"Oh, I am. My tide is finally comin' in."

The next night, Serena, Jamie, Ondine, Annie and Buddy had dinner at their hotel. They were staying at The Four Seasons.

Serena recognized the sound of Rico's horn before she saw his face. When she looked up to find her ex in a cheesy house band in a hotel dining room she had to resist the urge to gloat. He was the celebrity during the marriage. She was stuck in a tenement building with a whining kid while he shined in the world, though not half as brightly as she was shining now. Horrible thought, wasn't it? All that spiritual work unraveled in an instant. This was not at all how she'd expected to feel upon seeing her beloved again, but she was viewing him with new eyes and the truth was, he didn't look as good as she remembered. She didn't realize she was staring too long until Annie and Buddy turned to look.

"You all right?" Buddy asked.

Annie squeezed her arm.

"I'm fine," Serena smiled.

Jamie glanced over in Rico's direction, then back at Serena. "Wha's goin' on?"

Serena shook her head. "Let's just finish our meal and enjoy it, okay?"

They kept eating. Serena tried to stop staring at Rico. Ondine quipped about how Jamie was going to have to open for Serena soon. He frowned at her before catching himself and smiling. "Baby's got jokes, huh? A'ight then. That happens, you won't mind me cuttin' your allowance, right?"

Ondine didn't answer. She stared at her plate for the rest of the meal without another word.

Serena wrote her room number on a matchbook and had the waiter slip it to Rico. He called her late that night on the hotel's house phone. When he arrived at her door she greeted him with folded arms.

"What happened to my journals?" She tried to look him in the eye, but he pushed past her without answering. He sat down on the love seat by the window across from the bed. She sat at the foot of the bed and faced him. He leaned forward, resting his elbows on his thighs.

"How you doin', Serena?"

He was like a TV cop, interrogating her. She stared at him and crossed her legs. Wasn't it obvious how she was doing? Better than he was.

He exhaled heavily. She watched him, keeping his cool, as if counting to ten before exploding.

Serena wasn't going to get emotional. She would not get caught back up in what she had with Rico. Life was better now.

The silence went on too long. She got up and poured a glass of wine from a bottle she had delivered to the room.

"Want some?"

He shook his head. She sipped, sat back down and waited. Rico turned away from her. Serena saw that the glow that used to shine through his eyes and smile was gone. He seemed diminished. Had their break up done that?

"I wanted to tell you that I'm sorry," he said. "You know I never believed in violence... toward women, or anyone else. I snapped in the moment. And I'm sorry for hurting you."

There was silence again. Serena wasn't thinking about that slap. Hadn't thought of it in ages.

"I'd *really* like to know what happened to my journals, Rico."

He tilted his head back, recoiling. His eyes widened, then he glared at her.

"*That's* what you wanna know about?"

She was stoic.

"Are you kidding me? *That's* all you care about?" he yelled.

"You wanna tell me how she is, Rico, go ahead. But don't try to manipulate me."

He couldn't hide the shock in his eyes. Serena had no confidence in the past. When she'd confronted him previously, it had been with a measure of insecurity that was gone now.

He stood and walked out of the room.

She sat there and wondered if she should have said or done something differently. Serena *wanted* to connect with him in some way—even if only to have real closure. She'd communicated honestly, though, so she decided not to second-guess it. Maybe they weren't supposed to connect. Maybe it was too soon. If Rico didn't approve of her, so what? She didn't need his bloody approval anymore.

Although she was too anxious to sleep, she removed her clothes and makeup and got into bed anyway. She flipped through the TV channels looking for the BBC. British comedies always cheered her up, but dammit, she couldn't find one. She scratched her scalp. Despite her newfound bravado, there was a part of her that missed the companionship from the old life, when it was working. The conflicting emotions confused her. She loved her new life, but she missed Rico. She didn't want him back, but she wanted to be with him. What sense did that make? She wished she could fall asleep. The next day she'd have activities to distract her. Tonight, her mind was spinning. Was she doomed to be alone? Would she ever find love again? She didn't want to despair. If she could keep from *feeling*, then she could keep on with her progress and things would continue moving forward. Her focus and meditation were paying off. Her dreams were finally manifesting. Sadness could derail them. She wouldn't have that.

Someone rapped on the door. Bugger. *What if it's him? I look like hell nahw.* Her makeup was off and her eyes were wet, but she covered up in the fluffy Four Seasons robe and opened the door anyway. A white-coated waiter stood beside a cart.

She looked past him down hall. "I didn't order room service."

"It was sent as a gift, ma'am," he said.

She moved out of the way as he pushed the cart inside. Rico's raspy voice turned her around.

"'Member when I used to come home late and wake you and Artie up with ice cream?" he asked as he walked in.

She wiped her face and smiled.

The waiter sat the tray on the table and lifted the silver cover up. Two bowls of chocolate ice cream with a tray of hot caramel, whipped topping, and chopped nuts on the side. The waiter nodded to Rico and left.

"Yes. You'd wake us," Serena said, "Then we'd all sit in the kitchen and eat and you'd tell us who'd been at de show and brag 'bout how brilliantly you'd played. Then after a few minutes you'd say, 'Okay, well g'night now,' and you'd get up and go to bed. We'd be awake for hours, sometimes for de rest of de night."

Rico shrugged and sat down. She watched him dig into the bowl. Then she sat beside him, their thighs touching. She was close enough to breathe him in. How she'd missed that. It wasn't cologne; it was his *real* scent that she found so delicious. She could lick him all over.

"I vas cravin' ice cream," she said, wetting her lips. "How'd you know?"

"Just had a feeling." He didn't look up from the bowl. "You wanted to know about your stuff and we'll get to that, but first I just wanna say that," he cleared his throat, "she knows you don't want her, but it would help if she knew you at least thought of her sometimes."

Serena felt ugly. Leaving another person in such pain made her hideous. It wasn't on purpose, but he wouldn't understand that. No one could understand something so unnatural. She wished she could fake it. That would be the kind thing to do, but Serena couldn't be inauthentic with Rico.

She nodded. There was still love in his eyes, despite her defect. They both had them. She was a drug Rico wanted, though he knew he shouldn't indulge. She saw that he couldn't stop his heart from needing her anymore than she could force hers to do what it refused.

He finished the ice cream and fiddled with the spoon, scrapping the last drops from the bottom of the dish.

"They're gone, Serena. I had a moment and… they're all gone." His tone was matter of fact.

"What happened to them?"

"Does it make a difference? They don't exist anymore."

She didn't move. A wave of anger rose in her chest. Her neck and cheeks burned. She clenched her teeth and let it pass on through. What would she gain by reacting? It was interesting to learn that Rico could be driven to acts of madness—*meanness*, too. Made her somehow less of an ogre.

Finally she sighed. He looked at her and waited for her to say something. She kept silent.

"Well, congratulations," he said. "All that's happening for you must feel good."

He wasn't happy for her. She knew that tone. She'd had it herself in the past.

"It does," she said.

"Good."

"And how do you feel—about *your* situation?" she asked.

He smiled. "I'm doing okay. The tide's been out, as you would say, but it's coming in again."

"Is it? Hm. Not so easy doin' your life's work when dere's a kid makin' demands on you, ay?"

"She isn't a problem, Serena. She's great."

"What *is* de problem, den?" It was unkind to press him, but that didn't stop her.

"What do you mean?"

"Why're you doin' dis silly gig? It's beneath you." Soon as the words were out she regretted them.

"Think so?" He shrugged. Smiled. "I don't see it that way. Starting over out here is a challenge, but I love that. I'm down to play here as much as anywhere I've been in the world. And you know me, mami, happy to make dinero for what I'd do for free. It's not about flossin', Serena. It's about loving the journey whether the tide is in or out."

Hm. Good for him. There *was* a bit of the man she used to admire in there. She viewed success differently, though. She wanted the kind that was big and obvious and came with fat checks and financial security. She could appreciate the soulful artist thing, but he could keep that rubbish. She'd take the money.

"Guess we're opposites," she said.

He looked at her with eyes that were lifetimes deep. He didn't have to say anything, and it didn't make sense, but the *way* he looked at her told her he wasn't leaving that night. When she first saw that expression, ages ago, she knew he loved her, because it was the same look he had when he played his best. He'd take the trumpet from his lips and his whole being would shine with gratitude. Everything was right with the world.

Serena was grateful that he saw through her bitchiness. She wondered how he did, and why. She still felt something for Rico, but she wasn't in love the way she had been. She was in a liminal state, disconnecting, leaving the world she'd had and moving into a new one where he didn't exist. But it was a process, not an event, and the boundaries of each world weren't defined, though they were separate. She was pleased he'd come back to the room and happy they'd spend the night together. But she was grateful that he *hadn't* looked at her that way when she'd wanted him to, before she left, because then she'd still be committed to him; she wasn't any longer, and she was grateful for that too.

Twelve

Artie, 1990

Artie watched Rico walk through the door the evening he returned from San Francisco. Mingus's tail wagged and his nails clicked toward his master on the hardwood floor. As Rayana hugged Rico, Mingus pushed his head between them. His nose began bumping repeatedly into Rico's body and he made whimpering sounds he didn't usually make.

"Okay, boy," Rico said. "Basta. Enough." Mingus would not stop sniffing. Rico moved to hug Artie, but she smelled it, too, and pulled away from him. It wasn't just Serena's perfume, a spicy fragrance called Opium that Rico reeked of; it was also her natural scent. Artie hadn't smelled it since Rico gave the clothes her mother left in the apartment to the Salvation Army. She glared at him. Mingus continued sniffing, whining.

"No!" He tried to push the dogs face away with his hand. "Go to your bed."

Mingus would not move. Rayana stood looking at the three of them. Rico walked into the kitchen. Mingus and his nose followed.

"Why's he doing that?" Rayana asked, watching from the foyer.

"I don't know," Rico said. "He smells something. He's a dog."

Mingus kept sniffing and whining. It was like he was weeping. Rico grabbed his Kirin from the refrigerator.

Artie stood in the kitchen doorway. "I know why," she said. She looked her father in the eye before walking away. She went to her room and locked her door.

A few minutes later she heard Rico playing in the detached garage. He blew wildly. Sounded like shrieking. Like someone being attacked. But he was the bad guy. What was he wailing about?

Artie didn't come out of her room for the rest of the night. She didn't want to see Rayana. She wasn't going to be the one to tell her what was going on.

Rico knocked on her door later. "Mija? You have to eat something."

"Go back to San Francisco," Artie yelled.

"Open the door, Artie."

"No. You stink."

She heard his body rest against the wall. After a minute, his footsteps trailed away. She hugged her pillow. If he was seeing her mother and he didn't want to let her in on it, he should have at least been smart enough not to come home *reeking* of her. Or was that on purpose? Did he *want* me to know? Did he want Rayana to know?

She hated Rico that night. Why did he always underestimate her ability to figure things out? She used to think he was trying to protect her, but if that's what he was doing, he sucked at it.

When Rayana was shouting at Rico on the phone the night before, Artie could hear how she wanted him to *want* to come home to her. That he wasn't going to make it that night wasn't really what bothered Ray. It was that he didn't miss her enough to *need* to come home.

Serena had that same sound the night Rico made her miss her party. Maybe some of her mother's meanness was provoked by his behavior. Not that it excused her, but would Serena have been as evil that night if Rico had just come home when he was supposed to?

Artie heard muffled shouting coming from Rayana and Rico's

bedroom that night. And then Rayana sobbed. Much like the way Serena sobbed the night before she left them. But Ray hadn't done anything mean. She'd done nothing but love them. Artie covered her ears. She wanted to hurt Rico. She would have slapped him if she could.

The next morning, when she got up, Rico was gone. Rayana's eyelids were swollen into balls as puffy as the vegan macaroons she'd served at her dinner party. She hadn't dressed or taken a shower. It was obvious she wasn't going to work. She sat in the sunny kitchen nook, staring out the window into her back garden.

"Where is he?" Artie asked.

Ray shook her head. The shimmer in her light brown eyes was gone. Dulled, like two dirty puddles.

"He tried to tell me he wasn't over her; that he wasn't ready for a new relationship. My own fault for not listening," she said, the puddles leaking down her face. "Maybe I'm meant to be alone."

Artie couldn't think of the right words. She wanted to say that her father was a fucking bicho. A dick. But Rayana thought she was an angel and angels didn't say such things. She considered saying what they'd say at church: *Be positive. Don't affirm negative things*, but that seemed more irritating than soothing.

Instead, Artie hugged her. She squeezed as tight as she could. She tried to memorize everything about her sweet Rayana, because she knew that even though they loved each other, soon they wouldn't be together anymore.

It was a warm October day in LA. Artie sat in the sun and ate lunch alone at school. Her friend with the pink beads and braids was absent that day. Artie looked inside her binder at the note where Kendall had written his number. She'd stapled it there so she wouldn't lose it. His handwriting was neat. She wished they were in the same school. Kendall was the only person she wanted to talk with about Rayana, Rico and her mother. She couldn't be sure if she could trust him, but she thought it might be possible.

Except it wasn't. Rico decided to leave Los Angeles. They were moving to San Francisco. Artie had no say. And even though she would have preferred to stay with Rayana so they could cook and garden and throw fun dinner parties, that wasn't an option. With few words, Rico packed their stuff and their dog into the old BMW 2002, and they hit the 5 freeway.

"Papi's sorry for uprooting you again, mija." Rico reached over and caressed her shoulder.

Artie looked straight through the window. She said nothing.

"You okay?" he asked.

She didn't answer.

"Mija, I'm speaking to you."

"No," she snapped. Artie was done making things easier for Rico. He could suffer the ugly truth like everyone else had to.

Thirteen

Artie, 2004

Artie stares at Dr. Ligon and worries that something's wrong with her. Her eyes are bloodshot. Mascara is flaked above her cheekbones. Her hair looks greasy, pulled back into a sloppy bun. The white maternity dress she wears is a gauzy V-neck bearing cleavage and far more casual than her usual professional attire. She leans forward. Her swollen feet are flat on the floor. Her hand rubs circles on her protruding belly.

"Hey, should we talk about *you* today, Dr. Ligon?"

Ligon touches her lips with two fingers, and her eyes drift to the ceiling. She doesn't move for a moment. Finally, she exhales and shakes her head.

"That's not appropriate. I apologize if my appearance is distracting you."

"Is the baby kicking?" Artie asks.

Ligon shakes her head again. Her eyes water. "She's not."

Artie hopes it's just the hormones, but it seems like more than that. Strange being unable to express the concern she'd offer anyone else who looked so sad.

Dr. Ligon straightens up. "You talked a bit about Rayana and the New-Age church she took you to. Did the spiritual beliefs influence your reaction to things?"

"Hm," Artie says. "Not enough to matter. I thought most everything, including that stuff, was bullshit."

Artie, 1990

The headlights sliced through fog as the BMW 2002 chugged up a hill in Berkeley and stopped in front of a row house building. Rico peered out the window. "Like it? Lucked up and got us a sublet from a buddy who's giggin' in Europe."

Artie squinted through the glass. It kind of reminded her of brownstones back east the way the building was attached to the others, but this one was white and made of wood.

"You rented a place already?" she asked.

Without answering, he got out of the car and opened the trunk. Mingus whimpered. Artie wondered if Rico had been planning to leave Rayana all along. She threw open her door and shoved the seat forward so Mingus could climb out of the back. She took his leash and let him pee on the grass while Rico unloaded their stuff.

"I liked Rayana's house better than this bullshit," she said. "It's fuckin' freezing here."

Rico looked up from the trunk. "Artie, no me hables de que. I know you're upset, but watch your mouth."

"What are you gonna do, hit me, like your *puta*?"

"Don't test me, little girl, cause I can't promise you I *won't*."

She didn't recognize his tone. She looked at the ground and felt tears coming.

"It's warm inside," he said. "C'mon, I'll make us some rice."

"I hate how you make rice. It's not even healthy," she said, crying. "Rayana makes *brown* rice. It has fiber."

Rico put Artie's suitcase on the sidewalk and rubbed his face with his hands. He shook his head. It seemed like he was about to say something, but he didn't. He walked toward the house. Mingus pulled on his leash to follow, and tugged Artie with him.

He enrolled her in public school in Berkeley and drove her there the first day. She thought it looked weird. Makeshift. It wasn't even a real building. Just a bunch of trailers on a hill. Even the bathroom was in a trailer. But she liked being in the classrooms. The kids were multi-racial and multi-cultural, closer to what she was used to back at P.S. 41 in The Village. In L.A., her Catholic middle school was all black and Latino and she couldn't be herself, because she wasn't black enough or Latina enough for the other kids. She tried to fit in, by speaking and behaving more like whomever she was with. Kids were friendlier when she acted and spoke more like them, less like herself. In Berkeley the kids were from disparate cultures. There was no pressure to "act" like any one thing.

On Artie's first day, two pretty girls waved her over during lunch, which was in the classroom trailer because it was drizzling outside. The girls looked alike and they both looked a lot like Artie: caramel colored, with long, dark hair and big dark eyes.

"What *are* you?" Sushama wanted to know. She said she was black and East Indian; *Blindian*, she called it.

Alessandra was Brazilian. "Back in Brazil," she said, "if you're not *black*, black, you're white. But white kids called me names when I got here."

Artie suspected that they liked her because she resembled them. Shallow, she thought, but at least she had someone to sit with. And friendships had to start somewhere.

On a Friday night, when Rico was working and left Artie and Mingus alone, she got up the courage to call Kendall. She worried about it for days. *What if he's indifferent? Or what if he doesn't want to speak with me at all?* She'd been imagining what it would be like to kiss him again, and to have him hold her hand the way he had. She remembered how his breath smelled fruity and that he'd tasted like grape juice. Sitting cross-legged at the end of her bed, the phone was in her lap. She hoped he'd be glad to hear from her.

His mother answered. Artie told Vanessa who it was.

"Oh my goodness, baby. Are you all right?"

"Yeah. I miss L.A., though. And Rayana."

"Artie, she misses *you*. Ray misses you *very much*."

Something in Vanessa's voice said she was worried about Rayana. This worried Artie. She hadn't called Ray. It was too sad. She didn't want to make her feel worse. But she planned to reach out to her soon.

"Kendall's in his room, playing some video game," Vanessa said. "Hold on, baby. KENDALL," she yelled, "Artie's calling from up north."

He picked up immediately.

"How you doin', beautiful?"

Artie exhaled. Whew. She grinned.

"Hangin' in there. Things are okay, I guess." She hoped he didn't notice the goofiness in her voice. He called her *beautiful*. Ay ay ay!

"Cool beans. Hold on a second, can you?"

"Yeah."

Artie was a tad miffed that he was putting her on hold, but also a little thankful for a moment to calm down. She felt butterflies in her stomach and they were flapping their wings like mad. She thought of this boy *all the time*. She liked that he said, "cool beans," instead of just "cool." That was cute. *He* was cute. Then she heard the song. And Kendall came back on the line.

"Recognize that?"

"Yes," Artie smiled.

It was the Santana song that was playing when they kissed in L.A.

"That's hot, right? That's some slammin' shit right there. Rayana made me a tape. Been playin' it every day. And I think of you."

"For real?" Artie giggled. *Omigod.*

"Damn, you got the cutest laugh."

"Thanks." She felt herself blush. She hoped she wouldn't say something dorky and mess this up.

"I'm taking saxophone lessons. I'mma learn to play this song for you."

He wanted to play for her? Her heart beat faster. She tingled in private places. "Which sax are you learning?"

"Huh?"

"You know—tenor? Alto? Soprano?"

"Oh, you know about this stuff, do you?"

"My dad's a jazz musician."

"I knew that. But are *you* into it?"

"It's okay. I don't mind it. I'd rather listen to hip-hop, though, to tell you the truth."

"Oh yeah, saw you gettin' into those videos on *Yo MTV Raps.* Who's in your walkman these days?"

"Tribe Called Quest and Digital Underground. I like Salt-N-Pepa, and The Pharcyde, too, though. And Slick Rick."

"Okay. You like that funny stuff, huh? I like the *hard* shit. NWA, Ice Cube."

"Really? Well guess what—I got to actually *meet* Ice Cube when he was recording in New York, cause my father was gigging at the Greene St. Café and Cube was recording at Greene St. Studios."

He laughed. "You *braggin'* pretty girl?"

"What? No. I was just telling you…" She sucked her teeth.

"Just playin' with you." He laughed again.

"Very funny. Anyway, I love hip-hop cause it's fun and creative, but I've heard jazz like everyday for my whole life, so—yeah, I know about it."

"Cool beans. Ever heard Gato Barbieri's version of that same song?"

"Of course. From the *Passion and Fire* album. My parents had it on vinyl. They played it a lot. At night, mostly."

"Word? It's definitely hot. So which version you like better, Gato's or Santana's?"

Artie liked the Santana version better because that was the version she'd kissed Kendall to, but she wasn't about to say that.

"Um, I like the Santana version better," she said, "'cause it's *his*. He wrote it so it's his own emotion he's expressing. Guess that feels like it's more intense to me. But I like Gato Barbieri's version, too." She bit her lip. Was that a good answer?

"Wait, wait, wait—don't you think a musician can interpret and reinvent someone else's song—put their own thing into it and then be expressing something pure and deep too? I mean, yo, Billie Holiday didn't write 'Strange Fruit,' but we're still listening to it."

Artie took a breath. Damn. She wasn't prepared for all this. So Kendall was a thinker, huh? Wow.

"Good point. I guess so," she said, hoping he'd change the subject.

"Good. Cause one day, I'm gonna play you *my* version of that song, and I'mma rock your world, pretty girl."

Artie smiled. Kendall was full of himself, but in a funny way. "So you never told me which sax you were learning, but I bet I can guess."

"Ha. Think you got me figured out, do you?

"Tenor."

Kendall was silent for a moment. "A'ight, you bad," he said. "How'd you know that?" He sounded spooked.

"Your personality. Definitely tenor."

"Oh-kay. What does *that* mean?"

She cleared her throat before answering pretending she didn't want to say. "Nothing bad." It could be interpreted that way, though. As Artie understood it, big horn players were notoriously cocky.

"A'ight, whatever," Kendall said. "I like the Santana version best, because the first time I heard it, I was kissing you."

Artie fell back on the bed. That was the coolest thing a boy had ever said to her.

"You still there?" he asked.

"Yeah," she giggled.

"So what're we gonna do about gettin' together, pretty? I wanna see you again, and kiss you, and talk to you more. Gimme your number."

And so she did. She gave him her number and her address and he gave her his, and they made plans as best as a twelve and thirteen-year-old who lived four hundred miles apart could. Knowing that Kendall was in her life somehow made what *wasn't* in her life more bearable.

She still hadn't discussed her mother with Rico. She knew they were getting together, but since it was obvious that Serena didn't want to see her, it seemed pointless to ask questions. She could tell when Rico had been with her not only because she and Mingus could smell her on him, but also because he was different after he'd seen her. He smiled more. His eyes had more light in them; he was somehow more alive. This made him her adversary. Coño had no interest in being her mother, but bicho was willing to see her in secret rather than not see the bitch at all.

Artie didn't bring it up, but she knew that he knew she knew. Maybe that's why he said *I love you* every time he left for work. She believed him, yet she didn't trust that he wouldn't leave her for good one day. Serena had told her that she loved Rico more than she loved her, and Artie believed that Rico loved Serena more than he loved her, too. If they wanted to be together, and Serena didn't want Artie around, what would stop Rico from bouncing? At first Artie thought that might not be so bad. It would be nice if Rayana would take her, and she could move back to L.A. But from what she could tell Rayana didn't want her. They spoke shortly after she called Kendall.

"I'm so sorry," Ray said on the phone, "but I just can't—it's not a good idea for me to be in touch with you, Artie." Her voice sputtered. "It—it's not that I *want* to push you away. It's that I, I need time... To let go and accept that things didn't work out."

"But, just cause you and Papi didn't work out, doesn't mean I don't wanna be your angel. I still love you." When Rayana didn't say anything Artie tried not to cry. "Could I write to you once in a while?"

Rayana was quiet, aside from her sniffling. Artie swallowed. Her chest ached.

Finally Ray said, "That would be nice. Miss you, sweetie. I have to go."

It took some time for Artie and Kendall to figure out a way to see each other. Neither had a credit card, nor enough money to travel. Vanessa wasn't willing to drive Kendall and Rico said he had no reason to go down to L.A.

Kendall eventually found a way. He had an older cousin in his twenties, Troy, who was an aspiring filmmaker. Troy made a 16mm film that got into the Black Filmmaker's Hall of Fame Film Festival in Oakland. He'd be driving up there in early December and staying the weekend in a hotel in San Francisco. Kendall explained the situation and Troy said he'd be happy if he came. He'd appreciate the company at his screening. Kendall told Artie that Vanessa knew he was going to see her, and she was cool with it. She was relieved she didn't have to drive him up there herself.

Artie didn't bother to tell Rico her plans. He wasn't discussing *his* trysts with her, so why should she? She told Sushama and Alessandra.

"It's probably not *real* love," Alessandra said. It was after school and she and Sushama were sitting on Artie's bed. "The spirits could just be playing with you, 'cause you're gullible. But don't worry—fique tranquilo—I've been fooled, too."

"Me too," Sush nodded. "Boys are stupid and they can't even kiss right. They just want to slobber on you, feel your tits, and show you that their thing gets hard."

Artie stared at them. *Jealous*, she thought.

Alessandra nodded, and said, "And you can't believe a word they say."

"I'd rather practice kissing with another girl," Sushama said, "than waste my time with some middle school moron." She smiled at Ally, who frowned back at her. Ally turned to Artie. She was leaning against the wall with her arms folded, eyes glaring. She didn't hide the fact that she was sick of listening to them.

"You probably won't hear from him a month from now," Alessandra said.

"Yes. I. Will," Artie growled. "He loves me."

Alessandra and Sush smiled.

"Boys don't fall in *love* in middle school." Alessandra had a giggle in her voice.

"She's right. He's just horny," Sushama said.

"You don't even know him. He's not like the boys you know."

"*Really*," Sush said. She pursed her lips and twisted them sideways "Think you've met the love of your life, do you?"

"*Maybe...*" Artie rolled her neck.

"Lemme see your left hand." Sush held her own hand out to take Artie's.

"What for?"

"I know how to read palms."

Artie held out her hand. Sushama took it and stared at it.

"Hm," she said with raised eyebrows.

"What?" Artie studied her expression.

"This is your love line," Sush pointed out. "And this is your life line. Yours *do* start out pretty close together, actually."

"What does that mean?" Alessandra frowned.

"Means she's destined to find love early in life."

"Really?" Alessandra's eyes widened.

"Toldja," Artie said. She grooved her neck from shoulder to shoulder.

"I don't know though," Sush said. "I mean, twelve is a little *too* early, I think."

"I think so, too," Alessandra said, crossing her arms.

"If you meet him now, you'll be bored with him by the time you're fourteen," Sush said. "Don't you want some variety in your life?"

"Of course she does. The spirits are probably just preparing her for the *real* love she's supposed to meet when she's at least eighteen."

Artie reached into her nightstand drawer and produced a picture Kendall had sent of himself. She held it in front of them. *Bam*. It was a school photo, a 4 x 6 inch with a white border. Kendal was so handsome. And he looked cool, in his gray Kangol cap and his sly sideways smile. Artie spent many evenings staring at his brown eyes and those kissable lips—full and pink. She reached back into the drawer and pulled out a cache of letters (six of them) he'd written her.

"He *loves* me." The letters *had* to prove it to them.

"Lemme read them," Sushama said. She plucked the stack from Artie's hand.

"I wanna see, too," Alessandra chimed.

"Your ass needs to calm down." Artie snatched the letters back, gritted her teeth and leaned close to her friends. "I would *never* let someone read what Kendall trusted was private between me and him. What the hell is wrong with you?" Artie's tone was biting. It slipped out without her control. She realized that she sounded like her mother.

Sushama's brows moved together. Her eyes darkened. "Girl, you betta back up out my face. You lucky we even give a fuck about your stupid letters."

"What if he let *his* friends read *my* letters?" Artie said, softening. "I would hate that."

Sushama sucked her teeth. Whatever. Alessandra hugged herself and stared down at the bedspread, her eyes filling with tears.

The fact that they'd asked disappointed Artie. She liked Sushama and Alessandra, but they were silly. They had normal parents who took care of them, so they could *be* silly, carefree girls. Artie didn't feel she had that luxury.

"Why'd you even show 'em to us if they're so damn *sacred?*" Sushama asked, crossing her arms. Alessandra remained quiet. She looked upset.

"I showed 'em to you, 'cause you didn't believe that me and Kendall have a real relationship. Well, we do. But I'm sorry if I hurt your feelings. Shouldn't've snapped at you."

Artie was once every bit as nosey and she knew it. So, her friends weren't perfect. Neither was she. But they were good company when her father left her alone. And they'd have her back when Kendall came into town. She'd tell Rico she was hanging with her homegirls and hopefully he'd accept that as graciously as she accepted *his* lies.

Fourteen

Serena, 2004

Serena walks alone on the beach at sunset. Second time today. She hadn't planned on coming outside. From her flat she saw Jamie out walking and she rushed down to be with him. Before she could catch up a longhaired brunette approached him. They're walking together now.

She watches from behind. Will he hold her hand? Caress her back? The bastard is always chatting up someone. He hasn't made a move, but she's anxious as if he has.

What am I doin'? She turns and walks in the opposite direction. Tries to shake it off. He's going to do whatever he wants. Being clingy never gets me anywhere.

She's a little tipsy, which makes trudging through the sand harder. She could walk where it's flat, but the dry sand works her thighs harder and burns more calories. Probably have to walk all damn night to burn off all this wine, she thinks. But doing this is better than not doing it. Gotta do *somethin'*. No one's allowed to age in this blasted city. Even old birds like Serena are trying to look twenty-five. She sighs. Middle age sneaks up so quickly. Not long ago *she* was the one men desired...

Serena, 1990

After Jamie's tour was over, Serena spent a quite a bit of time traveling between New York and San Francisco. Seeing Rico was fun, more fun in some ways than being married to him had been. Technically they were still married, but this felt more like an affair. She would spend Friday and Saturday nights at the Four Seasons and leave early Sunday mornings in time to get back to New York to play her gig at the Gramercy Park Hotel. She had her advance and didn't *need* the job anymore, but she now she was developing a following. *Fans.* Why give that up?

Their ritual was they didn't see each other before the Friday night show. She'd show up in the audience at the Four Seasons during his second set. Sipping wine at her reserved table, which was candlelit and close to the band, she'd nibble kalamata olives and smoked almonds. She wore a tank dress in red, black or white. No knickers beneath it. When Rico blew his horn during his solos it was like no one in the room existed but her. He was playing for Serena, giving her the music like he was giving her himself. When the notes hit a climax, the applause made her blush.

It was delicious. Yet she felt sorry for Rico.

"You're too good for this gig," she told him in bed. "It's doin' nuffin' for your career."

"I don't do this gig, Mami, we don't get the rate on this room."

"Rico. You should be doin' more. You're a vorld class musician."

"I'm teaching, got royalties coming in now and then. I'm all right."

"Are you composing?" She played with the curly hairs on his chest. "D'you have time, wif Artie and all?"

"I said I'm fine. If you're really concerned, come back, then. Let's be a family."

Her eyes balked at that.

"Then shut up, Serena," he yelled. "If I'm cool with *this* right here, bein' all that's left of us, when you know I want more, then fuckin' leave me alone about all the other shit." He turned away from her.

This was untenable. She enjoyed their time together, but it was only for fun. When sleeping with Rico led to yearnings of anything more, she shook those yearnings off.

She and Jamie were making progress with her album. Musicians had been hired. Songs refined. The buzz was good. Benny at the label recommended that she go ahead and file for divorce. If she waited, he told her, she put her future income at risk. Serena never imagined that she'd be the one filing. She didn't know how to bring it up with Rico, because she knew it would hurt. Her lawyer forwarded the papers to him with no warning from her. She flew to San Francisco, as usual, the weekend after they were sent. He didn't show up for work at the hotel. She wanted to talk with him about it, but she didn't want to call the house. Artie might answer. She spent the weekend in San Francisco alone. It rained the entire time. Winter had set in and all the loveliness of fall was gone.

A vacation cruise line offered Jamie a ridiculous amount of money to headline a jazz cruise for three weeks. He told Serena he'd only have to play four nights out of the week and for the rest of the time, they could enjoy an all-expense-paid vacation. He'd worked her into his deal. The timing couldn't have been better. Though she'd done what made the most sense where Rico was concerned, she did miss him and she was sad to have hurt him. Being at sea for a few weeks would do her good.

When she found out they'd be docked in Bermuda for two days, she had to take deep breaths. It had been more than seventeen years since she set foot there. And aside from the occasional Christmas card, she hadn't interacted with her family for over thirty years. As far as she knew they were living as white. How would they react? Would they deny her altogether? She hoped to persuade them to come to her show. Let them see how brilliantly she'd done without them.

She didn't tell Annie where she was going, or her plan. It would only upset her. But she'd contact them when she got there. She looked up her mother Artimeza's information in Annie's address book.

When they docked in Hamilton she dialed the number, trembling in the salty air as she operated the rotary phone in a booth. She looked over her shoulder at the turquoise water glistening in the sun. Her heart pounded as she waited for someone to answer. Her brother picked up. When she told Brian who it was, he gasped.

"That's Serena, is it? No!" His voice warmed up quickly. "Vhere you callin' from, love?"

"I'm in Hamilton."

"Oh! Arryone'll vant to see you. I'm stuck at de house mindin' my kids and Phyllis's. She and Mother are at Deddy's road runnin' event. Can we meet you dis evenin'?"

It was odd to hear him speak of her parents so matter-of-factly. Her mouth got dry and she became light headed. She told him she was performing on the ship and invited him and the family to come aboard that night as her guests. He said he would be there and that he'd try to bring Phyllis and their parents as well.

Serena had her hair blown out straight in the beauty salon on the ship and she had her nails, eyebrows, and makeup done, too. She wanted to look better than she had *ever* looked, to show them that though she may not have been able to pass, she was beautiful nonetheless.

Before her set, she scanned the room, but she wasn't sure how they'd look after so many years. She didn't see anyone who resembled them as she remembered. The disappointment was a boon. While Serena was always emotionally sincere in performance, she was *particularly* emotional this evening. She connected more deeply with her songs, as if a layer had been peeled back. She was raw. That emotional availability was exciting to watch.

After the set, a couple approached her and while she had looked right past them in the audience the man embraced her and said, "Welcome home." When she took a good look at Brian's face, she was stunned. He wasn't *white*. His caramel complexion was lighter than Serena's, and he had "good" hair, but his coloring was like Artie's. If he thought he had a secret, it certainly wasn't safe.

Phyllis kissed her cheek. "Lookit you, with all that talent. Ah feel so prawd."

Phyllis was caramel-colored, too. What the hell was going on?

They sat and had dessert together. Serena asked why "Mother and Dad" hadn't come. With difficulty, Brian told her that his mother was still feuding with Annie and that she wasn't sure how Serena would receive her, so she elected not to come.

"Feudin'? 'Bout vhat?" Serena asked.

"My mum felt—," Brian began.

"—*Our* mum, Brian," Serena said. "She's *my* mothah too."

Brian looked at Phyllis, then back at Serena. He exhaled. "Serena, *Annie's* your mother. This is what they're feudin' about."

"No. Artimeza is my mother and she gave me to Annie, 'cause she didn't want me." Serena lowered her head and patted tears with a napkin.

Phyllis looked at Serena with warm eyes. "Why d'you think she would give you avay?" she asked.

"'Cause you were passin' and I couldn't."

"Serena. Lookit us, dahlin'." Her voice was tender.

Serena did, though she didn't have to; she'd already seen that she had reason to doubt what she'd been told.

"Annie said that to confuse you."

Serena felt dizzy. She didn't know what to believe.

"She told me that my mother and you, her older children, could pass, but I couldn't; so I hedda go to anotha school, and that's why I was sent to live with her."

"Annie *is* your birth mother, Serena," Brian insisted. "She was sent to de States to a home for un-ved mothers, and when she brought you back our mum took you for de first few years, 'cause grenny didn't want de family to be shamed."

Serena's mind was turning, trying to fit this information into what she knew, or what she thought. Tears fell too fast to bother wiping them. People could see. She felt exposed in the dining room. Jamie started toward her. She waved him away like a fly, excused herself, and fled into the bathroom.

In the mirror, mascara streaked down her cheeks. She literally did not know who she was anymore. Phyllis came in and embraced her.

"It was hard on us, too," she whispered. "We're sorry we never told you how much we missed you. You were our baby sister and we loved you, dahlin'."

A sob broke from what felt to Serena like the floor of her soul. No one had ever apologized. No one had bothered to tell her she'd been loved. That four-year-old girl was still inside her, still wounded. What might have turned out differently had this kindness come sooner?

So many things swam through Serena's mind—questions, thoughts she wanted to bring to the surface, but couldn't. Phyllis said nothing more. She held her. Serena welcomed the embrace, though she had *hated* this "sister" for most of her life, because in her mind Phyllis had been chosen and she had not. Suddenly Phyllis was her cousin? She *hadn't* taken the part of "mother" that was supposed to have belonged to her? So much to process. If it was true, she'd had *all* of her mother, all to herself, for most of her life. She should be happy. But the news was more upsetting than the lies she'd believed in all these years.

Fifteen

Artie, 1990

Kendall was set to arrive Friday evening. He'd be staying until Sunday night. Artie told Rico that she'd be at Sushama's that weekend. Not that he'd even be checking for her. He spent Friday and Saturday nights at the hotel where he played, and left her and Mingus home alone. *Irresponsible, selfish bicho.*

Sometimes she'd go to Sushama or Alessandra's house. If not, she'd visit with them on the phone. Rico would call her on Fridays at midnight, then return Saturday morning to take her to breakfast and to the kids' photography class he'd put her in at San Francisco Community College. But he'd leave her at class, and she'd be alone again until Sunday unless she hung out with the girls. He said she was a mature young lady and that's why he trusted her to stay home alone. Yeah right. He just wanted to be with his woman. Artie knew his behavior was shady and probably illegal. He also walked around naked at night when he thought she was asleep. Gross. Artie had slept with her door open, because there was a light in the hallway and she didn't like the dark. Until one night, she saw him walking to the bathroom and he was totally naked. From then on she had to keep her door closed. And she was scared of running into him when she had to pee herself. Why couldn't Rico be normal and stay with Rayana, so they could be family? And why couldn't he wear a robe at night so she didn't have to see his damn ding-a-ling?

"That is a fair question," Dr. Ligon says, bringing Artie back into the room and to the present.

"Ugh," Artie says. "I hated living alone with him. He did whatever the hell he felt like doing, like I didn't even matter."

Dr. Ligon is pale today. Her voice is hoarse. "Yes. A few things come to mind. I remember you telling me that he used to take you to the beach, without your mother, which seemed to make her jealous. Now the reverse, he spent weekends with Serena, and left you by yourself."

"But I wasn't jealous. Just mad. I mean, I was only a kid, he was supposed to look out for me."

"Yes. But look at the dynamic. Your father's behavior set up a competition. You mentioned a while ago that when you came home from the beach, Serena accused Rico of treating you like the wife. 'Going on dates.' There's a presumption of inappropriate intimacy. And she was onto something. Rico made you aware of his sex life. Walked around nude in the home he shared with you. I can't know what was going on in your father's mind, but his behavior points to provoking competition between you and your mother."

"Ew," Artie says. "Well I certainly wasn't trying to compete."

"Of course not. You didn't ask to be put in that situation. But you were, and you were powerless. That twelve-year-old-girl had a lot to be angry about. She needs to have a voice."

Artie sighs. "I tried the journal, but I don't know if it really did anything."

"Give it time. Your parents didn't give you the opportunity to express how their actions affected you, but you can, in a sense, be your own, *better* parent. Talk to your younger self. Let her tell you how she feels."

Artie looks at the drawing on the wall behind Ligon. Today, it's a woman hugging herself.

Artie, 1990

The Friday she was meeting Kendall, Artie was in her room trying on jeans in front of the closet door mirror when she saw that it was past six-o-clock and the TV was still on in the living room. Rico hadn't knocked on her bedroom door to say good-bye.

She opened the door and peeked into the living room. "Papi?" He was in pajama bottoms and an undershirt. He hadn't shaved. A bottle of Meyers Rum sat on the coffee table and he held a glassful in his hand.

"Mija."

"Not going to work?"

He shook his head. His eyes didn't leave the TV.

"But you never miss work. You sick?"

Again, he shook his head. His shoulders drooped.

"What's wrong?"

He didn't answer and he didn't look at her. She stared at him a moment before closing her door again. Something was up, but she had to get going. As she swept her hair into a side ponytail, she remembered that she told Rico Sushama's dad was picking her up. She was actually taking the bus to meet Kendall and his cousin at the Commodore Hotel in San Francisco. What if he wants to *see* Sushama's dad? Shit. Maybe he forgot.

She put on her pea coat and walked into the living room holding her overnight bag.

"Well, I'm going," she said. "Hope you feel better." She kissed his cheek. "Bendicíon."

"What?" He squinted at her.

"I'm going to Sushama's."

"No. Not tonight, mija. Sit down. Watch a video with me."

"My friends are expecting me."

"You'll see them next weekend." He sipped his rum. "Por favor. I need your company."

"Um, you leave me alone *EVERY WEEKEND.*"

"Why're you yelling?"

"I am *not* changing my plans." She slung her bag over her shoulder.

"I don't like your tone, mija. You're startin' to sound like your mother."

Did he really just say that shit to me?

"FUUUCK YOUUU!" she half sang, half shrieked in what she thought was G and E flat, but she wasn't absolutely sure. "You like *that* tone any better?" she yelled.

His eyes widened and he leaned back. She ran out before he could respond, but she thought she saw him smile, despite his anger.

It was raining. She didn't know that until she got outside. She would have grabbed an umbrella, but she couldn't go back now. She looked over her shoulder as she passed the next set of row houses. He wasn't following.

As she made her way down the hill to the bus stop she was getting soaked and feeling guilty that she'd cursed at him. She was angry, but she also wondered what was wrong. *Something to do with that bitch, I bet.*

Rico brought Serena's smell back into the apartment every Sunday. Sometimes he'd leave for work at the hotel with calla lilies. He knew Artie knew those were Serena's favorite. He didn't try to hide it. He wanted her to know.

She changed busses. The second was crowded with rush hour travelers. Riding the bus in San Francisco reminded Artie a little of New York. She liked the energy. She was standing in front of a family: a mom, dad, and boy a bit younger than she was seated between them. They were a unit. Just as Artie began to feel envious, the dad got up and gave her his seat. The mom handed her a towel. Artie was dripping.

"Don't you have an umbrella, sweetie?" the mother asked.

"I forgot it."

"Well, dry yourself off, hon. You don't wanna catch cold."

Artie thanked them and used the towel. They didn't even know her, but they seemed to care about her wellbeing. It crossed Artie's mind that their behavior had nothing to do with her. It was just how they were. And if that was the case, she thought, maybe her parents *not* caring about her wellbeing had nothing to do with her either. Maybe it was just how they were.

The family got off at the same stop Artie did. They had the towels because they were on their way to family swim hour at an indoor pool near the hotel she was headed to. And since they had a huge umbrella and she didn't have one, they decided to walk with her.

"You really don't have to do that," she told them.

They did anyway. She didn't get their names and they didn't ask hers. They just walked her to the door.

"Have a safe and lovely night, hon," the mom said as they left.

Artie watched them head down the sidewalk. At Rayana's New Age-y church she heard that the universe has ways of letting us know we're cared for, even when it seems we're not. Sounded like bullshit to Artie, but this made her wonder.

Kendall was sitting in the lobby on a red sofa. He looked right at her and smiled. She felt a surge of excitement in her belly that swelled up into her chest. She was about to burst. Wasn't he going to rush over, hug her, and lift her off the floor like in the movies? Nope. Kendall was too cool for that. He sat there and waited for her to come to him. At least he stood up and stretched his arms out when she got closer. They squeezed each other. It felt amazing even if it wasn't as dramatic as she'd hoped. Kendall was only in eighth grade, but to Artie, he felt like a man. *Her* man.

He carried her overnight bag into the room. Troy was brown-skinned and muscular with a glabrous head that looked like he buffed it with a shoeshine cloth. He was sitting on the end of the bed watching a music video without the sound. Light flickered on and off of his face. When he turned, he saw the overnight bag and jumped to his feet.

"Oh HELL no. I know you don't think your little pre-teen ass is *spending the night.*"

Artie looked at Kendall. He'd told her she could stay.

"I told Ken-doll you could hang out, but y'all are too young—I ain't tryin' to get arrested. I'mma take you over to the festival, we're gonna watch a movie, and then I'm driving your little fast ass home. Y'hear?"

Artie didn't say anything. She looked at Kendall again.

"Look here, dog," he said. "I brought sleeping bags, yo. And trust me, ain't my style to bust a move wit another nigga in the room. We'll be chill."

Troy didn't say yes or no, but Kendall left the bag in the room. Artie smiled hearing Kendall speak to Troy. He used a different language than he did with her. She liked that he could flip it like that. He was so fly.

The screening was on the campus of a community college in Oakland. It wasn't Troy's movie they were seeing. His screening was the next day, but Troy told them, "I'mma quiz y'all on the content so you better pay attention." Kendall gave him the finger and paid for Artie's ticket: their first real date.

They did not watch the movie. They sat way in the back, in an empty row, whispered to each other and made out. At one point, he stopped kissing her and looked her in the eyes.

"Something weird happened to me," he whispered.

"What? When?" she asked.

"Don't want you to think I'm buggin' or anything, but a voice spoke to me."

Artie's eyebrows shot up. "A *voice?*"

He nodded. "It told me that you're my wife."

Artie smiled. She did think that sounded odd.

"What did it sound like?" she asked. Her legs were tangled with his. She wiggled them free and put her feet on the floor.

He sighed. "I knew you'd think it was weird," he said. "It was a voice *inside* my head, yo. I mean, I didn't really *hear* it, but I *did*. Can't explain it, but it wasn't *my* voice. It knew what it was talking about, though."

Artie wasn't sure how she felt about that. She adored Kendall, but was he nuts? Voices? And marriage seemed pretty remote, though she'd imagined it herself, of course.

"How d'you feel about that?" she asked.

"Well, wouldn't be 'til we're older. But," he smiled, "I think it would be cool."

"Me, too," she whispered and grinned. Nuts or not, she had mad love for the boy.

They kissed again. She let him put his hands under her sweater. She was nervous; no one had ever touched her there. She liked it; it felt tingly. She was afraid someone might see, though. Kendall didn't seem to care. He was into it. Soon he pulled her hand down and rested it between his legs. She could feel the stiffness through his pants. She had to stop kissing for a minute because she was smiling so hard. Sush and Alley both claimed they'd touched a guy down there. Artie had felt so far behind.

"I wanna taste your tetas," he whispered.

That made her giggle, although it wasn't so much funny as it was overwhelming. He put his hand on top of hers and guided her to rub him. He moaned a little. She was sure other people could hear.

"Let's go outside," she said in his ear. "We can sit in Troy's car. I left my door unlocked."

He did get to taste her tetas. And he taught her to give him a hand job. He also put his hand down her underpants and touched her between her legs.

"You're crazy wet," he said. Then he hummed their Santana song. "Ba daaa da da da ba da daaa…"

He was a little off key, but she loved it. That Kendall appreciated old music and not just hip hop or R & B, was a turn on. He was different from any boy she'd ever met. He was fascinating. The way he touched her felt amazing. She couldn't *believe* how good it felt.

And then stupid-ass Troy flung the door open.

"God dammit, Ken-doll. Get up here."

Kendall stopped what he was doing, but he didn't move to the front. He put on the seatbelt and asked Artie to put hers on too.

"Damn," Troy kept fussing. "Barely out of diapers. Horny little fuckers."

He droned on lecturing them. Artie tuned him out as Kendall stroked her hand the way she liked. She felt at home with Kendall. She finally had someone who wanted to be with her more than he wanted to be anywhere else, and she felt the same way. There was nothing better. Artie was aware that she *was* young to feel all that she was feeling, but her heart was full of happiness, and she would follow it, because she believed that somehow her heart knew where it was supposed to be.

Sixteen

Serena, 1990

There were almost three weeks left on the cruise. Serena was aching to delve deeper into what she'd learned. Unfortunately, any excavating was going to have to be in person, and she couldn't get to the Bronx any time soon. Annie would not want to discuss it. She rarely talked about anything uncomfortable. She certainly wasn't going to speak about it on the phone. Considering Serena's rage, this was probably for the best, despite how frustrating the delay.

When she was a teenager, a friend of Serena's lied and betrayed her. In a rage similar to the one she was feeling, she bloodied the girl's nose. That same year, she threw a classroom chair against the wall. School officials put her in counseling. After two sessions, the therapist, a middle-aged redhead whose office smelled like cigarettes said, "This anger you're unable to control stems from your fury toward your parents for leaving you."

Serena slouched in her seat and stared at her fingernails. *They actually pay people to state de obvious?*

"If you want to get well," the woman said, "you'll have to let that anger go. You'll have to forgive them."

Serena sat up and barked at her, "I can't forgive something dat's unforgiveable."

She wouldn't speak to the woman again, and she was subsequently forced to leave the school. She and Annie left Bermuda shortly thereafter.

If what Brian and Phyllis had told her was true, then the animosity she felt all her life had been wasted on something that never even happened. Now she'd probably spend the rest of her life being vexed with Annie for *allowing* her to waste her life being vexed. If Annie had just told the truth, she'd have understood. She could have grown up knowing she was wanted. She knew Annie loved her, but it was never enough. Her belief in being abandoned pervaded everything.

The ship was still docked in Hamilton the next morning. She got off and began walking through the quaint city past blue-green water and pastel-colored colonial architecture. She wanted to see Johnny Barnes, a man she heard about who waved and blew kisses at people on scooters, and in busses and cars on their way to work. He'd been doing it for a few years, she learned, but he wasn't around when she was growing up there.

The breeze stung her cheeks and gave her gooseflesh. Why these cruise ninnies decided to dock in Bermuda in the winter, she didn't understand. Nonetheless, the walking was good. She vented at Annie in her mind and marched along a path past lush trees and green grass toward Crow Lane Circle. She saw him in the distance, a brown man with wooly white hair, waving at the cars and blowing kisses as they passed. His gray trousers were loose and he wore a navy windbreaker. As she got closer, she could hear him. "I LOVE ya. Mwah! I just love ya." She stopped and watched from across the street. He looked so happy. People smiled and waved back from their cars. Some beeped at him, too, as they passed. He did this five days a week, she was told. He was a retired bus driver. She wondered if she'd ever ridden his bus as a girl. He turned and noticed her. Blew her a kiss. "You are *beautiful*. I love ya," he shouted. She felt something warm envelop her, an invisible hug. She nearly cried. Was he a living angel? She smiled at him, blew a kiss back, and began walking in the other direction toward the city. Home was proving to be more welcoming than she remembered it.

Serena felt she could have walked all the way to St. Georges if the wind wasn't kicking up. She was headed toward the bus terminal when she caught a taxi.

The driver knew the house and its occupants and seemed suspicious that Serena never got out of the car. She wanted only to look at it. It had been painted a rich, clay-colored red since she'd seen it last. And its shutters looked new. She once did this same thing as a girl. She'd come by taxi on her twelfth birthday. She never knocked on the door. She simply stood and stared at the house for a long time. That morning she asked her Aunt, "You think she remembers? Do you think my mother's thinking of me today?" Annie hugged her without an answer.

When she spied on the house all those years ago, the shutters were open. She'd seen figures moving behind the sheer curtains on the window. Serena told herself that if they *were* thinking of her, they would look out, and when they saw her they would come to her with hugs and kisses. They would tell her they were sorry.

The shutters were closed now. She couldn't see a thing. No one noticed her. Not that she wanted them to. What would she say? She just wanted to see the home that she'd longed to be welcomed back to. Its image still haunted her. But she could leave the island knowing that none of the specters of her past were real, even if she couldn't make them disappear.

Serena didn't tell Jamie what was going on, but he saw her crying in the dining room the night before.

He came to her cabin and when she cracked the door open he pushed his way in, stumbling on her row of shoes lining the wall. "I ain't leavin' til you tell me wha's up," he said.

Serena was fond of Jamie, but she didn't believe for a moment that his real agenda was concern for her sadness. He'd made it no secret that he was itching to shag her.

"Jamie, please. I know what you vant and it's not happenin'."

"Tha's cold, lady. Jus' tryin' to be a friend." Acting hurt, he stared down at the cheap blue carpet. He was a terrible actor.

"Yeah. I don't need to get next to you right nahw, Ace-Bye," she said. "I needa figure my life out." She sat down on the bed's rumpled white blanket, and scratched the side of her head.

"So, 'm fittin' to help ya, dawlin'." He raised an eyebrow, smiled a wry smile.

"Oh Jamie, eeze me up, vould you?"

"Eeze ya up?"

"*Gimme a break.* And you need to stop disrespectin' Ondine. She's a nice garrl." Serena covered her face with her hands.

"We got a deal. She catches me, she gets a thousand bucks." He sat down beside her.

She eyed him from between her fingers. "Arry time?"

"Yup."

"That's sick. You're just—ya not right in de head." She swatted his arm.

"She knows I ain't changin' and she loves me just the same."

"Y'know what? Get out. Will you please?" She pointed to the door. "I'm *friends* wif her for fuck's sake."

He didn't move. Just looked at her. She turned away and faced the wall.

"So help her make some money," he said laughing.

"Get out!"

He shook his head.

"Quit badgering me, Jamie. It's not gonna happen."

"Maybe not t-night." He stuck his pinky in his mouth and sucked on it.

"What is it wif you? You just wanna do it, 'cause I don't want to?"

"Oh you *want* to, dawlin'." He grinned at her.

She scoffed. "Trust me, there are *many* things I'd retha do."

"Ya priorities' screwed up then," he said. "Like whut?"

She swallowed. "I'd like to get off dis ridiculous boat so I can find out who my deddy is, since I suddenly haven't a clue. I'd like to slap someone who lied to me. And I'd like to figure out why my life's been such a struggle when some people hev it so easy."

"Nobody has it easy."

"*You've* got it easy, ya fullish, spoiled white bye."

"Foolish? What? See, dere ya go. *'Life's so much easier for you white mu'fukas.'*"

"And it *is*."

"Serena, didn't you go to college? Weren't ya raised middle class? Life ain't no harder for you than it is for anybody else."

"Think you'd be sellin' so many records if you hed dark skin-n-nappy hair, you privileged idiot? You've no *idea* how much easier things are fa you."

"Oh, you must know that cause of your vast experience bein' a white man, huh?"

She sucked her teeth. "I'm not havin' dis argument wif you," Serena said, "So jus' stop. Get de fuck out."

"Look, I ain't tryin' a trivialize racism, but you ain't no poster child for the underprivileged, either. Life ain't easy *period*. For anybody. 'F you's white you'd have some other issue stressin' you. I am truly sorry you don' know who yo' daddy is, Serena, but y'know whut? Lotta folks don't know who dey daddy is. Lot of 'em better off for it, too. You got your health, got people who love you, y' got looks, talent, a career. Quit cha crying black girl. Shit ain't dat bad."

"Fuck you."

Jamie laughed. "Well bless your heart, but ain't feelin' you like dat no more, so I'mma pass. And for your information, dawlin', I'm from N'awlins."

"So?"

"My people *been* from N'awlins for at least a couple a hundred years."

"Bye, what do I care 'bout your people?"

"I ain't da *whitest* white boy, you ever seen. If y' know what I mean."

Serena did have an inkling. She'd figured there *could* have been *some* color in his bloodline *way* back somewhere as there was with many a white southerner, but she was shocked he'd admit it.

"My daddy's folks go back to the Creoles of Color. His daddy's great-grandmama was a Quadroon Mistress. We got a Daguerreotype portrait of her from the year 1850. Matter' fact, she looked a whole lot like you, gorgeous. One a the reasons I dig lookin' at cha."

"Yeah, okay. Thanks for de lecture, *brotha*."

He smiled. "No mo' pity party shit, y'hear?

"Jamie, I'm tired."

He hugged her and kissed her face. "Whatever it is, dawlin', it's just life. Don't take it so seriously."

Maybe she did take it all too seriously. That was the only way she knew. It took a moment before she realized that Jamie was kissing her neck and grabbing her bumpy.

"Jamie!"

"A'ight, fine." He stopped. "I'm goin'. Don't know why you keep— you know it's gon' happen, girl."

Serena shoved him out the door. Such an ass. But his humor helped her ride out the rest of the cruise.

Seventeen

Artie, 2004

Artie wakes up in the plush bed to crying sounds coming from the bathroom. She looks at the clock. After midnight. She yawns, hoping it'll die down. When it doesn't, she slides out of the sheets and into a robe. Lots of patients cry in this place, but Roxy's different. At eighteen, she's just a kid.

Artie knocks. "Hey lil' nut cake. Saved my Wolfgang Puck truffle from dessert. Want it?"

Roxy opens the door, sniffling. She's flushed and sweaty, in a black bra and panties, with her hair in a messy ponytail.

"Mad calories. Of course not, Artie-Fartie." She wipes her eyes with her fingers.

"Did your mom do something again, Foxy-Roxy?" Artie asks.

Roxy shakes her head. "It's Dr. Ligon."

"Oh. I'll miss her, too, sweetie. But she'll be back."

"She's in the hospital," Roxy says.

"Oh. She's in labor?"

"The baby's dead." Roxy turns away to grab some toilet paper. She wipes her nose.

"What?"

"Stillborn," she says.

Artie doesn't breathe for a moment. She watches Roxy sit on the bathroom mat and lean against the wall. Knees to her chest, she hugs her legs.

"They told me something was wrong," Roxy says. "I was supposed to tell her. She never liked me to talk about *her*, though. That's why I didn't do what they said."

"Roxy. *They?*"

"So?"

"So, maybe… You sure it's true? I mean, is there a source other than *them?*"

Roxy looks at her. "Think I'm stupid, Fartie?"

"Stupid? No. Crazy? Well…" Her head tilts from side to side.

"I wouldn't make this up. I know people who work here," Roxy says, raising her voice. "I know how to hack emails and computer files. You know I do."

Artie nods. "Okay." She exhales and sits down beside her. The hexagon tile is cold on her backside.

"She's been trying to get preggers for years," Roxy says. "Wanted a pea in the pod so bad she did six in-vitro cycles." She turns to Artie. "I knew when the pea was in trouble. They whispered in my ear and told me what to say." Her voice shakes, "But she didn't want me to listen to them and I wanted her to think I was getting better."

Artie rubs her back. "It's not your fault."

Tears slide down Roxy's face. "They said it *is*. They told me to tell her and I didn't. She's not coming back. She slit her wrists."

Artie feels like she's been punched. She swallows. "But, you said she's in the hospital. That means she's okay, right?"

"Alive, yes," Roxy says. "In a psych ward. They'll never let her come back here. I should have told her."

Roxy curls up on the mat.

"I understand how you feel, Rox. But they're wrong, it's not your fault." Artie pulls a bath towel down from the rack above, and covers

Roxy with it. She strokes her head, smoothing her messy hair.

"I'm really gonna miss her," Roxy says.

"I know. Me, too."

Roxy puts her head in Artie's lap and Artie cuddles her like a baby.

Artie asks the interim psychiatrist for an update on Ligon. It's their first session.

Dr. Schwartz scratches the stubble on his chin. "She's had a complication with her delivery," he says. "We don't know the details."

Artie looks him over. She met him weeks ago when Dr. Ligon was planning her maternity leave. He has black eyes, bushy gray eyebrows and a salt and pepper comb-over that fails to cover shiny pink gaps. He crosses and uncrosses his long legs so often, she suspects his balls itch. He asks Artie to tell him how she's feeling. She looks up and notices that the drawing on Dr. Ligon's wall has been removed. In its place hang soulless copies of Schwartz's diplomas.

Artie has nothing against him. The chemistry is just not right.

"I'd like to be released," she says.

Dr. Schwartz lowers his chin. His unruly brows become one.

"What makes you think you're ready?"

"I've appreciated my time here," she says. "I wasn't ready to see anyone or be back in my life. But now I want to be able to shave my underarms and cut my toenails. That's how I know."

He smiles. "Do you understand that there's more to being discharged than simply wanting to be? It's to your advantage to be evaluated over a period of time."

"How long?" She rocks in her seat and scratches her thighs.

"That depends. You might feel fine today. Next week something could arise to change that." He clasps his hands behind his comb-over. "I know it's not ideal to switch doctors abruptly and that you may be uncomfortable. I'm sorry about that. But—"

"—If I feel ill again, I'll come back. I checked myself in once…" She moves to the edge of the seat.

He clears his throat. "I know you'd like to be in control of when you come and go."

"I think I am, actually."

He leans forward. "You're *not* finished with treatment, Artimeza. You'll need a consult with the social worker. And I can't write a release evaluation. I don't think you're ready."

Her eyes meet his. "Look, I know Dr. Ligon is suicidal. In light of the fact that they made a mistake in hiring someone unstable to *treat* the unstable, I no longer feel confident entrusting this institution with my mental health."

"That's a hostile thing to say."

"Oh please," Artie says, standing. "Give me a hard time and I'm pretty sure I can sue for damages due to incompetent treatment."

Artie doesn't believe that she's received poor treatment, of course, but if her shrink is in the psych ward she can probably make that case.

She's not interested in going home. Kendall's at home, as far as she knows, and she isn't ready to speak to him, let alone live with him.

Rayana arrives days later to sign her out. Her eyes light up when she sees Artie.

"There's my angel." She squeezes her tight and for a long time. Artie watches her write, "MOTHER" on the release form under "relationship to patient." Ray catches herself and scrawls in "step" before "mother." She has to write tiny to squeeze it in. She looks at Artie and shrugs. Artie links arms with her and they walk out. She wouldn't have minded if Ray had left the form uncorrected. She *has* mothered her.

She's driven in Artie's 2004, turquoise Thunderbird convertible. Artie smiles at it. Bought it with money from a successful year shooting movie stills, it reminds Artie that she has a career. She has a life that will still be hers whether she lets Kendall back into it or not. Maybe it's only a little bit of a life, but it's something.

"I need to borrow this thing more often, love," Ray says as they approach with Artie's small suitcase. "Got so much attention on the way here, I felt like a hot babe."

Together they hoist the bag into the trunk and Artie kisses Ray's cheek. "Cool beans. You *are* hot, mami." And she is. Rayana has taken exquisite care of herself, mind, body and soul She's still vibrant and youthful at forty-five.

"I have to go to the psych ward at Hollywood Presbyterian," Artie says. "Do you mind?"

The joy on Rayana's face dissipates. She nods. After driving in silence for a few moments she says, "I thought you were feeling better, love."

"Oh—I'm sorry." Artie chuckles. "I should've explained. I'm just going to visit someone."

"Oh." Ray perks up again. "That's fine then. I'm free all afternoon. We'll get your manicure and pedicure, and wait'll you see the pretty flowers and scented candles I put in your room. You can stay as long as you want to, angel. Happy to have you."

Artie reaches over and kisses her on the cheek again.

When they get close to Hollywood, Ray asks, "So, you're visiting someone who was with you? Inside?"

Artie nods. She tries not to laugh when she imagines how disturbed Rayana will be if she tells her exactly which someone that is, but she can't help it. Soon she's laughing out loud. She doesn't say *why* she's laughing, but Ray laughs with her anyway.

Rayana decides to stay in the waiting room, since she doesn't know the patient. Fine with Artie; she doesn't know what to expect.

When she enters the room, Dr. Ligon's husband adjusts his wire-rimmed glasses. "No visitors," he snaps. "Didn't they tell you at the nurses station?" He's boyish looking, with black hair that skims the shoulders of his suit.

"No one was *at* the nurses station," Artie says. "I just saw her name outside the door."

Dr. Ligon is strapped to the bed, but she can lift her head. "It's okay, Bitao," she whispers. "She can stay. Look, she's an angel."

Oh boy, Artie thinks. The woman is in worse shape than she expected.

"No, it's just me, Dr. Ligon. Artimeza—Artie."

"Oh," Dr. Ligon squints at her. "But, you're glowing. I see your halo."

Mr. Ligon exhales with a huff. He moves his index finger in a circular motion near his temple area, indicating: *crazy*. Artie doesn't smile. He clears his throat and looks at his shoes.

"I'm glad," Artie says. "Good to be glowing, I think." She hopes she doesn't sound patronizing.

"Oh, I think so too." Dr. Ligon's voice is childlike. Her eyes are awe-filled.

"I have something to tell you," Artie says.

Dr. Ligon gasps, "A message."

"Christ," her husband moans. "Don't encourage this."

"No, it's just something *I* feel," Artie says. "Just a message from me."

Dr. Ligon looks at her spouse, then back at Artie. She smiles in a way that suggests they share a secret. "Yeah, okay," she says. "Go ahead."

"I know losing your baby was more painful than you could bear—"

"—Her name was Cora," Dr. Ligon says, raising her voice. "Short for Corazon. She was my baby girl. She was my heart." Dr. Ligon stares, intensely, straight ahead at air. Her eyes leak. She seems unaware of the tears.

Artie swallows and takes a breath. She has to quell her own urge to cry. "Cora... That's a pretty name. Even though you won't get to raise Cora, if you still want to be a mother you *can*."

Dr. Ligon's head turns to face the wall. "I tried harder than I've ever tried to do anything. She was my last try."

"But giving birth is just a small part of it. My mom gave birth to me, but that never made her my mother."

Dr. Ligon looks at her again. She nods. "I remember."

"Do you want to raise a child and love her unconditionally, guide her to be the best she can be?"

"I *wanted* to. But no one picked me. I thought Cora had, but she changed her mind."

"There are plenty of babies who need mothering, Dr. Ligon, and if you end your life too soon you'll miss an opportunity. If you want to be a mother, don't give up. *Mother* someone."

"Excuse me, but who the fuck are you?" her husband asks.

"Bitao, shhh," Dr. Ligon whispers.

"No. This is none of your business." He glares at Artie.

She ignores him. Dr. Ligon's yearning, crazed eyes give Artie a stark view of her raw heart. It hurts to look at her.

"But why didn't anyone pick me?" she asks, with a sob. "What's wrong with me?"

"What do you mean?" Artie asks.

"Before the babies come, they choose their parents. No one chose me. I thought Cora did, but she didn't stay."

Artie is stumped. She wants to tell her that no one wants her husband for a father, but she doesn't. Then a thought suddenly comes that surprises her. Words tumble out of her mouth that she's not sure she even understands. "Well sometimes, the babies come through a soul that they're only meant to be with for a short time and then they move on to the souls they've *really* come to be with. They know where they're going."

Dr. Ligon is quiet, absorbing this. Soon she nods as though she's understood.

Artie thinks she looks a bit more hopeful and she's glad for that, but she wishes she'd written down what she just said. It sounds something like Rayana's church-speak, but Artie doesn't remember knowing this stuff. She speaks again, "Cora's purpose may have been to open you up to another soul that's on its way to you. Or it may have been to teach you something about your own soul."

After a moment, Dr. Ligon nods again. Artie thinks the words that have come out sound wise, but they're not *her* words. It's like when she was recovering from the breakdown and she cried for days then realized, *somehow*, that her hardships were her soul's journey. The wisdom was from someplace else. She remembers how Kendall told her a "voice" in his head had spoken to him, but it wasn't *his* voice. That's what this feels like. Someone else's voice, someone wiser than she is, speaking through her. She waits a moment to be sure it's finished.

"Thank you for working with me, Dr. Ligon," she says, moving closer to her. "The way you got me talking and the way you listened, and gave me exercises, it really did help."

Ligon nods. "We were meant to meet. I believe that's why I can see your shimmer. It makes sense now. We've met before. In the other realm."

Her husband walks out of the room shaking his head.

Tears course down Dr. Ligon's face. "Thank *you* for coming to help *me*." She smiles.

Artie takes a tissue and wipes Ligon's face. She's in restraints, and can't wipe it herself. Then there doesn't seem to be anything more to say and it's time to go.

Eighteen

Artie, 2004

While riding back to Rayana's, Artie wonders about the desire to give up and die. Does it open a door to the spiritual realm? Like Ligon, Rico said odd things when he tried to die.

Artie, 1990

Troy drove Artie home after the screening at The Black Filmmakers Hall of Fame Film Festival in Oakland.

"I'm coming in," he said. "Your father needs to know what y'all are up to."

Artie squeezed Kendall's hand and felt sick to her stomach. She lied about where she was going *and* she was messing with a boy. She was really in for it now.

They entered the row house and then the living room. The TV was still on, but Rico wasn't on the sofa. Mingus came to the door. He barked a bit and then he whined.

"Papi?" Artie called. His bedroom door was open. He wasn't in there either.

"Can I use your bathroom?" Troy asked.

Artie exhaled. Rico was out. Whew. Saved!

Then she saw the note on the coffee table.

Dear Artie,

Papi loves you. None of this has anything to do with you. I'm not angry with you. I just need peace. Forgive me.

Love, Papi

"OH SHIT," Troy screamed from the bathroom.

Artie ran down the hall. "Papi! Papi!"

Troy came out and closed the door. "Hold her back while I call 911," he yelled to Kendall. Troy's hands were on his face, his nails digging into his cheeks.

"What did he do?" Artie lunged for the door. "PAPI!"

Kendall grabbed her. Mingus growled, then bit him on the forearm. "Aoow!"

"No Mingus," Artie said. "It's okay, boy."

Nothing was okay. The skin on Kendall's arm was broken. He needed antiseptic. Artie took his hand. Shaking, she pulled him into the bathroom.

Rico was passed out in the tub. Naked. Instead of looking at him, she focused on an empty amber-colored prescription bottle on the shaggy blue mat. "I'm sorry I cursed at him earlier. And I want him to be okay, I do, but why does he have to be *naked*? I don't wanna see all that." She turned away and got the Bactine for Kendall.

Rico was fine, physically, after his stomach was pumped. Troy missed his screening at the festival the next day, because he was at the hospital with Rico and Artie. A social worker asked for his help. Troy didn't know what to do. Kendall called his mom collect from a pay phone. She contacted Rayana, who flew there immediately.

The nurses would only let Artie sit with Rico for brief periods. She sat in the waiting room in Kendall's arms most of the time. He held her all day and he told her that he'd make sure she was okay no matter what happened. He'd take care of her from then on.

Artie appreciated that, but she couldn't trust that *anyone* would take care of her. People were selfish. Unreliable. She wondered if while Rico was taking his clothes off and taking those pills, he'd thought about how she'd feel, or what might happen to her. Doubtful. He hadn't considered Artie much since they left New York. Back then he did things with her and treated her like she was important. Lately, he treated her like shit.

Artie was allowed to sit with Rico in the room, alone. They wouldn't let Kendall go in with her. The first time, she sat for fifteen minutes. He was weeping, and all he said was hello. He wouldn't talk or make eye contact. The room had no windows and only one chair. It was tiny and dark with a dim overhead light. There was a TV, but it wasn't on.

The next time she went in, Rico started babbling. "I was her spirit guide in our past life," he said. "Serena didn't believe in anything good. I tried to show her what *was* good, but she only saw the negative. And you, you were one of her guides, too. You came back in this life to help me help her."

Artie wondered what the fuck he was talking about. She wished he'd stop. He was on some kind of drug that made him loco. If he kept talking about that bitch, she was apt to crack him over the head with the chair she was sitting on. *I came to life just to help that woman?* Coño!

When Rico was released, Rayana stayed with them in Berkeley for a month. Artie spent a lot of time with Sushama and Alessandra, and Ray spent a lot of time with Rico. He needed her help. For reasons Artie didn't understand, she was willing to give it.

Rayana talked Rico into moving back to Los Angeles with her. Months later, at the end of Artie's school year, that's what they did.

Artie, 2004

Artie watches the way Ray's head lilts from side to side as she drives, as if there's a song in her mind.

"My psychiatrist said that Rico's behavior toward me was sexually abusive."

Ray turns to her, wide-eyed.

"Hearing him having sex," Artie says. "Seeing it. Seeing him naked. That's considered abuse. It's damaging."

Rayana turns back to the road. She exhales. Nods. "I'm sorry that happened. That was a difficult phase. He wasn't well, mentally."

Artie snorts. "That's an excuse I've heard before."

"It's a context, Artie. You have to look at things in context if you want to understand them, if you want to recover. Do you want to recover? Or do you want to stay damaged?"

Artie looks out the window. They pass a block of mom and pop shops with colorful, hand painted signs. Ray turns off the boulevard into her tree-lined Inglewood neighborhood. The canopies of the Magnolias are wider and denser than when Artie first called this street home.

She sighs. "Tell me your formula for happiness again?"

"Two things," Rayana says, "The ability to forgive, and a commitment to building relationships up rather than tearing them down. If your life isn't working, there's someone or some*thing* you need to forgive."

Artie smiles sadly. Ray parks in front of the house in the same spot where Kendall's mother's car was the day he first kissed her.

"Guess my life'll never work again."

"Give it some time," Ray says. She pats Artie's thigh.

Artie believes in Ray's formula, but there's no pill she can take, or book she can read, or prayer she can pray that will make forgiveness take place. You have to want to forgive. What she wants is revenge.

Nineteen

Serena, 2004

Serena sits alone in the hot tub at Burke Williams, a spa in Santa Monica. Since the incident, water—being in it or around it—soothes her.

Spa visits are part of the maintenance that keeps her body fit. Imperative not just for the music business, but also 'cause someone's always chattin' up Jamie. She walks every day, lifts weights three days a week, eschews white sugar and white flour, eats organic, drinks green tea, exfoliates, bleaches her teeth, dyes her hair, wears hats and sunscreen, takes vitamins and herbs, gets acupuncture, microdermabrasion, manicures, pedicures, eyebrow waxes, leg, bikini and underarm waxes, facials, massages...

It's exhausting.

Red wine's supposed to have health and anti-aging benefits; that's the only alcohol she drinks. A bottle a day's probably too much, but Christ, she thinks, could I *be* enny bloody healthier?

She didn't drink as much back in New York. It was Jamie's idea to have a place here. He saw the towers fall from their loft. Still anxious a few years later, he wanted out. He's taking a break from touring to be a beach bum. Bought himself a small building on the boardwalk in Marina Del Rey where it meets Venice. They each have their own flat, and there's a recording studio on the top floor.

Serena and Jamie don't call themselves a couple, though they are one. They don't live together, exactly, yet they *do*. Serena pretends it's okay, but it isn't.

Before it started, she thought their flirtation might lead to *something*. A brief romance at best, she figured. Whatever this is, however, has persisted well beyond a decade.

Serena, 1990

The cruise ended in Florida and they flew back into La Guardia airport. At the baggage claim, Jamie ignored Ondine and wouldn't leave Serena alone.

"Whatchu doin' for Christmas?" he asked. "Or should I say *who* you doin'? Hidin' a man up in the Bronx?"

Serena was watching the carousel for her bag when she saw Ondine cut a look at Jamie then turn to grab her own luggage.

"Your charm may get you laid, but lack of chivalry's gon' get ya *left*, Ace." She pointed to Ondine.

He turned and watched his girlfriend struggle with the large black suitcase. "Be there in a minute, babe," he yelled.

An elderly man stepped in to help Ondine. Once they set the bag on the floor, she turned and stared at Jamie. Her expression was one Serena would not forget: utterly fed up with being disappointed. Done. Poor Ace-Bye didn't get it. He turned back to Serena and winked.

"She's a'ight. So, I'mma see you in a couple weeks? We goin' back in the studio right after New Year's, so don't catch no cold or nothin'."

"Enjoy your holiday," Serena said. "Betta buy dat garrl somethin' aspacially nice."

He leaned in to kiss her on the mouth. She gave him a cheek. Ondine was watching behind them. A nice gift wasn't going to be enough.

In the taxi en route to the Bronx Serena tried to imagine what Annie would say. Would she deny it? Cry? Beg Serena's forgiveness? It began to snow on the Major Deegan. By the time the cab pulled up in front of the narrow three-story house, the small front lawn was blanketed in white. She stomped snow off her shoes before entering the front door and wiping them dry on the matt. The mantle clock chimed. Annie came from the kitchen to greet Serena in the foyer. Her hair was pinned back and she wore a crew neck sweater and an apron around her waist. Her eyes were red and sunken as if she were tired. Her face was sallow. Serena wondered if she had a cold.

"We missed you, darling. The house was so quiet without you," Annie said.

She reached out to offer a hug and Serena stepped back.

"What is it?" Annie asked. "What's wrong?"

"I need to talk to you alone."

"Oh. Well, we're smack in the middle of preparing Buddy's Christmas puddin'. You know he's been soaking those currants and raisins in rum all year long."

"Annie, I'm tellin' you, you don't want Buddy to hear what I've got to say."

Annie crossed her arms. Her smiled faded. "Darling," she shouted toward the kitchen, "be a dear and shovel the walk, will you, love? Snow's piling up."

"I will not," he answered. "Nothin' gon' keep me from makin' this puddin'!"

"I've been to Bermuda." Serena took off her wool coat and slung it over the staircase railing. With the oven adding to the temperature, her black turtleneck was suffocating. She stared steadily at Annie, and wiped perspiration from her forehead.

"Buddy!" Annie yelled. "If you don't do it now the snow will be too heavy later."

They could hear him suck his teeth and slam the oven door before coming through the foyer. Cursing Serena under his breath, he stomped upstairs toward his warm clothes.

Annie walked into the kitchen. Serena followed. The classical radio station played a Bach organ sonata. Annie pointed to the table while she refreshed a pot of tea with hot water. Serena sat down and didn't speak until Annie pour herself a cup.

"I spoke wif my so-called siblings," she said.

Annie folded her hands. "You should have told me you were going. You went into my address book?"

Serena nodded.

"You had no right," Annie said, shaking her head.

"*I* had no right? You serious? Are you my mother?" Annie banged a hand on the table. Her cup rattled and the tea splashed about.

"You ran off and spoke with those people about me? How bloody ungrateful? I took you off that little island and showed you there was a world out there. You got an education, you traveled, I paid for singing lessons, piano lessons, nice clothes, money for college; *anything you asked for*," she shouted in Serena's face. "I struggled for you. You had a good upbringing. I've *always* looked after you and supported and encouraged you in everything AND DID NOTHING FOR *MYSELF*!"

Annie's stentorian shouting was apoplectic. Serena leaned back; afraid the woman might hit her. She never had. Not like her first mother. Thirty years later, Serena still recalled the sting of Artimeza's spankings, and the terror.

"Then it's true?" she asked, her eyes welling up. "Y've lied all this time."

"Get out. You ungrateful, self-centered bitch. Get out of my house."

"Vhere'm I supposed to go? There's a blizzard."

"That is not my concern. I want you out of my sight."

Serena took a paper napkin from the table, dabbed her tears, and then blew her nose. Her head throbbed above her eye sockets. She stood up, left the room, and retrieved her coat from the staircase railing. Her luggage was where she left it, by the front door. She removed the gifts she'd picked up for Annie and Buddy on her trip, and left them in the front parlor where the mantle clock was bling, blang, blonging as she walked out.

Buddy was not shoveling when she reached the walkway. No one was on 230th St. in the cold, wind, and wet snow, except her. As she struggled up the hill with her bag toward White Plains Road and the elevated train, her feet froze and she slid repeatedly on the icy sidewalk. She thought of ringing Jamie, but decided against it. She knew of a residence hotel in Greenwich Village not far from where she used to live. She rode the 2 Train down there, checked in and stayed alone in a small, albeit warm room until after Christmas.

When she finally did ring Jamie, he sounded drunk. He cried on the phone and slurred his words. Something happened with Ondine, but he wouldn't say what. He lived on Astor Place, walking distance from where Serena was on West 12th Street.

She arrived at his loft and saw that it was huge—two floors. An eclectic art collection filled the walls. The paintings and photographs, some of them antiques, had display lights illuminating them. The space was also littered with ripped up sheet music, dirty dishes and sundry take-out boxes. Wine bottles littered the coffee table, dining table, and the floor. Ace-Bye was barefoot in a soiled white T-shirt and gray sweat pants.

"We had company on Christmas, me and Ondine," he said, scratching the stubble on his face. "Both our folks were here from N'awlins and the girl disappeared for like a hour! Know where I found her? On the fuckin' roof swappin' spit with Benny."

"*Our* Benny? From de label?"

He nodded. Sniffled. "Can ya-belee-dat shit? With our mamas here and e'rything. Y'know I gave Ondine's folks money to pay off her school loans? Moved her up here. Wanted to marry that girl." His voice cracked.

He grabbed up a handful of sheet music confetti strewn on the sofa, and sat down.

"The songs I been writin' were all for her." He dropped the torn pieces of paper onto the floor. "Hadda put her ass out. She's gone back with her mama-n-daddy." He put his head in his hands. "What'm I supposed to do now?"

"She does one thing and you throw her out?"

"It was Benny," he yelled, lifting his head. "Not some random mufucka I'd never haveta see... She wanted to go anyway."

Serena moved a bottle aside and sat cross-legged on the floor. Her jeans were loose as pajamas. She'd barely eaten in days. "The way you are is hard on a garrl, Jamie." She spoke gently. "Most women wouldn't tolerate it."

He rubbed his face. "She knew who I was. We had an agreement."

"C'mon, nawh. Even if she knew, no one wants it in their face."

"Least I'm honest about it. Shit. Other dudes'll straight up cheat and tell a chick she's the only one. Can't help the way I am. Don' mean I don't love deep, though." His face was flaming. He let out a sob. "Will anyone ever *get* me?"

Just then, Serena looked up at the wall and for a moment thought she saw *herself*. It was an old photograph; so old it was on metal, and the woman looked eerily like her—similar shaped face, features, and long, thick hair. It was startling enough that she took it as a "sign."

Serena would kick herself for it later, but she thought *she* could understand Jamie. She was going through so much, with her burgeoning career and falling out with Annie. An open relationship seemed okay. No man was entirely faithful, she reasoned. What was so egregious about a man who admitted it?

Their arrangement was that Jamie L'Heureux could do his thing, though never where they lived. And she didn't want to see him with other women, not even flirting. She was free to be out there as well, if she cared to be. But wondering what he was up to, where he was going, and who he was talking to, took all the energy she might have had to chase another man.

Not long after she moved in with Jamie, she wrote this letter:

January 19, 1991

Dear Annie,

Just a note to let you know where I am and that I'm fine. Hope you're well, too. I want you to know that though I was angry, I love and appreciate you very much. Sorry if my inquiry has made you feel otherwise. You were good to me all my life and I don't deny that. However, I would like to hear the truth. If you are my mother, I believe an explanation is a reasonable request. And please, may I know who my biological father is? This is important to me. I hope you'll be in touch.

With much love,
Ree

Serena's CD was released later that year, and for a jazz album it was a stunning success. She sent Annie a copy. There was no response. A time that should have yielded immense joy was achingly empty. Moving in with Jamie didn't fill the space left by Annie's absence. Serena wanted to share the experience, to make her mother proud, but Annie would have nothing to do with her.

In late October, a birth certificate showed up at Jamie's loft. It was different from the one Serena held a copy of all her adult life. This one listed Anna Ward as her mother and the father as "unknown." It said her birthplace was Goshen, New York, USA. The certificate Serena had named John and Artimeza Bullock as her parents, and noted Bermuda as her birthplace.

She didn't understand. Was the first one forged? And "unknown?" Surely Annie had to have known who the father was. Shortly after Serena received the birth certificate Annie rang her up. She wanted to meet. Elated, Serena said she would come home, but her mother didn't want that. She would come to Serena's flat in Manhattan.

She buzzed downstairs. Serena opened the door to the flat and waited in the hall facing the brushed nickel lift. She adjusted her hair to one shoulder. It had been pressed. Her makeup was simple—mascara and lip-gloss. She picked a piece of lint off of her black tank dress and she scanned the matching tights for any imperfections. The loft was spotless. Jamie's art collection and photographs dazzled on the walls behind her. She took a deep breath and let it out slowly, steadying her nerves.

When the elevator doors slid open and Annie stepped off, she looked directly at Serena, without smiling. Her Scottish tweed suit was the kind she used to wear to work, and she had on a short black wig.

"That hairstyle is lovely on you," Serena said. She was about to call her Auntie, but she stopped herself. "And you've lost weight, haven't you? Y'look fantastic."

She hugged her tightly. Annie flinched, as if she didn't want the hug. Serena released her. She bit her lip and tried not to cry. She led Annie inside.

"Jamie's in the studio. Sends his regards."

Annie looked up and all around, taking in the space—the large windows, high ceilings, the antiques, artwork, and the grand piano.

"Mm, mm," she grunted, repeatedly. "Lovely. Just lovely."

"Thank you," Serena said. "I bought a much smaller place downstairs. I rent it out and live here wif Jamie."

"You've done well for yourself, Ree," Annie said.

Serena tried to smile. "Vould you like tea?" She pointed at the glass and stone coffee table, where a pot and cups waited.

Annie moved to the sofa. Before she sat, she stared at the portrait of the woman on the wall who looked like Serena. "Well that's uncanny, innit?" Annie sat and continued to stare at it. "Who is she?"

Serena joined her, kneeling on the floor beside the coffee table. "Jamie's great, great grandmother—somethin' like dat. I know. We look related."

Annie poured herself a cup of tea. "Who knows? Maybe you are." She looked at Serena again and cleared her throat. "The birth certificate you received is a copy I saved of the original," she said. "The one you had before was issued when you were adopted by my sister. Your grenny, who was quite religious, insisted upon that. You were born in Upstate New York at a home for un-wed mothers where I was sent to avoid shaming the family. I always intended to leave you the original, and I sent it because I'm dying and I don't want Buddy to find it first."

Serena froze. "Dyin'? What?" She held her stomach as if she'd been punched.

"Never mind that," Annie said.

"But, what's wrong—"

"—Let me finish, dammit." Annie paused to take a breath. She let it out. "I tried to give you the opportunity to believe you were from respectable people. I know what I told you was hurtful, but I tried to love you enough to make up for it. Pardon me if that wasn't the case."

"That's not what I—." Serena tried to touch her, but Annie knocked her hand aside.

"—I'm not through," she growled. "Before working at the dress shop on Front St. I was a chambermaid at The Princess. My sister had always been the one admired and flattered for her looks. When I went to work at the hotel, *I* received attention for the first time. Men from all over the world noticed me. Some said I was beautiful. They wanted to spend time with me. After I had my heart thrashed by more than one gentleman who said he'd be back for me, but never even sent a letter, I began to understand what these men really thought of me." She was quiet for a moment. Her dark eyes shined with tears. She looked away and sipped her tea. "I stopped feeling. I knew they didn't feel for me either, but I decided it was enough that I was… *desired*. Heaven forgive me, I *enjoyed* that." Her eyes met Serena's. "I haven't the faintest clue who your father is. You wanted the truth: there you have it. Hope you prefer it to the tale I told to protect you."

Serena digested this in silence. It *was* in fact, better than the lie. She felt no judgment toward the promiscuity, though it was a bit astonishing. She'd always believed Annie to be quite prim. Who knew their sexual appetites were so similar? She finally stood up and was about to offer a hug when Annie removed her wig to reveal a baldhead.

"I have stage III breast cancer," she said. "The last round of chemotherapy was unsuccessful. I don't expect to survive it."

Serena felt her legs buckle.

Serena, 2004

Annie's death remains painful thirteen years later. Serena still sees her. She feels her, and even talks with her. Sometimes in dreams, sometimes she dreams while wide-awake. She imagines her sitting across the hot tub, her body submerged in the water. Her face glows with health. Her hair is full.

"How are you?" Annie asks, her light brown cheeks flushing from the heat.

Serena stares at her. "Feel like I did when they dumped me in your driveway. I seem to feel that way a lot."

"Good God, get over it." Annie tells her. "That's a lifetime ago,"

"True. But every loss digs de feelin' deeper. Gets vorse instead of better."

"Is that right?" Annie asks. "That's why you stay with that hellion who doesn't honor you?"

"Jamie? What do you mean?"

"You're frightened of loss. Can't lose what's not really yours, can you?"

Serena hadn't put that together before. Hm. "Your'e right. He's *not* really mine," she says. "No one is. You vere all I had."

"I can't change what happened when you were a girl," Annie says. "Only you can change how you live with it now. Stop punishing yourself, Ree."

"You let me think I was noffin'. Thrown away like a woffless bit a rubbish."

"No. That's what *you* did to *your* daughter. I didn't throw you away the way you did little Artimeza. I took you back."

Didn't matter that Annie was her mum and took her back. Serena didn't know that then. The fact that she thought they didn't want her was what stuck. She wants to tell Annie that. But a couple of young women step into the hot tub and Annie's head disappears under the water.

Twenty

Artie, 2004

The first night back in her old room, now Ray's guest room and office, Artie sits on the white bed quilt and cleans her beloved camera. She's found a microfiber cloth that she left in the nightstand drawer years ago. She doesn't remember bringing the camera to Ray's. Kendall must have dropped it off. She loves the feel of its weight in her hands and the coolness of the metal against her skin. With newly manicured hands she wipes down the extra lenses, as well. "Nikki" is Artie's favorite camera, a Nikon F3/T she received for high school graduation. She was told it was from Rico, but that wasn't true.

Artie, 1995

It was a week after graduation. In a tank top and shorts, Artie leaned back against the brass headboard and played with the exposure settings on her new toy. Mingus lounged on the floor beside the bed. She heard the pin key twist in the doorknob. Kendall entered, closed the door, and locked it. He put a finger to his lips. *Shh.*

Mingus got up, stretched, then wagged his tail and licked him on the chin.

"Rico didn't give you the camera," Kendall whispered. "Overheard my mom talking to Rayana. It's from your mother."

"What?" Artie asked, getting under the covers. "Why didn't they tell me?"

She wiggled out of her shorts and underwear.

Kendall took off his T-shirt and undid his belt. "Ray said that Serena sent the camera to your grandmother in New York and asked her to give it to you for graduation. Rico didn't tell you, 'cause, according to him, 'that bitch is unreliable and inconsistent.'"

Kendall stepped out of his jeans and climbed into the bed. Artie snuggled into his arms. He smelled freshly showered and donned his signature scent, Dial soap.

"He's just trying to protect me," Artie said. "It's okay."

Kendall kissed her forehead. "Even if she is unreliable, they should still tell you the truth."

"The truth isn't always so great."

"I disagree. 'No lie can live forever,'" he said. "Member we saw that MLK quote posted outside the church? That shit is true. And if the truth's gonna come out anyway, might as well be honest from the jump."

Artie sits up. "Yeah, well you don't need to be honest *all* the damn time."

"You mad at me, baby?"

"Stop telling me when you think some other girl is cute. I didn't need to hear that shit at lunch today."

"Baby. I don't love anybody, but you. I'm a dude, though. Dudes can't help lookin' at other girls. It's how we're wired. I'm not gonna do anything, but I gotta be honest with you about it. It helps me."

"Well it doesn't help *me*."

Kendall shrugged. "*Not* pimpin' ain't easy."

Artie rolled her eyes and pulled her underpants back on.

"Whatchu doin'?" Kendall asked.

"If I had a dick it'd be limp right now."

"Oh, come on, baby…"

Artie, 2004

Artie shakes her head. Fool. How did we stay together as long as we did?

She admires the camera as she finishes wiping it down. When she received it, it was already a used model, from the eighties, and she couldn't imagine why Serena picked *this* particular camera, or how she could have known how perfect it was. Artie worked with it all through her photography studies at NYU and she continues to shoot with it. She owns newer cameras: a Hasselblad, a couple of digital SLRs, and even a collectible Leica, but she loves Nikki the Nikon like she's a living soul.

There was a time wherein she fantasized that Serena had changed. Imaginary Serena cared about her. Imaginary Serena had made attempts to contact her, but Rico had thwarted them. Artie knew it was make-believe, but Nikki was her magical possession, her link to this higher version of "the bitch." She relished the delusion. What *wasn't* delusional was that the camera took her finest photographs. She had the best luck with it, and it was as much a part of the essence of her work as her own eye was. She'd photographed Willie Nelson on a movie set once with his raggedy-ass guitar, "Trigger," that was held together with bolts and crazy glue. People on set snickered and speculated about why he didn't get a new one. Artie didn't have to ask why he didn't replace Trigger. She knew that he never would, just as she'd shoot with Nikki until one of them couldn't anymore.

When Artie and Kendall were living in New York she photographed

Serena with Nikki. It was '97 and Kendall was at the New School, immersed in jazz studies. He took Artie to just about every jazz club in town. One of them, The Jazz Standard, was right around the corner from the place they rented on lower Lexington Avenue. One night, Kendall was studying, and she went with Alessandra for dinner. Ally was also in New York, at Columbia, studying filmmaking with Milos Forman. Artie shot stills for her when she made short films.

They chose Standard only because it was close, but when they walked in, Serena was at the piano. Artie froze, staring at her in the blue-tinted light.

"What is it?" Alessandra asked. "You look upset."

Artie shook her head and let the hostess seat them. Alessandra knew who Serena Ward, the well-known singer, was, but Artie had never mentioned that she was her mother. Years earlier she told Sush and Ally that her mother was dead.

Even though her mouth watered from the smell of garlic and grilled fish and she was starving, Artie left Ally at the table and began shooting while Serena performed. She opened the lens way up, slowed down the shutter and used available light. It wasn't bothering Serena or the other musicians, and it was a way for Artie to unleash her emotion in a constructive way. That is until her waitress, a tall woman with a big afro, who looked like a model, hissed at her to stop.

"She's my mother," Artie snapped, as if this gave her license to break the rules.

The waitress gave her a heavy-lidded, look. "Miss, I'll have to have security handle you if you don't sit down. And the cover charge won't be refunded."

Artie sat down.

"She's not your mother," Alessandra whispered. "Are you crazy?"

"Okay," Artie said.

Alessandra tried to chat with Artie during the rest of the set. Artie wouldn't talk. She listened. Serena was so talented, her voice powerful and filled with pain. Artie wished she knew what that pain *was*. But she didn't. She didn't know Serena.

An inexplicable burst of courage helped Artie pull Ally back to Serena's dressing room after the set. Though she wasn't sure how the woman would receive her, she was fairly certain she'd admit to being her mother.

Artie had grown up in the seven years since they'd seen each other. She was nineteen.

Serena was putting her leather coat when she opened the door. Her mouth fell agape. She covered it with her hand.

"Oh my God. Artie," she said. A smile came moments later.

Artie smiled back. She figured Serena knew she was in New York, because she'd sent a note to Annie's address letting her know she was graduating a year early from high school and on her way to NYU to study photography at Tisch School of the Arts. Buddy was still in the house so even though Serena wasn't living there, she still got her mail. She must have received the note, because Nikki showed up not long after.

Serena kissed Artie on the cheek and touched her other cheek with her hand. It was the warmest gesture Artie could remember receiving from her. *Is she really glad to see me?* She wondered. Serena's signature cloud of spicy perfume, Opium, transported Artie back to the stress of East 13th St. Artie doesn't recall kissing Serena, or even touching her. Maybe she did. Maybe she was too stunned. What she does recall is the two of them standing there looking at each other, Serena's eyes laden with pathos like her singing voice.

"Vell," she finally said, her Bermudian v's for w's still distinct.

"Hi, I'm Alessandra." She extended her hand. "Artie's friend since childhood. Amazing to meet you." Serena shook her hand. "Can't believe you're her mother. Wow." Her wide-eyed astonishment made it painfully clear that Artie never mentioned her. "My mother played your first CD constantly. It was magical."

Serena nodded. She looked at Artie. "Would you garrls like to hev a drink? My treat."

"Okay," Artie said. She was trembling. The night felt like a scary dream, yet she didn't want to wake up.

They sat at a table near the bar.

"Hahw do you like NYU?" Serena asked, staring at Artie.

"It's cool." She touched the camera to be sure it was still hanging around her neck. "I have some amazing instructors—"

"—I feel *so old*," Serena blurted. She shook her head and sighed.

Artie stopped speaking. Serena didn't seem to be listening anyway. She *was* looking at her, though. She seemed to be studying her face.

"But, um, you d-don't even look your age," Alessandra said, giving Artie a sideways look. *Mia Madre.*

Serena must have sensed how ill at ease they were. She smiled. "Artie, you're just too grown-up. And too beautiful."

Her tone was playful, yet adversarial. Artie was nonetheless moved to know that Serena thought she was beautiful, even if she didn't seem comfortable with that. Awkward as it was, seeing her mother and something of herself in her face was more gratifying than she could have predicted. She hoped Serena felt that way, too.

The pretty waitress with the afro brought their drinks. She wouldn't look Artie in the eye.

Artie expected Serena to comment on the camera, since she was wearing it around her neck. She didn't. Artie told her she was glad to be back in New York, it still felt like home. And she explained that Rico had gone on tour with a Latin pop star to be able to afford NYU. The sacrifice was implicit. Serena knew Rico had contempt for pop music. She didn't comment.

She said, "I'm glad you're pursuin' photography. I saw your talent, even when you were a little garrl. You were always an ah-tist."

Artie appreciated this, though she didn't say so. She was afraid to express her emotions. They might boil over and scald someone. There were things she wondered about, but didn't have the courage to ask. Serena's second and third CDs did poorly. Her label had dropped her. How was she coping with that? And with Annie's death? Serena loved Rico and Annie *most*. Now she had neither. Though Artie still thought of her as "the bitch," she sensed that Serena's life wasn't flourishing. There was something stagnant about her, no sense of enthusiasm. As if she were a ghost moving through the motions of a past that she knew led nowhere special. Artie was thriving. Because of that, she resented Serena a little less.

When the check came, Serena snatched it and stood abruptly. "I'll bring it to de bar and take care of it on my vay out." She was eager to escape.

Artie wasn't sure how to say good-bye. Serena kissed her quickly, and with less warmth than she'd greeted her with. They made no plan to stay in touch.

The night left Artie bruised. Serena still didn't want to know her. And that still hurt. To numb herself she decided to think of Serena as a relative she'd known when she was younger, but wasn't close to anymore.

Later, when Artie looked at the photographs she'd taken of Serena, she noticed the absence of light. It wasn't that there was *no* light source at all; it was that Serena seemed to have no luminance of her own. Artie believed that most people had a barely perceptible light that emanated from them. It attracted and combined with other light sources and you could actually capture that connection in a photograph. Other photographers were quick to tell her she was crazy, but Artie saw what she saw. People who carried that light popped when she shot them. And some just didn't sparkle no matter how well you lit them. Nikki got this. She was a magic barometer that detected where radiance existed and where it did not.

When Artie looked at her treasured photo album and the *old* pictures, Serena's light was there. Somewhere along the way, she'd flickered out. Even though Artie was haunted by things Serena had done, and things she hadn't done, she still rooted for her. She hoped she'd get her spark back.

Artie, 2004

Not anymore.

She looks down at the camera in her lap. She notices now that there's film inside. A roll was shot, but never removed. Her stomach turns queasy as she remembers now that *she* was the one who brought the camera here. It was that night. She'd somehow driven herself to Rayana's and stayed a day or two before accepting that she couldn't function. She remembers shooting the pictures. She wishes she could block the memory out. Artie doesn't have a dark room at Rayana's anymore. She can't develop and print them herself. She *could* drop the film at the lab. Or she could toss it in the trash. What good could come from seeing the photographs? Her rational side says there isn't any, of course. But her crazy side is louder at the moment.

Twenty-one

Serena, 2004

Serena takes a seat at the bar alone. She comes to Hal's, a black-owned watering hole in Venice, for the jazz and people watching on Sunday and Monday nights. Once in a while she sings, but mostly, her bumpy's propped on a stool in red lipstick, a dress, and heels. She takes in the musicians, the paintings on the walls, the colorful patrons, and she *drinks*, of course. This is her spot.

The music is pure melodic grace this evening. A young jazz harmonica player amazes the crowd; transcending preconceived ideas about the places this (lowly) instrument can take them. He hits notes and curves lines in ways that pull Serena into her own heart. This sublime art form has helped keep her going. Jazz nourishes her soul. Only thing that could make her fancy frequenting Hal's any more is if she could get here and back via subway. How she misses New York.

Lately, she comes half hoping to run into Rico again. Every jazz musician in town comes through at some point, so she's told. She needs him to listen—to believe her. If he does he might convince Artie, and then maybe, one day, there could be a rapprochement. They may never be friends, but she hopes to shed her enemy status one day.

Rico won't take her calls. When she rings him he either hangs up, or sends her to voicemail. She could've pressed charges when he struck her.

There were witnesses. The least he can do is listen. Maybe he *has*. She's left voicemail and email. If he passes the information along to Artie it's not like he'll report back to her. All Serena can do is wait.

She didn't know who that bye was. How could she? She'd never met him. Before that night, she'd been in L.A. less than a year's time. She hadn't got 'round to meeting all the local musicians yet. Hal's was an unsung song. She'd discovered it only a week earlier when Jamie brought her in for supper. Hal Frederick, one of the owners, was so friendly it made her instantly at home.

The following visit, she went unescorted and a young man was playing with his quintet. She sat right where she's sittin' now and thought the bye and his band mates were brilliant. Babies, too, the lot of 'em under thirty. They played some original compositions, which she found charming. Then at the end of their set they played Carlos Santana's "Europa," and Serena went mad, cheering and dancing like some callow groupie.

The song is one of her favorites. She thinks it's just about the sexiest piece of music ever written. Ah, the memories it evokes... She and Rico listened to the Gato Barbieri version so often they wore the record out in the late eighties. One thing she's never been fond of, however, is the song's subtitle: "Earth's Cry Heaven's Smile." *What de hell did Santana mean by that?* She doesn't really know, but she's decided it means that human suffering amuses God. This evokes anger, because it *does* feel like heaven's havin' a laugh at her expense. Quite often, in fact. Nevertheless, she loves the composition.

As she watched the handsome tenor player blow the fat out of one of her favorites, it struck her that he was wearing his sex appeal like a neon sign. The combination of the music, the eye-candy, and a couple of glasses of vino, made her giddy.

Did he look at her and smile? Perhaps it was her imagination, but it appeared as if this sexy bye was playing directly to *her*. She looked around to see if anyone noticed. No one seemed to recognize her. Must be because she'd just had her hair cut short and dyed that very day. It was chic. Made her eyes and cheekbones pop. Jamie was out doin' whatever the flip he does and she wanted some attention. She put on dangly earrings, a clingy beige knit dress, some painful, but spectacular Via Spiga sandals and fire engine red lip-gloss. She wasn't planning to pick anyone up, but she was looking to get her flirt on.

He must have announced his name when the set ended, but she was paying her bill and didn't catch it. She still had no notion of who he was when he came and sat beside her and told her she was sexy. She withheld a grin and thought she'd like to climb into his young lap and French kiss him, but instead she told him she was old enough to be his mum.

"Whoa—that accent makes you even hotter," he said, shaking his head. "If you're really that old you must be aged to perfection, lady." He slid her a slash of a smile and rested a hand on her back. "Like fine wine."

It was a disastrous attempt to be smooth. And yet, it was flattering to be hit on by a young, handsome man. She got the feeling he didn't recognize her. Surprising, because while she wasn't exactly a household name, she was undeniably known in the jazz world. Surely he'd heard of her. The lights were dim at the bar. He just hasn't had a good look, she thought. Her hairstyle was different. She'd only been photographed with her dark hair either in a bun or wild and long. It was close-cropped now and nearly blonde. She'd also filled out a bit since the last album and since Flo had stopped visiting as frequently. Serena had always been lean, but she was more muscular now that she'd been weight training. And she was fuller on top. People thought she'd had her girls done, but she hadn't. He was staring straight into them when he asked for her name. Paid no attention when she gave it to him.

"You are stunningly beautiful," he said. What are you drinking?"

Something about him reminded her of Rico. Maybe it was his white guayabera—identical to one Rico used to wear. He looked a bit like him, too: dark, curly hair and black eyes. And, she found, that like Rico he was self-absorbed. Talked about himself non-stop for at least forty minutes while they shared a bottle of pinot noir. He banged on about his tour to Japan, and his CDs, his publishing, his grant and his bloody, boring success. She couldn't get a word in, so she kept sipping 'til she found herself considerably smashed. She'd had enough of him by the hour's end, but she'd driven there and though she didn't live far, she could barely drive *sober;* so she made the mistake of asking him for a lift home.

If only she'd called a cab.

Instead of being a gentleman, the wanker felt her up in the car. His fingers tickled her nipples. She stopped him, though she didn't hate it. She thanked him for his interest, but assured him, "I'm far too drunk to properly appreciate dis, Ace." He seemed to accept that she parried his advances, and he proceeded to drive her home. But then she wasn't able to properly explain how to get to her flat. They headed down Washington Boulevard, then up Speedway, which was the right street, but it was dark and she was inebriated; she couldn't find the back of her bloody building. After a couple of attempts, he gave up and drove her to *his* place, which wasn't far. He said he'd go online and look up how to get there. His hand caressed her thigh.

"It's okay if you're drunk," he said and flashed his straight, white teeth.

He sounded sweet. Sounded like he really wanted her. It was nice to be desired. Maybe she *would* give him some, she thought. While she was trying to remember if she'd checked her underarms and if any gray hairs might have sprouted since her last bikini wax, she fell asleep. And then suddenly he was opening her door and trying to coax her out of the seat. Her body longed to stay put. The car was one of those monstrous SUVs. Who knew they were so damn comfortable?

He somehow flipped her seat back and she found herself reclining. The sunroof was open. She could see the stars. He eased on top of her, buried his face in her bosom and began sucking one of her breasts. She was stunned—it happened so quickly, like he was in some mad rush. Then he moved down, pulled up her dress and tugged at her knickers furiously. He was giving her a wedgie. He began to look farcical as he grew aggravated struggling with them. She realized he was trying to rip them. What made him think that was acceptable? They were Escada. She asked him to stop. Not that she wasn't a wee bit excited for him to proceed with his plans, but she was concerned about those little gray bastards. Jamie didn't mind them and she *was*, after all, almost fifty. *Still,* she, thought, *I'd rather not startle the bye with geriatric pussy.* But then he did manage to get the knickers off without ripping them and it was too late to worry about what he might find.

Horn blowers have exceptionally well trained tongues.

She would have said his name out loud if only she knew what it was. And was she ever grateful. He hit just the proper spot with just the proper pressure. Startlingly skilled. He was a nimble wanker, too. In what seemed like one smooth move, he shed his trousers and spun his body 'round so that his below the belt business was pointing in her face. Quite convenient. And mutually satisfying for about a minute, but then the unthinkable happened: up came supper. Ghastly. This had *never* happened before, but she was a bit queasy to begin with, and he was well endowed. Her gag reflex kicked in and BLECH. All over her dress— food mixed with wine stinkin' like a fetid puddle in Hell. Then she began to sweat. Profusely. In seconds she'd be drenched. Christ, she thought, fine time for a bloody hot flash.

She heard the boy say, "What the fuck?"

Then she looked up and saw someone through the open car window holding a camera.

"Oh shit," he squealed.

Then the figure disappeared. It came back moments later and tried, repeatedly, to smash the windshield with what looked like a tripod. The glass merely cracked, but that was no less terrifying. The figure was a woman and she was patently intent on killing them. The bye got out of the car to restrain her. And only then did Serena realize who she was, and whose *he* was and what an utter mess she'd found herself in. Surely forces beyond her control had conspired against her. This was far too heinous to have been a random coincidence. Earth's cry, heaven's smile, indeed. The gods, or perhaps the demons, were havin' a jolly laugh at her expense and she didn't appreciate the blasted joke.

Jamie's always tellin' her to lighten up. Says she takes life far too seriously. But what can she call hers, if not a disaster?

Twenty-two

Artie, 2004

Artie's been using the same lab on La Brea in Hollywood since before she left for college. There are a couple of grizzly old-timers who've known her since she used to take the bus there after school with Kendall.

As she picks up her photos, it occurs to her that it might have been a bad idea to have them developed here. Maybe it's made them uncomfortable? No one will look her in the eye. At the counter, Sandy, a middle aged lady with a buzz cut and tats looks down while entering Artie's invoice information on the computer. She doesn't engage as she normally does. Sandy and the other customer service person must have seen the salacious pictures, Artie thinks. They don't know how to act, or what to say. Usually, they make chitchat, ask how she is, how Kendall is, but they're quiet today. Gray, frizzy-haired Pete rings up her order. He smiles sadly and hands over her package. "Be well, sweetheart," he says, and goes on to the next customer. *Is he feeling sorry for me?*

Artie usually examines her photos before she leaves to be sure they're printed properly, but today she rushes out. She doesn't look at them in the car either. She drives with the top up, back down toward Inglewood without touching the envelope. She's afraid to. It's torturing her, imagining the images; remembering looking through the lens at Kendall in the sixty-nine position with Serena. Her heartbeat is racing.

She's wigging out. Maybe I need to get back on that damn Paxil, she thinks. It does take the edge off, but it makes her fat. A joint would help. She knows where Rico keeps his stash. That'll have to do.

"You're totally stoned, aren't you, love?" Ray asks, looking at her from the doorway.

"Damn," Artie says, sitting on cross-legged on the bed, blazed. "How could you tell?"

"Girl, please. I work with teenagers."

Artie leans against the wall and watches Ray as she lights vanilla scented candles, puts on her CD and settles down on the bed, too. She's brought in a bottle of champagne and two elegant flutes. She deftly opens the bottle, with a gentle pop, and pours them each a glass. Ray is like a fairy, Artie thinks; the way she makes ordinary moments magical.

"You're amazing," she says, gingerly taking the glass. "Thank you."

"My pleasure. I'm glad you're here," Ray says. She sits near the end of the bed.

"Please don't tell my dad about the weed, okay?"

"Oh," Ray says, her eyes meeting Artie's. "It's *his?*"

Artie turns her head to stare at the candle flame. She takes a sip of champagne.

"Artie…" Ray sighs. "If he asks, you know I won't lie to him."

"Hopefully he won't ask." Artie sets the glass on the bedside table. She fingers the stem. Ray's loyalty to Rico is irritating sometimes, but Artie admires their relationship. They still hold hands, go on dates, travel together, and generally adore each other. It's more than luck. Over the years she's watched Ray *tell* Rico what he was to her. For example, instead of complaining when he was a jackass, she would focus on times when he wasn't and she'd say, "Oh, baby, you're so good to me," or, "You make me happy." Eventually, strange as it sounds, he *became* consistently good to her and he *did* make her happy. He does. It's an approach that takes more patience than Artie feels she'll ever have.

"I just needed to relax," she says. Artie looks at Ray, whose legs are stretched across the width of the bed. "I'm kinda startin' to lose my marbles again." She combs her fingers through the hair on the top of her head.

"Uh oh. Sounds like you ignored the memo on forgiveness." Ray winks. "Works better than drugs and the benefits lasts longer."

"We can't all be saintly, like you."

"Saintly?" Ray raises her eyebrows. "That, I'm definitely not." She lets out a giggle, sips her champagne. "I just try to have peace of mind, Artie. It's preferable to stress." With one hand she gathers her long dreadlocks off of her back and pulls them into a twirl that hangs down one side of her chest. She closes her eyes and hums along with her CD.

Artie watches her. It's literally *Ray's* CD. She wrote and performed the songs. They feature jazz guitar, and a voice free of anguish. They're New-Age-y, praise-the-Universe kind of songs that sell at her "New Thought" church and online. Artie would be tempted not to listen if it wasn't Ray, but it *is*. She admires how the woman knows what she wants to do, and she does it.

"You're good at being happy," Artie says.

Rayana opens her eyes. "Thank you. But happiness is a choice, love, and it's a constant effort. I find myself angry and sad as often as anyone. Only difference is I'm committed to choosing happiness."

"I've never seen you miserable or crazy like me."

Rayana tilts her head. "That's selective memory. You've seen me through *all* different phases. I just don't *stay* in the negative places too long. But I certainly visit."

"Hmphf. I do more than *visit*," Artie says. "I bring all my shit and move in."

"You just need to learn to release things, angel. You're not bound by the past if you release it."

"I don't agree," Artie says. She stares at the train of bubbles rising in her glass. "I think things happen and they shape you. That's what makes us who we are."

"No. The *choice* you make about what happens is what shapes you."

Artie scratches her head and looks at Ray. *Huh?*

"You think your past makes you who you are and you think your past was unhappy, so *you're* unhappy. The past is over. Let it go. Move on."

"How? It's not like I can erase it from my memory."

"Release it, is what I mean. Disconnect from it. You were already who you are before you came here. And you'll still be who you are when you leave. You're a wonderful, creative, *eternal* being. Nothing can kill your soul. So nothing that happens can permanently harm it."

Artie stares at Ray. "That's a nice theory," she says, "but no one knows for sure what happens to the soul. And the past creates the future here on planet Earth. This isn't heaven, Rayana, it's life."

"The *present* creates the future, Artie. You can't control the past, but you do have control over yourself and your choices right *now*. You can control what you say, what you think, and how you respond."

"If something terrible happens that hurts me, I can't pretend it doesn't hurt."

"But you can let what hurts pass *through* you," Rayana says, getting louder. "You can choose not to own it and invite it to *live* with you forever. You hold on and think that something that hurts is a part of you, but it only stay a part of you because you hold onto it. Let it go."

Artie gulps some champagne. "Let it go *where*? I just don't think it's that easy. I think things happen to people that wound them, and some of those wounds never heal, and that makes them who they are. I think that's life."

"For *some* people that's life. That's not how it *has* to be." Rayana can see that Artie's doubtful. "Have it your way," she says. "But just consider the possibility that that's not the truth; it's just a belief you have."

"Yeah, alright." Artie snorts. "I'll consider it."

154

"I can do without the sarcasm."

"Shh," Artie says. The envelope with the pictures is on the bed. She grabs it and hands it to Ray. "What is this?"

"I shot them that night," Artie says. She leans back on the bed. "I had my camera and instead of opening the door and bashing their heads in with my tripod, like a normal person, I shot a roll of film."

Ray looks at the pictures. Artie's closes her eyes. She draws her knees to her chest and listens to Ray flipping through the prints.

"Have you looked at these yet?"

"I'm afraid to." Artie opens her eyes. "I want to, but…" Her eyes puddle up.

Ray sighs. "Wish you wouldn't do this kind of thing to yourself. You need to be building your life back up. This is breaking it down, Artie."

"*They* broke it down, not me."

"Stop focusing on them. What are *you* doing to yourself?"

"I can't help it." Artie holds out her hand. "Give them to me."

Ray stares at her. "No."

"Give 'em to me, Rayana."

"There's nothing to see."

"Give them to me!"

"They didn't come out, Artie. There's literally nothing to see."

Artie snatches them from her and rifles through them. Shiny, black nothing after nothing. She snorts. There are only ten prints though she shot a roll of 24-exposure film. There're only ten, of course, because none of the others had any image at all. Those that *have* any detectable image are so dark, she can't make out anything but a little light coming in the window and the reflection from the lights on Kendall's dashboard. Artie takes a sip of champagne. She feels like an idiot. Either Nikki the magic Nikon refused to record the event, or she just messed up. The film was the wrong speed for low light. The exposure wasn't set properly. There was no flash. Of course nothing came out. That wasn't the goal, now that she thinks about it. She just wanted them to feel exposed.

"At the lab, I thought they were feeling sorry for me," she says, smiling. If they were, it was only 'cause my pictures suck. I have the munchies," she says. "Whatchu got to eat?"

Rayana sticks her hand out, to take the pictures. She's not smiling. Artie gives them over and Ray walks out of the room.

Artie follows her to the kitchen. Ray lights a burner on the vintage stove, puts the photos into the flame and says, "Bye-bye."

The small fire mesmerizes Artie. It blusters, emitting noxious chemical smells, and sets the smoke alarm shrieking. As it burns the photo paper looks like mesh before transforming into ashes. She's not sure why Ray's done this, but it felt good to see them burn, even if there was really nothing to see. Maybe it'll help burn the memory away, too.

Twenty-three

Artie, 2004

Rico's out of town gigging, and Rayana isn't big on treats. Soy ice cream is not what Artie had in mind, but it's better than nothing. She shovels spoonfuls out of the container into her mouth.

"We never talked about what was going on with you and Kendall before that night," Rayana says as she peels a grapefruit and watches Artie eat. "Were you getting along?"

"I guess," Artie shrugs.

She knows Rayana is waiting to hear more, but she just wants to dig into the container and lick the sweet, cold cream off the spoon.

"Well, I was wondering, because you had a suitcase packed already. But when you got here that night you said you'd driven home, seen them in the driveway and drove off right after. So I was wondering why you had the suitcase already."

Artie's eyes drift up to the ceiling as they do when she's thinking. "Oh." She looks back at Ray. "Alessandra was in town for work, and me and Sushama were gonna spend the weekend with her at the Four Seasons and do the spa thing. But Sush talked Ally into going to this Brazilian Lesbian club and doing the gay thing and I wasn't up for it. Kendall pissed me off so much that morning. I was too anxious to party. Can't dance when I'm stressed."

"Did you have an argument?"

Artie breathes in and out. "He told me *it didn't mean he didn't love me*, but that he wanted permission to sleep with prostitutes. Can you believe that? Pendejo."

Rayana is quiet for a moment. She looks down at the grapefruit, avoids Artie's eyes, and continues to peel it.

"Why do you think he wanted to do that?"

"Why do *you* think he wanted to do that, Rayana? Does it matter? 'Cause he's an asshole, that's why. Told him I was sick of him making me feel like our marriage was depriving him of something, and that if he thought it was gonna be better with some nasty ho he should do what he hadda do. But then later, when I was with my girls, I wished I hadn't said all that. I wanted to take some of it back. So when they went to the club I went home."

Artie scrapes the bottom of the soy ice cream container. Though she tries not to let the sadness settle into her, it does. She never felt like she was *enough* for anybody, but Kendall. She wasn't enough to make Serena love her, wasn't enough for Rico to want to stay alive for, and she wasn't Ray's real daughter, so she wasn't enough for her either. With Kendall, for a time, she'd felt she had someone she would always be most important to.

She swallows. An ache has swelled inside her chest.

Rayana looks up. She clears her throat.

"You two had been with each other, *only each other*, since middle school, right?"

"Yeah." Artie looks at her. "So?"

"Did either of you ever sleep with anyone else during high school or college?"

"We got *married* in college, Ray. You were there, remember?"

Rayana covers her mouth with her hand as if to trap errant words.

"What? What are you getting at?" Artie asks.

Rayana shakes her head. Nothing.

"Tell me what you're thinking, dammit."

"He never sowed his wild oats," Ray finally blurts.

"So? Neither did I!"

"I'm not defending him, angel. Just speculating about his interest in other sex partners. "

"He's fantasized about being with other people, ever since we were kids, but he always promised he wouldn't do it," Artie says. Her face is wet with tears now.

"Maybe he felt like prostitutes wouldn't really be cheating."

Artie looks at her. *What the fuck?* She wipes her face.

"Because there'd be no emotional investment," Ray explains.

"Whatever." Her nose is running. She inhales forcefully, sucking it back up. "I never deprived Kendall. He got *plenty*. And he got anything, anywhere he wanted. We did it outdoors, in cabs, at the movies, on planes, in the ocean, in swimming pools, on the terrace of our apartment in New York, in the elevator, on the roof, Anything you can think of, we did it—rough, kinky, oral, anal. And he has a big dick—*you know how much that shit hurts?*"

Ray holds up her palm. "Okay, okay. You made your point."

"Sorry, I know you'd like to believe I'm all sweet and angelic," Artie says. "But the truth is, I fucked the shit of out of him from the time I was *thirteen years old*. I think he's got a lot of goddamn nerve. Almost got me arrested once, cause we did it on the back of a city bus and the driver saw us. I actually pulled up my skirt and sat in his lap on a *public bus* because that was *his* fantasy. I did all *kinds* of crazy things for him. And now he wants to screw prostitutes? And my *mother*? Fuck him!"

Rayana covers her mouth again.

"And I'm not naïve. I know that cause we've been together since we were kids it would be unlikely that we'd go the rest of our lives never sleeping with anybody else, but I certainly didn't want to know about it. And if he just *had* to sleep with another woman, my fucking mother was a really bad choice."

A chuckle bursts from behind Rayana's hand. "I'm sorry," she says. "I don't mean to make light—but that is so very true."

"It's really not funny, Ray. God dammit, don't you have anything fun to eat? Doesn't Papi have any chocolate?"

Ray sighs. "He might. Look around."

Artie gets up and moves toward the cabinets next to the stove.

"I apologize for laughing," Ray says. "It's just—Kendall told me he had no idea who she was. And if he's lying, and he *did* know, he was just beyond stupid and if he's *not* lying, I think he just had some unbelievably bad luck."

He didn't know who she was? This is news to Artie, but she doesn't want to deal with the conversation anymore. She's foraging in the cabinets now... walnut pieces and some coconut, but no chocolate. She keeps digging. Rico is notorious for stashing Hershey Bars. She's not giving up.

"Did Kendall tell *you* he didn't know who she was?" Rayana asks.

Can't she see I don't want to talk about this shit anymore? She's pulling drawers open and rummaging through them. It occurs to her that she's "snooping," but Ray isn't stopping her and she can't stop herself. "If I don't find some fucking chocolate, I'm gonna punch something."

Rayana is still working on her grapefruit. "You pre-menstrual, sweetie? I have some herbs I can give you for that."

Artie takes a deep breath and continues with her search mission. "I haven't talked to Kendall since that night. I don't know *what* he tried to tell me. He sent a couple of letters, but I didn't read them."

In the back of one of the drawers, she lifts a large cookbook to see what's in the plastic bin underneath. She freezes as she sees a gray envelope with SERENA written across it in black magic marker. She stares at it for a few seconds before putting the cookbook back and closing the drawer. She turns to Rayana.

"Can't find any."

"Ralphs is open. Want me to take you?"

Artie shakes her head. "I'm just gonna go to bed."

"I was going to the store anyway. Need some soymilk for the morning. Sure you don't wanna come?"

"I'll stay. But if you feel like bringing back something full of fat and sugar, I won't mind."

Rayana smirks. "I'll see what I can do."

Artie waits until she hears Ray's car pull out of the driveway before going back into the drawer. She's not thinking about chocolate anymore. When she pulls the envelope out, she sees that it's sealed. She looks at it, front and back. I shouldn't do this, she thinks. It isn't mine. This is a violation of Rico and Rayana's privacy. She puts it back in the storage bin, under the cookbook, closes the drawer and walks away. After a few steps she stops. *Who am I kidding?*

When she gets the envelope out she tries to pull it open without ripping it. It isn't going to work. She looks over at the O'Keefe & Merritt. One of the flat burners still has the pile of ashes from the pictures on it. Another holds a red kettle. She lights its flame. When it starts to whistle and steam pours out she holds the glued part of the envelope to the vapor until it loosens and she can open it without tearing the paper.

Inside she finds an un-opened greeting card and a bunch of postcards, six of them, written to her from Serena. They're dated May and June of 1995 and postmarked from New York. It's like discovering a time capsule. Her chest pounds as she takes the envelope back to the guest room. She closes and locks the door.

Artie recognizes that these postcards are the free kind you see in inexpensive restaurants; the ones with ads on them that live on a special display back by the payphones and restrooms. A couple of them are the exact same card advertising flavored vodka. There's one for hip-hop gear, a cell phone company, a cable TV movie, and a brand of perfume. She flips them over and arranges them by date.

May 23, 1995

Dear Artie,

Just received your letter and wanted to say <u>well done</u>! Graduating a year early is something for which you can be very proud and NYU is a GREAT school, especially for the arts. I am pleased for you and sincerely happy to hear that you've stuck with your photography. You showed such talent for it as a child. Thank you for reaching out. I have wanted to be in touch, but didn't have the courage. I'd like to support you in your work, if I may, somehow. Being an artist is something I understand better than I ever understood being a parent, and since it's too late for that, I would, if you'll allow me, like to encourage you in your art. Will write again. Definitely want to see you in New York.

Warm regards,
Serena

May 31, 1995

Dear Artie,

Hope you received my card and the camera and that you were not put off that it is an older model. It's from 1987 and a photographer mate of mine who shoots album covers told me this was a wonderful model and even better than what they make today, in his opinion. He used it when he was in school and after school when he shot for The City Sun, a local black newspaper. He said the camera is very special and he promised me you would like it. I really hope that you do. I believe in your talent and look forward to seeing what you do in your career. Please let me know when you'll be arriving in the city.

Warmest regards,
Serena

June 5, 1995

Dear Artie,

Hope you're receiving my cards. You can send a response to Uncle Buddy's address or to me at 7 Astor Place, New York, NY 10003. I live very close to NYU, so it will be easy for us to meet when you arrive. Hope the camera is working out. I would love to have a photograph by you. I will have it framed if you'll send me one. If you can spare any photographs of yourself I would like very much to have one of those as well. Aunt Annie had a baby picture of you, which I found in her Bible after she passed. I was glad to find it, because I didn't have any. When you come, I would like to talk with you about Aunt Annie and about some other things about my family history that you should know, because it's your history as well. Hope your last days of high school are enjoyable.

Warm regards,
Serena

June 10, 1995

Dear Artie,

I am having a tough day today. Though Annie passed away a few years ago, sometimes I feel raw as the day it happened. I have found myself feeling angry with her lately. I had found peace at her passing, but now, I find myself thinking about things she did that I can't forgive even though I know I should.

This resentment is such a burden, but can't seem to make my heart let it go. She once told me that the most important relationship you have in life is the one with yourself, because that's whom you'll be with for eternity. She told me it didn't matter if my relationship with her was not perfect, because it was only temporary, but the one with myself would never end, so I should focus on that more than on any other. I used to have a relationship with myself through my journals, but I lost them and have been out of touch with "me" for a long while. Will have to re-connect. I can guess that you are probably as angry with me as I am with Annie. I want you to know that I'm sorry for my failings and for all the times I was unkind. I don't say this because I feel I deserve your forgiveness, or even because I think I'd be a better mother now, but only because I want you to be freer of resentments than I am. Holding them robs you of happiness and you deserve to be happy.

Sincerely,
Serena

June 13, 1995

Dear Artie,

I am disappointed that I've not heard back from you and confused because the note you sent a month ago seemed to suggest that you wanted to be in touch. But then, I can't be sure that you're receiving my cards. Maybe I have your address wrong? Anyway, if you're getting them and just don't feel like responding, I understand. Maybe when you wrote you were ready to connect, but have since changed your mind. I shouldn't have waited this long to try to be in touch. What can I expect?

My emotions are raw 'cause I'm grieving again. I grieved intensely for a year, then I was better and now losing my mother has hit me hard once more. Your father had taught me that grief eventually transforms itself, but he neglected to mention how unpredictable it is. It can come back and strike you hard when you're not even thinking of it. Maybe it's confusing to you to for me to refer to Aunt Annie as my mother. I would rather explain this to you in a conversation that I hope we'll have one day.

Sincerely,

Serena
June 17, 1995

Dear Artie,

I am at a place on 9th St in the East Village called Around The Clock that has these free postcards. I am always here having a drink when I write you. Must seem odd that I write the cards rather than a regular letter—just a quirk of your eccentric, nearly middle-aged mum. I drink a lot lately, like a fish, to numb this grief.

My third album came out this week. I am not terribly excited about it. Only the first one, so far, was really me. It was my autobiography, as my hero Charles Mingus would say. The subsequent two are okay musically, but they aren't quite genuine or inspired. I think I was not ready to write something substantive on these last two. An artist should wait until she has something to say, not just say anything for the hell of it. The people at the label wanted to fit me into an idea they had about what I should be and I wanted to please them, but in the process I lost my authenticity and made something "to sell" rather than something to communicate. You're an artist and I hope for you that you'll always find outlets that allow you to express the real you and not the you that someone tells you will make money. Money ebbs and flows and it's lovely to have, but you can't get back the time you waste creating rubbish that you could have spent creating art.

Yours,
Serena

Rayana knocks. "Open up, sweetie. Got you some M&Ms."

Artie isn't sure what to do. She's not ready to come out of this space she's in. She wants to re-read the postcards and savor the words. And there's something she hasn't opened yet. It looks like a greeting card. Ray knocks again.

"I know you're not asleep. The light's on... What are you doing?"

Artie's chest tightens as she stares at the closed door. These things were kept from her and it's not right.

"What's going on? Artie, I know you hear me."

Finally, she springs up from the bed and throws open the door. Her jaw is tight as she glares at Rayana.

"What's wrong?" Ray asks.

Artie points to the bed at the cards sprawled there. The envelope with "SERENA" written across it lays there too. Rayana steps in, puts the M&Ms on the dresser, and leans against the doorframe.

"You and Rico should have given these to me."

Rayana nods. Her head hangs forward.

"He had no right. I knew about the camera. Kendall heard you talking to Vanessa about it."

"Artie—"

"Who the hell was he to decide I couldn't hear from her? It's not like *he* was gonna win any father of the year awards. Who was he to decide?"

"Artie, he—"

"And you knew that was wrong. Why didn't you stand up to him?"

"It wasn't all his fault."

Artie stares at Rayana and catches her breath. "Kendall told me he heard you say that Rico said he didn't want me to hear anything from Serena 'cause she was unreliable."

"That was partly true," Rayana says, nodding. "It was his choice not to tell you about the camera."

"What part *wasn't* true?"

"Well, he spoke about it hypothetically. He said *if* she did try to reach out again that he wasn't sure he wanted you to be subjected to her, because she couldn't be counted on. That was his experience with her. She was flaky. When he said it, she *hadn't* tried to make contact again. When she did, I didn't tell him."

Artie blinks. *Ray* did this to her? "Why not?" she asks. Her face is on fire.

Rayana's smooth forehead tenses into a matrix of lines. "I just... couldn't at the time. She *had* her chance to be your mother and she didn't want it. And by the time she sent the camera and the cards, *I* had been your mother for almost six years. You were mine. And I wasn't gonna let you down. I thought she *would* if you gave her the chance... I was trying to protect you."

Artie regards this diminished version of Rayana, "Any other shit hidden away that I should know about?"

"I always planned to give them to you eventually. But I let too much time go by. Then didn't know how."

Artie can hardly stand to look at her. "You made a really big mistake," she says. "I would have never thought... I'm going to sleep."

"I'm sorry, Artie." Ray hugs herself. Then she taps her fingers rapidly against her mouth. "I hope you'll forgive me."

"I hope so too."

As Artie burrows under the covers she thinks that she'll never again believe that anyone, no matter how "spiritual," is closer to being perfect than anyone else. All people are flawed. It's what makes them human.

She breaks the seal on the card that hasn't been opened. There's a Hallmark graduation greeting inside. She doesn't bother to read it, but at the bottom she finds Serena's handwriting:

Congratulations and the very best wishes to you.

With warm regards,
Serena.

P.S. Recently read a quote from a spiritual teacher who said, "From your father you learn the things you must do. From your mother, you learn who you are." I have much to tell you about who you are. I look forward to seeing you in New York.

Artie also finds ten, nine-year-old hundred dollar bills inside the card. She stares at her mother's handwriting for a moment, then rests her head against the wall and closes her eyes. She wonders what might have gone differently if she'd received all this when she was supposed to. They might have spent time together in New York and become close. Or maybe they would have fought and not been close at all. Artie might have punished Serena for the past. Or she might have found a way forward, a way to begin a *new* relationship. She'll never know. As missed opportunities go, this one feels monumental and cruel.

Twenty-four

Serena, 2004

Serena wakes up startled. She's been dreaming. She was in Bermuda, standing on the green of a pristine golf course near the sea, and singing a song she composed. No one was around, but she was excited about her melody. She wanted someone to hear it. Annie appeared several yards away, driving a golf cart. She was in a big white sun hat and a white dress. She looked young and healthy and she was driving straight towards her. Serena was happy to see her and eager to share the song. But Annie was speeding so fast, Serena had to jump out of the way. The cart zipped by and Serena sang. Annie wasn't listening. She was singing her *own* song: "Dust yourself off..." She sounded like Mary Poppins. She looked back as she kept zooming forward and singing, "And wash yourself clean, dear!" The cart was headed toward the ocean. Serena ran after it, but she couldn't catch up. It barreled into the water. Serena followed in after it as Annie and the cart disappeared under the waves. Serena began to swim, but she felt something grab her hips and yank her back. She woke up.

Jamie has slipped under her covers. He's spooning her. They sleep together most nights, usually downstairs in his king-sized bed. But she stayed in her own place tonight, because he was still out when she got back from Hal's.

He's naked. Smells like scotch and cigarettes and his willy is hard. It pokes into her backside. She doesn't feel like doing it, but she'll let him. It's part of their arrangement.

He nudges her onto her stomach and enters her from behind. He doesn't bother to caress her breasts, or kiss her neck, or tell her that she turns him on. Doesn't even check to see if she's wet. She *isn't,* and it hurts a little. Serena gets no sense at all that Jamie's even thinking about *her.* Probably imagining some young girl he saw while he was out earlier.

The sex has been like this on and off for a while. He usually prefers it from behind. And if he does face her, more often than not, his eyes are closed.

Serena tries to detach from how she feels. Small. Like she doesn't matter. She falls back into a dream state and sees herself disconnecting from her body. She levitates away from the bed, and finds herself aloft, looking down. She hears the clinking of porcelain china and turns to see Charles Mingus and Annie sitting at a table floating near the ceiling. They're having tea. Serena glides up to an empty chair and joins them. With big, puffy hands Mingus pours her a cup. His dark eyes shine and stream energy at her. She drinks it in. Behind him, she sees a window, through which she watches herself making love with Rico. They're in the shower at the Four Seasons in San Francisco. Her legs hug his waist; he nails her into the wall with pounding thrusts. Their eyes are locked; their bodies a synchronized duet.

"Now *that* was heat," Mingus says, his voice gritty. "Not like that bullschitt down there." He guffaws.

Serena nods. "Rico loved me." She runs her tongue along the rim of the porcelain teacup. "He wasn't thinkin' of anyone else."

"Oh, rubbish," Annie says, clanking her cup on its saucer. "It was better, but not perfect."

Serena looks at the lackluster sex beneath her. Jamie banging away.

Her face in profile, one half pressed into the mattress, the other staring up at her with a sad eye.

"Why do you settle?" Mingus asks.

"You're punishing yourself, dear," Annie says. She sips her tea.

Serena faces them. "Am I?" She looks back down at herself with Jamie. "But we adore each other in some vays. We look out for each other."

His lips pursed, Mingus arches a brow. Annie takes her cup and pours its contents down the front of her white dress. Instead of tea, it's soapy water. She rubs her chest and bosom, over the dress, making suds. Serena hears the oscillating of a washing machine. The whole room begins to fill with water.

"Your bodies don't sing together," Annie says, soaping herself. "Sweet songs danced in your minds—missed the way to your hearts."

Serena repeats those words silently, to remember them.

"But he's a nice companion sometimes," she says after a moment. "And he pays our expenses. He takes care of me..."

Below, she sees herself and Jamie underwater. He's still thrusting and her eye is still open, like a dead fish's. The water continues rising.

"You're kept? Not bad for a penance." Mingus begins tapping a rhythm on the table.

Annie frowns at him. Serena listens closely to Mingus's taps. She knows she's dreaming. She wants to stay in it long enough to catch the song that's there. She wants to remember. The water is now at their feet and still rising.

"Don't listen to him," Annie says. "You don't have to do penance. You can dust yourself off and start clean." She soaps her neck now.

Serena looks at them. She drinks some tea. But it's not tea. It's bad wine, like vinegar. She swallows it anyway. The sound of the washing machine grows louder. The water in the room has risen to her knees.

"Penance? I'm doin' penance?"

"You wronged someone," Mingus's eyes twinkle. "You'll treat yourself like schitt until you suffer enough."

"Dust yourself off. Wash yourself clean," Annie shouts. Now she spreads the bubbles down her shoulders and arms. But the water rises to cover them. The bubbles disappear right away.

"Wait, do you mean I can wash away what I did? How?"

"Don't make schitt, make art." Mingus leans close to her with a penetrating gaze. His rhythm taping hand is under water now. She feels his breath on her face.

Serena wants to tell her hero that she's gone back to real work, writing meaningful songs, songs she hopes Artie will hear, but the water has covered her face.

She's awake again. Jamie moans and shudders. A moment later he stops moving. His weight presses her down. She's disappointed that the dream is gone. It was good being with Mingus and Annie. And there was more to say.

Jamie pulls out and rolls away. She hopes he'll say or do something affectionate. He falls asleep quickly. She kisses his shoulder and keeps her lips pressed there. She finds his toes and touches them with her own. Tiny bits of connection are better than none.

She knows this situation is crushing her, but she can't leave. When she hints at it he pays her more attention for a while. He doesn't want her to go. Being the source of someone's pain is a kind of hell Serena can't bear again. She kisses his shoulder once more and listens to the rhythm of his breath rolling in and out and the waves doing the same outside.

Twenty-five

Artie, 2004

Beneath The Underdog, is on the bookshelf in the guest room, which was Artie's room before she left for NYU. She pulls it free. Though she never met Charles Mingus, his face, with its handsome, heavy features, full lips and intense expression seems as familiar as if she knew him personally. Serena used to scat, copying his bass solos. Badoobadoobadoobadoo doom doom babazoobAAAaaaaoooom doom doom... His autobiography belonged to her. Artie saved it when Rico was packing their apartment on 13th Street. He threw it in the trash, and she took it out, because she was curious about Serena's interest in Mingus. And because, as a twelve-year-old, she thought it was cool that their dog was named after him. She read the book as a young teenager and she was delighted with its many dirty parts. When she re-read it in her late teens, she found that most of the women in the book seemed unrealistically accommodating, happy to be Mingus's whores, fucking him *and* taking care of him because he was "so sexy," and such a "genius." Artie wondered what Serena thought of this type of woman. Did she recognize herself in any of the characters? Was that what attracted her to the book? Or was it her desire to know Mingus? Serena had lived in Rico's shadow as if he had a right to eclipse her. How did she feel about that? Artie knew her mother wanted a career of her own, but she also liked being Rico's woman. Maybe she sabotaged the marriage because getting out was the only way she could have a career. Artie wishes she could ask Serena about this and many other things she'd like to understand.

The postcards, which she's been reading over and over, are the first glimpse into Serena's thoughts that Artie's had since reading her journals. In the cards, she's not evil or competitive. The cards suggest that Serena *didn't* hate her, at least when they were written, but what she did with Kendall—if that wasn't hatred, what was it? Artie longs to understand. Yet at the same time, she wants to make Serena suffer. She was willing to soften her focus on the childhood wounds, but this latest transgression… Serena is going to pay for that.

Artie won't come out of her room today. She isn't ready to deal with Rayana after last night. And she isn't ready to jump back into her own life yet, either. She decides to avoid the day by re-reading tales of Mingus's sexual escapades. Maybe there are clues to Serena's behavior within the pages? Reading about Mingus's randy romps is amusing, but it also makes her want to climb the walls. She hasn't had any of *that sort* of attention in months. Scary to be so alone. Scarier still is the fact that she can't imagine herself with anyone but Kendall. She's never *been* with anyone but him. She's had a couple of sexual dreams, but she was alone in them, masturbating. Depressing. Artie wants to be with *someone*. But she doesn't even know how to date. Maybe *she'll* have to try prostitutes.

A knock on the door startles her. Rayana hasn't come to check on her until now. She's probably been afraid to face her. It's almost five o'clock and Artie hasn't eaten anything except M&Ms. Still, she hesitates. She's not dressed and she doesn't want to talk to Ray yet. But the knock comes again. Artie takes a breath. She will try to be kind and polite.

She opens the door to find Kendall standing there holding a sandwich on a plate in one hand and a glass of grape juice in the other. He's wearing jeans, a white-collared shirt and his vintage gray fedora.

"Delivery," he says with a smile. His eyes are sad.

He smells of too much patchouli and there's sweat on either side of his nose.

"She shouldn't have let you in," Artie says.

"Take the sandwich, baby."

"Don't tell me what to do."

She's in her underwear and she doesn't like that she was tricked into letting him see her. It used to arouse Kendall to see her in dishabille, and while she once enjoyed this it's no longer his privilege. She's not sure that she still has this effect on him, though.

"Ray said you didn't eat today."

"Oh please. Like you give a shit. Have you eaten… anyone's *mother* out, today?"

He hangs his head. "Can we just talk, please?"

"I'm not interested in anything you have to say."

"I haven't had a chance to talk with you and my life's been in limbo for going on three months." He pushes past her into the room.

She turns around and catches him checking out her rear view.

"*Your* life? Kendall, you broke my heart. And it nearly killed me. Do you understand that?" She covers her body with her arms.

He sets the dishes down on the nightstand.

"Did you read my letters?" It sounds like he's scolding her.

"Anything you'd have to say in a letter would be to make *you* feel better. Wanna feel better? Go to therapy. Go to church. Suck on a crack pipe for all I care, Kendall. But-leave-me-the-fuck-alone. Get out of here."

He sits on the edge of the bed and stares at the floor. "I didn't recognize her. I'd never been with her before and haven't seen her since. It wasn't intentional. Wasn't an affair." He looks up to meet her eyes. "Please, please forgive me."

She moves onto the bed, slides her legs under the covers. She takes the glass and sips the juice. If he's expecting this to change things, he's stupid.

"You're sexy," he says, eyeing her like a puppy dog drooling for a treat.

She pulls the comforter all the way to her neck. Her eyes slice him up.

"Can't blame me for trying," he shrugs. "Missed you, baby."

"Sexy, huh? Obviously, I'm not all that. I didn't meet your *needs*. Right? Wasn't that the problem?"

Kendall sighs. He takes off his hat and sets it on the nightstand. There's sweat on his forehead.

Artie takes a bite of the sandwich. Tofu cheese? Ugh. But she *is* hungry.

Kendall rubs a hand over his curly hair. "You gonna come home?"

She chews and swallows, looking at him. "Why?" she asks. "The hookers and people's middle-aged mamas aren't enough company?"

"Stop. I don't want anyone but you."

She turns away. "This isn't something you can fix with words."

"If you want to come home, I can move into the studio 'til we work things out. I want you to get back to your work and I know you can't really do it here. You have a job coming up."

She looks at him.

"Alessandra finally got Troy hired on one of her productions and they start in less than two weeks. They want you to shoot stills."

"Where are they shooting?"

"Here. LA. The main location is on the boardwalk in Venice."

"Is Alessandra in town?"

Kendall shrugs. "Got the news from Troy. He's directing. Wanna do it?"

"If Ally asks me to. If the money's okay."

"Cool beans, cause someone called from production and I told them you'd take it if they'd pay your rate."

"Since when are you my rep, Kendall?"

He wipes his forehead with his sleeve. "Money's starting to get tight, baby. Your bills set me back. I'm trying not to run through *all* that grant money, so if you could kick in your part of the mortgage in the next month or two... I've been covering everything myself since the end of March."

Artie looks at him sideways. *Is this fool serious?* "And whose fault was that, pendejo? You want me back to help with the mortgage?" She smiles. "*That's* why you came over here?"

Kendall exhales and massages the bridge of his nose. "Sell the house. I don't care," she says.

"I want you back because I love you. I want our life back. You decide you don't want that, fine. We'll sell it. But in the meantime doesn't make sense to let the bank foreclose on it, does it?"

"*This* is your attempt to get me back?"

He's silent.

"You're a dick."

Kendall coughs and clears his throat. His voice shakes. "You know I've loved you my whole life, Artie."

"And just look at the good it's done me: I got a trip to the nuthouse, and the privilege of paying bills. You're a real catch."

She reaches into the card on the nightstand and hands him the ten, hundred dollar bills.

"There. You won all that money, broke my heart, and you can't pay the damn mortgage?"

Kendall stares at the bills in his hand, stunned. He blinks. "Only got a fifth of the money so far, Artie. Your bills ate half of that, taxes took a chunk, and I'm trying to save *some* for our future."

"You got your money. You don't need me." She rolls to face the wall.

Kendall sniffles. "I'm not leaving unless you come with me." He sniffles again.

She turns to look at him. "What the hell are *you* crying about? Are you kidding me?"

He wipes his nose with the back of his hand. "You're a different person. And it's my fault. I had a beautiful, sweet woman who loved me. And I messed it up."

"Would you please get out of here?"

He moves toward her. There's fear in his eyes as he embraces her. She tries to push him off. His arms are strong. He squeezes tight and kisses the top of her head, then her face, and her tears. She knows he's going to try, but he won't be able to fix her.

The room is dark when she wakes up later. Kendall is under the covers, wrapped around her with his clothes off, the way they used to sleep. Nothing is resolved. But her *body*... He's awake too. His fingers are on her breast and he begins kneading her nipple.

"The very first time I came inside you," he whispers, "we were here. I was trying to be quiet, but I couldn't." With his other hand, he moves into her panties. He feels her pubic hair.

"God damn, girl. Did you grow a Chia Pet down there, or what?"

She cracks up. "Shut up."

He dips a finger inside the Chia Pet, and then strokes her. It feels good. She's very wet. She has been all day. It's that damn Mingus book with its dirty parts.

"Remember, baby? That first time?"

Yeah, she remembers. So what? She wishes Kendall would just shut the fuck up. His dick bumps into her ass. She reaches back and strokes it. He moans. She squeezes and strokes and feels him get harder, growing thicker and longer. He stops talking, thank God. He's breathing heavily in her ear. And then...

"Aah, oh yeah, that first time I busted a nut inside you, the shit was so awesome. Remember how hard I came?"

She laughs.

"What?" He nibbles her earlobe.

"*Shut. Up.*"

He pulls her panties down. She crosses her legs.

"C'mon, I wanna lick your pussy."

"No."

"C'mon, baby, please. Lemme taste it."

She shakes her head. When she closes her eyes she sees his car, the open window, his face between Serena's legs. No. She guides his finger back to her spot. He rubs it patiently. The release is nothing spectacular, but it's better than doing it herself.

He opens her thighs and begins to ease his body between them.

"Wait. You need to use a condom."

He freezes. "Fuck. I don't have any."

"I don't know where your shit's been. It's not happening without some latex on it."

"Come on, baby, please. I haven't been with anybody. I swear. Please."

"Hell no."

"Oh God, oh fuck, please, then suck me, baby, *please* suck it."

She sees his car. She's walking up to the window... She spits in her hand and wraps it around him and strokes. He's still begging her to suck it when he comes.

They used to mess around clandestinely in this room when they were teenagers. Kendall made so much noise she had to muffle him with a pillow. Mingus was usually on the floor, snoring through whatever they were doing. He'd wake up when they stopped for food.

"I miss the dog," Kendall says, as if reading her mind. "Feels weird to be in here without him."

Artie misses him, too. His legs went bad and when he couldn't walk anymore Rico and Rayana called them in New York to tell them they had to put him down. They lit candles, got drunk, looked at pictures of him and cried.

"If we break up," Artie says, "and I find someone new, I'll have no history with that person."

"You don't have to find someone new."

"How do we unravel our lives?"

"We won't," Kendall says. "You *are* my life."

"But what if we have to?"

"Go to sleep, baby."

Twenty-six

Serena, 2004

It's early morning. Serena and Jamie walk barefoot on the beach in silence. He holds her hand. They're each in their own thoughts, yet together. He leads her closer and closer to the water. Soon a wave comes in and covers her feet. She runs to dry sand.

"It's freezing."

"Refreshing," he says. He walks backward, looking at her, until the water is up to his knees.

"Come," he waves. "Get wet with me, dawlin'."

She shakes her head.

"You can't be scared of the water. You grew up on a island."

"Not *skurd*. Just not comfortable."

"It's okay once you're in." He walks out farther, soaking his long shorts. "I'll buy you a wetsuit for next time, but for now, just go with it."

"Polluted, innit?"

He ducks his whole body under and comes back up. "A bit," he smiles. "Probably not enough to kill us, though. Come play with me."

She smirks. How he manages to be delightful and annoying at the same time is still a mystery. She moves toward him in her bike shorts and long sleeved T-shirt.

"FUCK! Jamie, it's too cold."

She's up to her hips. He pulls her close and kisses her. Without warning, he pulls her under. She screams as she comes back up and swats him.

"Get ready," he yells. "Here it comes."

As the wall of a wave comes in, he dives into it. She follows. It pulls Serena up, and flips her over. She's gliding, unsure of where she'll end up. When she finally lands back at the shore. She can't stop laughing.

"Shit's fun, ain't it?" he says as they climb toward dry sand.

Her eyes sting and she tastes salt on her lips. She feels young. "Wow," she says. "Wish I had a towel, but, yeah."

He lies in the sand. "Towel? We can dry out here."

"Aw, Jamie, come on."

"*You* come on. Live a little."

Serena sighs and sits down.

He props himself up on one elbow and squints at her. "Think you might try to be happy today?"

She stares at the ocean. "I'm okay."

"Girl, please. Been mopin' around for months. If the work is gettin' you down, your ass needs a break. Stop takin' the shit so seriously. Have fun."

"Fun? Pain inspires me. I don't write happy songs."

"Yeah, well you should."

"Did you know Elvin Jones died?"

"What's that got ta do witchu?" He tugs at his shorts, sticking to his bum. "Lighten up, will you? Let's go dancin' tonight."

"I didn't even hear about it. Missed the obit in *The Times*; it was on a Vansdee. I got an email forward wif a rant by Carlos Santana about how Elvin's passin' was ignored."

"We haven't done salsa since we left New York. That was always fun, right?" He dusts the sand off his feet.

She stares at the water. Jamie squeezes her thigh.

"I wanted to be a genius. Like Elvin Jones," she says.

Jamie laughs. "Okay."

"Seriously. Used to think I could be. But I got caught up in 'schitt' as my Mingus vould say… He said his abilities as a bassist were de result of hard work, but his talent for composition came from God." She looks at Jamie. "I want that; that feeling that somethin's comin' through me, from God."

"Girl, *every* artist wants that. Includin' me. And most of us have it, least once in a while, includin' you." He squats then stands up.

She doesn't move or look at him. Tears spill onto her cheeks. "Maybe. There have been a *couple* of inspired songs. Not enough, though." She smiles sadly. "Truth is, it would be nice to blame de universe for what it didn't do, but I really can't."

"Let's go. I'm startin' to itch."

She doesn't move. "I'm not convinced that it does come from God. I believe in inspiration, but I think inspiration comes after de hard work. I mean, would Mingus've been able to create those compositions without all those hours on de bass?" She wipes the tears from her face.

"Holy Mother of God. What is wrong wit chu?" He squats down again and looks at her.

"I'm afraid I never worked hard enough, when I should have." Her heels dig holes in the sand. "And nahw it's probably too late." She wipes more tears. "I wasted time writin' bullshit. For de label."

"You're complainin' 'cause you had a record deal?" He stands up again. Shakes his head.

"No Jamie. I know I was lucky to make money, but I lost sight of what I really should've been doin'. I'm almost fifty. And I still haven't done anything half as good as de artists I admire. I used to think I would, but now I don't know. And if it's not gonna happen—why should I be here?"

He rubs his temples. "Dawlin', it'll come. Just keep at it and it *will* come."

He takes her hand and pulls her up. He looks her in the eyes. "I *need* you here."

She tries to smile.

"You're havin' a crisis, baby, but it'll pass. You'll write somethin' that'll make up for everything. And in the meantime, nobody's gon' be mad at you if you let yourself be happy once in a while."

The sand is hot on her feet as they walk home. She wishes she could tell Jamie that someone *is* mad at her. But then she'd have to tell him why and he might be mad at her too.

He does buy Serena a wet suit and their morning body surfs become a routine.

In the afternoons, she takes her notebook out onto the balcony while she works on lyrics. Watching the waves and the way they roll, crash, splash and fizzes makes her think of how life itself ebbs and flows. Calm periods follow stormy ones. The tide of success comes in and rolls back out.

She's been working for a couple of hours one day when she sees Jamie walking down the boardwalk toward the building with a black lab puppy on a short leash. She hopes he hasn't *bought* this animal.

He brings it upstairs. As soon as the puppy lays eyes on Serena, his little ears perk up and he runs right to her. He jumps into her lap and licks her on the chin. Brilliant.

"The *last* thing I vant is a blasted dog, Jamie." She says this, but she's smiling at the cute baby.

"But, look, he wants *you*," Jamie says. "I think he knows you're his mama."

"I don't have time for this. I'm tryin' to work."

"Oh c'mon, woman." He kneels in front of her and the puppy licks his nose. "He won't take up that much time. Whatchu think a the name Treble?"

The phone rings. She hands the puppy to Jamie and moves inside.

When she says hello, the person on the line is silent. The caller ID is blocked. She can hear breathing and music playing faintly in the background. Hip hop. She says hello again and the party hangs up. Serena's stomach drops. Just a wrong number? Maybe. But she has a heavy feeling.

The puppy scurries inside toward her. Jamie follows.

"Treble? Sounds too much like *trouble*," she says. "Take him downstairs, J, I'm busy."

"But I bought him for *you*, dawlin'. To lift your spirits." He picks him up.

"I'm workin'!" She goes back out onto the balcony and returns to her chair.

"Treble" starts to whimper as though he realizes he's being rejected. Jamie puts him down and he runs straight to Serena, again, lands in her lap and barks a squeaky baby bark.

She finds herself walking him at the crack of dawn. And again mid-morning, late afternoon, evening, and before bed. He pees on her white carpet and he wants to play all the damn time. He turns out to be sweet, spoiled, loving, too cute and a huge distraction even with Jamie taking turns watching him. He demands so much attention that he slows her down more than her depression did. She *is* fond of this puppy, but she's annoyed with Jamie for getting him. She suspects he's done it because he doesn't believe in what she's working on. He's *said* that he does, but his actions... She's struggling to finish her compositions and get on with recording them and he acts like she has nothing better to do than play all day.

The puppy is much like the black Lab she had when she was with Rico. He even has the same sweet, funny personality. She can't help but call him Mingus. He looks like a Mingus, too, not a Treble. Jamie's says he'll think about it.

While they're down in his flat, Jamie plays Mingus's, *Oh Yeah*, the album on which he sings and plays piano rather than his usual bass. Serena sips a glass of wine, and listens in the living room, while the puppy gnaws on a chew toy on the floor nearby. Jamie putters in his kitchen, making gumbo. That old portrait hanging behind the piano beckons Serena's eye. She used to resemble the woman, Jamie's father's great grandmother, but not as much now that she's older. This ancient, younger version of Serena has eyes that follow her and seem to communicate disappointment. Serena would like to splash her face with a glass of wine.

Mingus's "Devil Woman" begins to play as Jamie enters the living room. He smiles at Serena, then gets down on all fours with the puppy and looks him in the eyes. "Yo, lil' dude, ya like this tune?"

The track is bluesy. Mingus sings of wanting to get himself a "devil" woman. Says an angel won't do him no good.

The dog tilts his little head and seems to truly listen for a moment. Then he falls onto his back with his little paws in the air and he does a sort of happy dance-wiggle on the floor. Serena and Jamie turn to each other and laugh, falling hard for this four-legged time eater.

Jamie stops laughing. "Serena, I want you down here with me and Mingus more. He needs to know he has a family."

She smiles at him. The youthful face in the old portrait seems to smirk. *Family? You can't give him that. Even if you had any eggs left, they're cooked.*

Later, Jamie carries the crate into his bedroom.

"Oh, come on, Jamie. Not in here. Please."

"What you talkin' 'bout, woman? He's our baby."

It's Jamie's room. His condo. His world.

"Great," she says, climbing into the bed. "First it's de crate in de room, next it'll be a big dog wif his paws on de sheets."

He turns out the light. "But right now, it's just us dawlin'."

His hand moves between her legs. She's had a Brazilian wax and his fingers explore her smoothness. She's not the least bit aroused. He pushes the sheet back, spreads her legs and strokes her with his tongue. Still nothing. Fucking menopause.

"I'm gonna make you feel good," he whispers.

"Earth's cry, Heaven's smile," she whispers back, too softly for him to hear.

Twenty-seven

Artie, 2004

Artie slips into bed and feels the smoothness of one hundred percent silk sheets against her body. She mentioned the facility's plush linens, and earlier in the day Kendall surprised her with these. According to him they're better than Egyptian cotton. And he even made the bed, which he never does unless he has to. Their house is otherwise pretty much the same as she left it, except that most of her plants have yellow leaves if they're alive at all. She hears Kendall brushing his teeth with the bathroom door open. She faces the opposite way and rests her cheek against the smooth pillow. He rinses and spits and the bathroom light goes out.

"Mmm," he says, sliding into bed beside her. "These feel sexy, huh babe?"

Artie doesn't answer. She breathes deeply, steadily and hopes he'll think she's asleep. He moves closer. Within seconds, she feels a poke in her butt cheek. She exhales with a huff. "What are you doing?"

"What do you mean?" He squeezes her around the stomach and kisses the back of her head.

"Don't do that."

"But, I thought... I mean—"

"No." She wriggles away, toward the edge of the bed.

"Artie."

"Don't touch me." She sits up and looks at him, even though it's too dark to see his eyes.

He rolls onto his back. "How are we gonna…? We should at least try. I bought condoms."

She stands up. Her long nightdress skims down her legs. "If you're gonna pressure me, I'm leaving."

He sits up. "No, please don't. Come back to bed, baby. We can just cuddle. We don't have to do anything."

After a moment she climbs back into bed. He snuggles around her.

"I just want us to reconnect, babe," he says.

"Could you please just back up?" she asks.

He rolls away. Moments later, she hears him sigh sadly.

She gets up and moves to a chair across the room where her jeans are. She pulls them on.

He sits up. "What are you doing?"

"I can't do this. I'm the bitch now, because I need space to heal?"

"Okay. Don't leave." He stands up in his underwear. "I'll go downstairs. I'll stay down there as long as you want me to. Just please don't leave. I don't think you're a bitch."

He puts on a robe, grabs his pillow and a blanket from the closet and he's gone. She hears his footsteps going down the stairs to his studio.

Surrounded by sad, neglected plants hanging from the ceiling, and on the shelves in her home office, Artie types on her desktop Mac. She doesn't find any "Serena Wards" listed in Los Angeles. She types, "S. Ward," which brings up a few addresses and phone numbers. There's one in South LA, but the age is too old. There's another in Redondo Beach that's too young. An S. Ward on Ocean Front Walk in Marina Del Rey is listed as age forty-eight. Artie hears her own heartbeat. *Wait a minute,* she thinks, *the shoot is near there, isn't it?* She clicks on her calendar and looks up the location for Alessandra's movie. 2001 Ocean Front Walk. She clicks back. S. Ward's address is 3100. Wow. She begins to write the phone number on a yellow legal pad.

"What are you doing?"

Artie jumps. "Jesus. Don't sneak up on me." She turns to see Kendall standing behind her. "Why are you even up here?"

He casts his eyes down at the floor. He's dressed up in a black polo shirt and slacks, clean shaved, and he smells like patchouli oil.

"We planned to go out to dinner, tonight," he says softly.

"I made rice and beans this afternoon. I left you some on the stove." She looks back at the screen and finishes copying the number.

He exhales and stokes her hair. "Please. I wanna take you out, Artie."

She rubs her eyebrows. "Where are we supposed to be going?"

"That Cuban place on Washington near the beach."

"I'd rather go to Hal's."

"Hal's?" His voice goes up a couple of octaves. "Why there?"

She turns to him and shrugs. "I like the food, the art, the music. What's your problem?"

"Oh," he sighs. "I was just there for work."

"Look, we don't have to go anywhere. There's food on the stove."

She turns back to the computer. He leans in.

"What are you—? S. Ward?"

"Leave me alone."

Kendall is silent. "Get dressed," he says after a moment. "We'll go to Hal's."

They sit across from each other in a spacious booth toward the back. A jazz trio, piano, bass and saxophone, is playing in the front near the bar. Artie wears her long hair loose, and she's in a dress and heels for the first time in months. She eyes the large paintings on the walls, portraits by a local artist. She finally looks across the table at Kendall and notices that he's staring at the front door. His forehead is tense.

"Did someone put a hit on you?"

"What?"

"You're looking at the door like someone's gonna come through and shoot you."

Kendall passes a hand over his face. He smiles at her. "Sorry, baby. You look gorgeous. Sorry."

Artie smiles, but she doesn't feel it. She bites her lip and tries to think of something to discuss. "I read the script for Ally's movie," she says. "I liked it."

"Oh yeah? What does Sushama play?"

"She's a waitress whose boss dies and leaves her the boardwalk café where she works. Prime real estate. The man's son comes from New York, pissed that she's received his inheritance. He thinks she was screwing his father and he contests the will. They hate each other, of course, but she ends up teaching him about who his dad really was and they fall in love. Predictable, but cute."

Kendall shakes his head. "Mammy shit."

"How do you figure?"

"Isn't the guy white?"

"So?"

"So the black woman teaches him about his dad and helps heal the guy's relationship?" He rolls his eyes. "I'm sure it'll do great. The mainstream loves clinging to mammy."

"Y'know what? I don't critique your work, so shut up about mine."

He looks at her. "How am I critiquing *your* work? You didn't write it."

"The role was written for a white woman and Sushama lobbied and won the part, okay?

"Okay, sorry. Maybe I was wrong. Calm down," he whispers.

She picks up a piece of bread from the basket and holds it like she's going to throw it at him.

"Please don't do that," he says calmly. "I know you're angry, but think about where you are and what you're doing."

She stares at him. His eyes are concerned. For her. She feels other people in the restaurant looking. She puts the bread down, picks up Kendall's car keys and walks out.

She waits for him in the car. They're quiet for a while as he drives.

"Thanks for trying," he says, finally.

She looks out the window. "Sorry."

"Would you think about doing some counseling with me?" he asks.

"I hate this car," she says. "It wastes gas. Why do you need such a big-ass car?"

He sighs. "Before we got the townhouse, when you got mad at me, I would go outside and sit in it. It was our extra room, remember?"

Artie looks at him. He shrugs. She turns toward the window and smiles. Months ago, they would have laughed together at this. She does miss laughing with him.

The shoot starts a few days later. Artie is happy to be away from Kendall and on set with Alessandra, Sushama, and Kendall's cousin Troy, who's directing.

Casting Sushama in a role written for a smart, sexy white woman isn't a problem because Sushama is smart and sexy herself. Casting an actor who doesn't find her sexy *is* a problem, though. Artie stands behind the monitor with Alessandra and Troy on the first day, as they watch a scene with Sushama and the handsome, up-and-coming actor.

"Dammit. I told you there was no chemistry," Alessandra says.

"Shh," Troy says. "He's talented. Just give him a chance."

"This isn't fucking rehearsal, Troy!"

Sushama is bisexual. She has a penchant for boyish girls. But she's also attracted to men. The actor, however, is so turned off by her that he winces when they have to kiss. It's hard to know if this is because he's gay, a bigot, or if he just lacks skill, but it's definitely not going to work. Watching, Alessandra bends over as if she's been kicked in the gut. She holds her head in her hands and glares at Troy before calling her boss at the cable network. They have to recast.

Days later, Artie and Sush are in the middle, because Troy bitches to them about how difficult Ally is and Ally complains to them about what an egotistical dope Troy is. So when they're on lunch break, which is catered at tables outside, Sush is trying to get Alessandra off the subject of Troy bashing when she suddenly shouts, "Ally look!" She points to the nearby boardwalk. "Didn't we *do* that guy in New York?"

Artie doesn't even bother to look, she thinks Sush is bullshitting, but Alessandra glances over.

"Lower. Your. Voice," she growls. "I'm right fucking here. The whole crew does not need to know our business."

When Artie finally looks up from her burrito she sees a tall, broad shouldered white guy in a "Kerry 2004" T-shirt, walking a black lab puppy. It makes her think of Coney Island and Mingus. He's hidden under a scully and sunglasses. How can they tell who he is?

"You met him too, Artie," Sush says with her mouth full. "That time I came to New York for Ally's short and we went to Nell's, that club on 14th Street. Remember? We met him on the dance floor and he bought us drinks and he wanted all three of us to go home with him, but Artie, you wanted to be *true to your man*, the lying motherfucker, so you didn't come."

"He's a *cheating* motherfucker, not a *lying* motherfucker," Artie says.

"Whatever. You missed a good time, cause ol' dude was fly. What was his name again? He's a musician or something. "

"Jamie L'Heureux," Alessandra whispers. "He's a singer-songwriter-piano player— hot in the 90s. I mean it, Sushi. Keep-your-voice-down."

"*That's* who he is?" Artie's heart flutters. She *does* remember meeting him at Nell's. She also remembers reading, years earlier, about Serena being involved with him. Wow.

"Well he was thoroughly entertaining in bed," Sushama says. "And for *me* to say that, you know his ass had to be exceptional. Dude liked to dine in the lush oases as much as I do." She licks her lips and winks.

"Oh, project in your stage voice, *please*." Alessandra says. "There're some surfers out there who didn't catch that."

Sushama cuts Alessandra an *I don't give a shit* look. "Hope he strolls his sexy self back this way so we can say hello."

"Don't you *dare* remind him how we know him," Alessandra hisses. "Our scandalous ho-ing days will not be discussed on my set."

Artie laughs.

Sushama shows Alley her palm. *Talk to the hand.* "He could dance his behind off. Had a huge one, too, especially for a white guy. Remember Al? It almost looked fake."

Alessandra pushes away from the table and storms off.

Sushama chuckles. "Wasn't all that big, really." She winks at Artie. "Just love messing with her. Who is she to tell me what I can talk about? She's not the boss of me."

"Well, she is producing this film. That kinda does make her your boss." Artie finishes a bottle of Evian.

"Whatever. I'm not ashamed of *my* scandalous ho-ing days. Still have 'em when I'm lucky."

"You need to stop," Artie whispers. "She's nervous about her job, Sush. She's already scrambling 'cause of Troy's debacle. Damage her reputation and she might not get another chance, y'know?"

Sushama pouts. "You sound like the voice of doom. Both of you. No fun."

"We're fun. You just need to have some sense of propriety."

"And you need to get laid. You and Ally. Miserable, celibate bitches."

Artie locks eyes with Sush a moment before looking away. "Well," she says, "can't argue with that, but I still don't think you should gossip about Ally's sex life on her set. It undermines her authority."

"Okay. Let's talk about *yours*, chica."

Artie snorts.

"What does *that* mean?" Sushama laughs.

"Not worth talking about."

"Exactly why we should." Sush leans toward her. "You're still pissed cause dude did something to you that you never did to him, right? Do that shit back and you'll feel better."

"I don't think it's that simple."

"Sure it is. But it has to be better than an ordinary screw. Has to be an exquisite affair where the lover is mad about you, and teaches you positions from the Kama Sutra; wines and dines your ass, sucks your toes, eats your nectar, and gives you gifts, bubble baths and massages on top of mouth-wateringly delicious, finger-lickin'—."

"—Jesus, Sush." Artie swallows. She glances around at the other tables— extras, production assistants, crew guys. She lowers her voice. "I've thought about it, but I've never stepped out like that."

"You'll be fine," Sush says. She sips her iced tea.

Artie whispers. "I do wonder what it would be like with someone else, though."

"And I so want that for you, chica. Having only *one* sex partner your *whole life*?" She shudders. "It's unnatural."

"No it isn't," Artie says. "There are plenty of people who do it."

"Bullshit. They're lying."

"That's not true, Sushama."

"It is. Think about it. You might LO-OVE chocolate ice cream, but if you never got a taste of another flavor in your entire life how're you gonna be *sure* chocolate is all that? At some point, aren't you gonna wanna try some vanilla or strawberry? Just to see?"

Artie glares at her. "I might *want* to, but if I took a *vow* that I *wouldn't*

I'd do my best to forget about the vanilla and strawberry and appreciate my god damned chocolate."

"Okay. But what if—"

"—Shut up, Sushama."

Artie gets up, grabbing her plate and moves past the table to a trash bin. Sush follows.

"Go away," Artie says.

"I'm sorry." She gently straightens out one of Artie's braids. "You're my girl and I'm not trying to upset you. I want you to be happy."

Artie dumps her stuff and turns to face her. "I've been tempted by other flavors, okay? But I loved Kendall more than I needed to taste them. He didn't love me like that."

"He *does*. He loves you, sweetie," Sush says. "He always has, and always will—it's in your palm, remember? Guys are just different. They can cheat and still love you."

Artie turns to look at the ocean. She's at work, she cannot cry.

The black Lab puppy appears, running past them on the boardwalk all by himself. His red leash drags on the concrete. Seconds later L'Heureux appears, running after him.

"Mingus! MINGUS," he shouts. "COME BACK HERE. BAD DOG."

Artie gasps. She watches, astonished, as L'Heureux steps on the leash, grabs the dog up and trots away.

"Same breed *and* he's got the same name?" Sushama says. "Weird."

It's not weird to Artie. The Ocean Front Walk in Marina Del Rey is the right one." She takes a deep breath in and blows it out. *I said I was gonna make Serena pay*, she thinks. *I'm a punk if I don't do it now.*

Artie, 1999

The trio met L'Heureux at Nell's in New York five years earlier. The three of them were shaking their booties in designer jeans to a hot Latin song when he came up to Artie, uninvited, took her hand and started dancing with her. He didn't ask. If he had she would have told him she *couldn't,* because that's what she thought. Though Rico played Latin music and knew how to salsa, Artie never learned much. He tried to teach her, but it was when she was young and they never kept it up after leaving New York. She and Kendall grew up freestyling to hip hop and slow grinding to R & B. They never got far with couple's dancing, though. One private lesson for their wedding dance and that was it. Artie felt inept on the dance floor. But L'Heureux took her hand, led her, and she danced as if they'd been partners for years. He whirled her around and pushed and pulled her gently leading her where she was supposed to go. It was effortless. She was unnerved by it, although it was fun. She looked around worried that one of Kendall's boys might be in the club and tell on her. She was also disturbed because she moved *so well* with him. He led like a pro. It was as if she couldn't take a wrong step. She didn't understand how this could *be.* She hadn't practiced these moves before and she didn't know the man at all, yet it felt like she *did* know him. It felt like she was remembering dancing with him. She knew who he was, of course. There was a fuss when his first CD came out and she'd seen him perform live at the Knickerbocker, a jazz supper club near NYU. But she didn't *know* him, and yet there was this odd familiarity and exciting chemistry.

During a slow song, he stared into her eyes. She evaded his, glancing around to see if anyone was watching. When she looked back his dark eyes beamed straight into hers again. He seemed to be trying to communicate something to her, something important without words. The staring felt a little ridiculous, like he was "acting." It was bit over the top, but intriguing.

Kendall was practicing with his quintet that night and he didn't like the idea of her hanging out with Sushama and Alessandra at a club. He knew they attracted a lot of attention. *Y'all look like super-model triplets,* he said. The three of them were slim, with long, dark hair, clear, golden-brown complexions and large, dark eyes. They *did* get a lot of attention, but Artie was uncomfortable flirting with guys, not only because she wasn't available, but also because she'd been with Kendall so long she really didn't know how.

When the slow dance was over, L'Heureux said, "I wanna take you somewhere else for a drink, dawlin'. Have you all to myself. You too fine to share with all dese folks."

"Oh, I can't," she said. "I'm here with my friends." She pointed at them, dancing together. She caught their eyes and waved them over. And that was it. They pulled him to the center of the floor. Alessandra swayed her hips. Sushama turned her butt to him and backed it up into his crotch. Artie stood aside and watched. He invited the three of them upstairs, bought them drinks at the bar, and then he sat on a loveseat in the lounge between Sushama and Ally. Artie sat opposite them on a chair with her arms folded. Her friends plied him with questions about his albums, what was next, and where he was touring, all the while smiling, touching his arms, his chest and his thighs occasionally. He lapped up the adulation. Artie clenched her teeth.

"Why don't y'all come back to my place," he said. "Free drinks and I got a slammin' view."

"I'm down," Sushama said. Ally was into it, too.

"I have to go home," Artie huffed. "I have a husband."

Ally and Sush didn't know this, but, when they went to get their coats, L'Heureux hailed a taxi for her outside. "You're the most beautiful girl in the world," he said. "I'll never forget our dance."

She had goose bumps as he handed her cab-fare, kissed her on the lips, and put his card in her hand. For a moment she wished she could tell him to ditch those chicks and come with her.

It was the only significant romantic encounter she'd had with anyone besides Kendall. Ever. In the days that followed, she thought of their dance, of his touch, his eyes. When she made love to Kendall, she imagined L'Heureux. She never called him, but she did look obsessively for web pages on him and found, to her horror, that he'd been romantically linked with Serena. The interview on the web page she read said he produced her first CD and that they were living together when it came out.

Artie couldn't believe it. She and Kendall had the CD somewhere among the hundreds they owned. She rifled through rows of them, found it, and saw that L'Heureux name *was* there. She never paid attention to who produced it. When it came out, she was still a kid and anything related to Serena was painful.

They couldn't be together anymore if he was out at clubs and taking girls home, she figured. Could he? It didn't matter. It was disgusting to have a crush on a man her mother had slept with. And though she enjoyed the way her heart raced when she read about him or saw his picture, she let it go.

Artie, 2004

It's mind-boggling now. She and L'Heureux, Serena and Kendall. *What is it with me and my mother and men?*

Even Alessandra and Sushama are incredulous when she tells them over drinks in Ally's suite that night.

"There's no WAY," Sushama scoffs. "The bitch is like fifty years old. Just cause he named his dog Mingus? She could have told him about the dog years ago and he just used the name."

"She wasn't fifty when they met, she was in her mid thirties and she was hot."

"I think Sushi's probably right," Alessandra says. "Serena was a beautiful woman, but I find it hard to believe that they'd still be together."

"Look, I cyber stalked her," Artie says, crossing her arms. "And there's an S. Ward living at 3100 Ocean Front Walk, right down the boardwalk from set."

"Damn," Sush says.

"Alright," Ally shrugs.

"Maybe he's not with her just for her looks," Artie says. "Don't be so shallow. But apparently she's still hot. Ask Kendall."

The girls don't say anything for a moment. They look at each other, and then back at Artie.

"Okay, we'll see, my love," Alessandra says. "He either is or he isn't. Guess you'll know soon enough."

"There're lots of reasons people stay in relationships. It's not just about looks," Artie says. "Everybody's pretty in L.A. You need more than that to keep a relationship going."

"I just don't see him with one woman," Sushama says. She finishes her wine. "Much less the *same* woman for so long. Dude likes multiple partners."

"That was five years ago, Sushi," Alessandra snaps. "He could have outgrown it, like most of us do."

"Speak for yourself," Sush says. "I bet he's polyamorous."

Ally yawns. She picks up their wine glasses and carries them to the kitchenette. "Love you guys, but call time tomorrow is 6am. Ciao."

Neither Sush nor Artie moves. Ally leans back against the kitchen counter and crosses her arms. Sushama gestures *one minute* and looks at Artie.

"Okay. Suppose he *is* with her. What are you gonna do about it."

"…Not sure yet," Artie says.

"Wrong answer."

"Sushama," Ally says, "Leave her alone, or take it outside, please."

Sushama flicks her eyes at Alessandra. "In a second."

"I know what I think I *wanna* do," Artie says. "But I'm not sure I can go through with it."

"I know," Sush nods. "That's cause you've always been a good girl. But what has it done for you, but make you crazy?"

Artie hates feeling sorry for herself, but that's how she feels as she drives home. She *has* been a good girl. She's tried not to do deceitful things. But that hasn't stopped them from happening to her. What *is* the benefit of doing the right thing?

When she gets home, Kendall is waiting for her in the living room, snuggled into the sofa, watching TV. She's annoyed that he's upstairs, in the house. With hopeful eyes, he hands her a piece of paper. She looks at it. It's from a medical lab. Test results. He has no sexually transmitted diseases. She hands the paper back.

"Congratulations," she says.

"That's it?"

"I don't know what you expected, Kendall. I need more time."

He looks at her. "Time for what, Artie?"

"...You got to try something new. I haven't yet."

"Yet?" He puts his head in his hands. "Forbidden fruit leads to many jams," he says.

She smiles. "Okay."

"Drove past that church we used to run by during high school. That's what the message board said today. That shit is so true."

She chuckles.

"I don't want you to love someone else," he says, sounding like a little boy.

His face has that luminance it's had since she's known him. There's an inner light that draws her to him even when she wishes it didn't. She has the urge to hug him and tell him it's going to be okay. But she can't be sure of that. She still wants to hurt him. It may be wrong, but it's there. The good girl was bullshit. Wasn't she? *Maybe I'm good and bad. Maybe everybody is.*

Twenty-eight

Serena, 2004

Serena bumps into Artie's boy in the wine and nuts aisle at the Trader Joe's. As their red carts clank, between the Cabernets, Merlots and Pinot Noirs stacked on one side and almonds and walnuts on the other, he peeks at her from under a gangster-style fedora.

"Sorry, ma'am," he says, his eyes twinkling.

Before she can respond, he recognizes her. And in seconds, fear drowns out that confidence in his eyes. His shoulders tense, his head drops, he wriggles past her and wades away up the aisle.

The encounter results in Serena losing a day's work on her music. It's already hard for her to concentrate. It has been since that night. All kinds of things distract from the writing. For example the check is late from her tenant in New York and she has to call to complain about it. Or she loses her glasses and wastes time trying to find them. By the time she *does* find them, she feels pressure to focus *only* on the songs for the rest of the day, because it's imperative that she makes progress. She can't allow herself normal activities, like cooking a meal, calling a friend back east, or watching a movie. Work, Work, Work! Forces against her are intent on keeping her from living a real life where she can actually *live*. It's a period of punishment and she deserves it. So she accepts the sentence. When her time's been served, she tells herself, the Universe will release her. She'll complete her album and life will flow again—new activity—a record deal. She'll go on tour, God willing. *Somethin'll get goin'. Somethin' has to.*

Days later, Serena sits out on the balcony with her journal, watching the activity on the beach below. A mother carries a baby on her shoulders. A young couple holds hands. People connecting like human beings are supposed to.

Jamie stopped going on the morning swims with her, of course. Though it was his idea to make them a daily routine, Serena knew it wouldn't last. Even in her libido's better days his attempts at intimacy have always been short lived. No warning. He and Mingus just didn't come home one night. His car wasn't there the next day. Serena didn't waste time with tears. She put on the wetsuit he bought her and she made the best of swimming alone. The honeymoon is over yet again, and she draws deeper into her own life. Hardly a monumental adjustment, since she doesn't share a space with Jamie. Hers is hers and his is his and sometimes they spend time together, but often they don't. It's fine. When she's lonely, she has her journal to mull things over in. Often, what she muses about leads to song ideas.

> *You came to take a ride*
> *I let you down*
> *I should have been your guide*
> *Could not be found*
> *The time went by so fast*
> *Wish I could change the ugly past...*
> *Sweet songs danced in our minds*
> *And we held hands*
> *We should have stayed in entwined*
> *I stopped the band*
> *Then lost you in the dark*
> *And missed the way back to your heart.*

While fiddling with this ballad, sadness overwhelms and distracts her.

"How can I ever have peace when I've caused so much anger?" she writes. And just as she's about to put the pen down, something, *someone* answers. It's as though the pen is moving on its own.

"You really wanna find peace, baby?"

She's startled. What de hell? Her journal is asking questions of *her* now? And calling her "baby?" I've gone mad for sure, she thinks. Nonetheless, she writes, "Yes." And she waits. The pen moves again.

"Beautiful, baby. About time. Fill your heart with a deep love for that soul and her anger will spontaneously disappear."

Bugger! Serena can't believe this is happening. A higher being is *not* flippin' communicating wif me. *Is it?* She's heard of automatic writing, but in all her years of journaling it's never happened to her. Maybe it's the lunacy of menopause? She thinks she must have read this spiritual advice somewhere, though she doesn't recall where. It's certainly the right bit of information at the right time, however, because *this* I can do. I can work on my own heart. And even if Artie's anger *doesn't* "spontaneously disappear," can't hurt to bring love into my heart.

She closes her eyes and begins to meditate. An image comes to mind. Artie is sitting down on the beach and Serena is up on the balcony waving to her, blowing kisses, and radiating loving energy like the angel-man Johnny Barnes does in Bermuda as he waves to people on their way to work. Serena imagines that Artie's back is to her, but she feels her energy. She senses it, receives it.

What Serena feels isn't a typical "motherly love." She can't define it that way. Yet, she does have a feeling of profound connectedness for having made the child. But what *is* love? She has to think about that. There are so many forms. When she thinks of Artie, there are several elements that together create a composition of love: appreciation for what she's learned from her is one. She's discovered things about life and about herself through what she has and hasn't done with Artie.

She appreciates the immortality Artie provides by being in the world. There's fondness for the memories she has of Artie's sweetness—her personality was full of warmth and kindness when she was a girl. And there's admiration for the gifts she knows Artie has, though she hasn't been there to experience them. There's also the love she *wishes* she'd given; the sense of worthiness Artie deserved because she was here. It's the sense of security Serena longed for as a girl—the love she thought her own mother withheld. Serena tries to feel each of these loving thoughts as deeply as she can as she sends this energy to Artie, waving, blowing kisses, and shining kindness from her eyes.

Afterwards, she goes back to her journal.

"Despite my mistakes, she's been one of my best teachers. Learning how I failed teaches me compassion for those who've failed me. It's all a blessing in the end, isn't it? Even the things that seem disastrous."

The pen writes on its own again: **"Fantastic. You figured it out, baby. Proud of you. Now that's what Serena needs to put into her music. That's her song! Don't let your girl be afraid to express in her very own way. Let her be as inventive as she wants to be, even if it sounds absurd. Celebrate the struggle, cause it's given her something to say."**

Serena stares at the page. She re-reads what she's written, knowing that either she's a lunatic, or there really *is*, in fact, a spirit communicating with her. Both possibilities are cause for concern. She realizes, though, that whatever (or whoever) it is means to encourage her and she does feel comforted; more than she has in a long time. By going deep to find love for Artie, perhaps she's discovering a treasure for herself, too.

Twenty-nine

Artie, 2004

"I went to the set and I ran into Roxy near the boardwalk early in the morning. She was wearing a red jumpsuit and she was stealing red vines licorice from the craft services table. I didn't stop her, but I asked why she was doing it. She told me they kicked her out of the hospital because she turned 21 and her mother stopped paying the bill. She was living on the beach. I was furious. I told Roxy I was gonna find the bitch and beat her fucking ass. How dare she treat her daughter like that? But Roxy seemed to have peace about it. She said she would be okay, that she'd find her own way in the world. She wasn't angry. 'And don't you be angry, either,' she said."

Artie writes this down because she hasn't had a dream she's remembered in such detail in quite a while. She thinks about it as she dresses in layers for work.

She's still thinking about it when she arrives before call time and she's the first to pour a steaming cup of coffee at the craft services table. She sees L'Heureux coming towards her, shirtless, with his black Lab puppy. She's shivering her ass off in long underwear and a sweatshirt and he's half naked. Showing off those rock hard abs. *They are easy on the eyes.* She covers a smile with her hand. Though she hasn't spotted him for days, she's expected him to show up. She's willed it, in fact, by picturing it repeatedly, making up scripts about what she'd say and what he'd say.

As he moves straight toward her, she picks up her coffee to take a sip. It scalds her tongue. *Ow, shit.* She sets it down. Crosses arms. Uncrosses them. *Why can't I act normal?*

"Those cameras aren't heavy 'round your li'l neck, dawlin'?" he asks, grinning. His teeth are perfect. Gleaming. He's not wearing the scully, just the shades. His dark hair has the sheen of lacquer. His six-pack is awe-inspiring.

She swallows. "Not really," she says. *Do I sound casual?* Her heart thumps. "I'm used to it." Her voice comes out higher pitched than usual. She turns to watch the puppy, clumsily pulling on his leash. He's trying to get closer to the craft services table and the bacon that's on it. As Artie watches him, she taps her lips with her knuckles.

"What kind are they?" L'Heureux asks.

She doesn't look at him. "One's a Nikon DX-1, it's digital, and the other is a Nikon F3HP, an old film camera."

"Why the two kinds?"

She laughs. "Why all the questions?" She glances his way for a split second before turning to pour milk into her coffee. Her hand trembles. When she finally looks at him, he lifts his shades to the top of his head, grins, and stares at her in that probing way of his.

"Good to see y'again dawlin'," he says.

Flutters and tingles. Holy shit. He's trying to see deep into her, like he did years ago. It's too much, too soon. She bends down to pet the puppy. He gnaws on her fingers with pointy teeth.

"So you *do* remember me," she says. "Wasn't sure if you would."

"Didn't I tell you you were the most beautiful girl in the world?"

She tries not to grin. *Ay ay ay. Am I turning red?* She glances up at him quickly before returning her attention to the floppy ball of fur. She removes her fingers from his mouth and he licks her on the chin.

"You did," she says. "And that was really… sweet. Thanks."

When she looks back at L'Heureux, he tips his head and eyes her in a way that puts everything in the background out of focus. It's all about her.

"Be honest, though," she says, "you've said that to more women than you can count, haven't you?"

"I said it to *you* on 14th Street in Manhattan."

Breathe. "Well, you have a good memory. That's cool." She meets his eyes again, and feels something stir inside her. A magnetic pull. She'd latch onto him right now if that weren't a crazy thing to do.

"Not really, dawlin'," he said. "You were just unforgettable."

She knows better than to take him seriously, but she does. She lets out a giggle.

He nods. "Y'know, you look *very* much like someone I know."

And just like that, Artie's a pricked balloon. "Oh," she says. She's unsure if this means he knows her relationship to Serena, or just that they look alike, but she's not "unforgettable" for any good reason.

"The resemblance is kinda scary."

Scary? Maybe he *doesn't* know who I am, she thinks.

The first A.D. yells, "STAND BY FOR REHEARSAL."

"Excuse me. That's my cue." Artie moves to the set to shoot the rehearsal, a scene with Sushama and Ben, her hot-young-new-fresh co-star.

She uses both cameras. Alessandra wants everything digital and delivered on a disc, no processing, but Artie prefers her images on film, glorious *film* so she shoots a few with Nikki too.

Once rehearsal is over and the movie camera is rolling Artie has to stop, and when she does, L'Heureux is still standing by craft services. He's signing an autograph for Van, a pretty Vietnamese-American P.A. who's gushing. He's enjoying the adulation. Asshole. Artie mentally smacks herself for feeling jealous. Their eyes meet and she hopes he can't tell. He finishes with Van and racks focus back to her.

"Lemme see that." He reaches for the camera. She hands Nikki over. He focuses the lens and takes a shot.

"Make sure I get a copy of that," he says, handing the camera back.

"We'll see how it comes out first."

"Fair enough. Why 'on't you come by on your lunch break. My place is right down Ocean Front Walk," he points. "Ya could hit it with a beach ball from here." He takes out his wallet and hands her a card with the address. "You gotta see her."

"I don't think that's a good idea," Artie says. She feels her jaw clenching.

He squinches his face, baffled. "Why?"

"Just not interested." Her hands have become fists. She remembers her dream. *Don't you be angry*, Roxy said.

"Did I miss somethin'?" he asks.

"I don't wanna see her."

L'Heureux shrugs. "A'ight. 'f you change your mind—"

"—I won't," she says. She tries to hand the card back, but he doesn't take it.

"Y'outta re-think that, dawlin'. You'll definitely find her interesting. Promise you that."

Artie shakes her head.

"Suit yourself." He sounds annoyed. "But just so you know, you can see her from the window. Blinds are open during the day."

Strange, she thinks.

He smiles. "Girl, you ain't got a clue what I'm talking about, so how you gon' not be interested?"

Artie flicks her eyes away.

"A'ight then." He shakes his head. "That closed minded shit ain't a cute look."

Fuck you, she thinks, frowning at him.

"Ha," he says, pointing a finger at her. "Now *that* look is kinda hot, though." He chuckles and walks away pulling Mingus, who walks backward several steps watching Artie. He squeaks high-pitched puppy barks at her, as if he's trying to tell her something.

Sushama approaches. "What's shakin' chica?"

"That is one arrogant mothafucka."

"Mmmm," Sush says, watching him walk away. "That's a tall drink of water on a hot-ass day is what *that* is. When y'all gettin' together? Did he remember me?"

Artie just looks at her.

Surely Serena doesn't sit in the window all damn day. Maybe it's a picture or a painting of her he's talking about? She's dying to know, but she doesn't want to go down there. At lunch she tells Sushama and Alessandra what he said and Sushama offers to go take a peek. Alessandra makes her bring Van, the cute production assistant, so she won't get "lost." Sushama pretends to be irritated, but she loves the attention.

Artie waits inside the restaurant next to set, where lunch is being catered. Alessandra has moved across the room for a "meeting" with Troy. Right. After all her ranting about him she's practically sitting in his lap. Her hand is on his thigh. Artie smiles. *Scandalous ho.*

Less than five minutes have passed when Artie's cell phone rings.

"You won't believe this," Sush says. "It's amazing, you *have* to see it."

"What? What is it?" Artie asks.

"Some sort of antique photograph. On metal, I think, and it's *you*."

"Me?"

"Yes, you. It's—Oh, hi! We were just admiring your—Click. Sushama has hung up. Artie's too anxious to eat. She walks outside. After a few minutes Sush comes skipping toward her trailed by Van, who stomps into the restaurant.

"You were right about 'the B,'" Sush says. Definitely still in the picture."

"What happened?"

"We were looking in the window and she came out onto the balcony upstairs. She looks effin' awesome for fifty, by the way."

"She's forty-eight. What did she say?"

"She'd look good for thirty-eight. She's bangin'."

"What did she *say*?"

"I mean, if I didn't know she was your mama—."

"—Sushama!"

"You're way hotter, though. She asked what we were doing and I told her we were admiring the portrait and she said in her fake accent, 'Does this look like a bloody museum?'"

"Her accent's not fake, she's Bermudian. So the portrait looks like me?"

"That's the crazy part." Sushama puts both hands on Artie's shoulders. "It doesn't just look like you," she says. "It looks like it *is* you."

Artie feels electricity dust up her back, neck and skull. She shakes her shoulders.

"Seriously," Sush says. "It's wicked old, like from the 1800s or something, but Artie, it's *your* face, your hair, even. It's freaky."

"Huh," Artie says. "Maybe Serena got a picture of me. Maybe my dad sent her one?"

Sushama shrugs. "But why would it look like an antique?"

Artie wonders about that, too.

She shoots a rehearsal right after lunch and when she's done she looks at the card L'Heureux gave her.

It takes several rings before he answers and then a few seconds for him to speak.

"Artimeza Reyes?"

"Changed my mind," she says.

Silence.

"You there?" she asks.

"I'mma have to call you back." He hangs up.

What the—? Is he angry that I sent Sush down there? She wonders, unsure of what to do. She could go and look at it on her own, but what if Serena's outside? *So what if she is?* She's the one who did something wrong, not me. She should be more worried about what I might do to *her.*

He wasn't kidding when he said you could hit it with a beach ball from set. It takes less than two minutes to get there. The modern, gray, three-story building is mostly glass in the front, and there are native grassy plants and polished gray stones in the small yard that's enclosed by a brushed nickel fence. Artie doesn't see anyone outside. She leans against the fence and peers into the picture window at the street level. First thing she notices is the elegant Steinway. But behind the grand piano on the north wall is a whole plate daguerreotype, lit like a museum piece.

Artie learned about daguerreotypes while studying at NYU, though she hasn't seen too many. She can't get any closer without jumping the fence, but she takes out the long lens in her camera bag. The magnification allows her to see the features clearly: the full lips, the delicate arch of the brows, the dark, almond shaped eyes, the dimple in the chin; all eerily similar to hers. Even the shape of the face and the length and wave of her hair are like Artie's. Bizarre. But it *isn't* me. It's an authentic piece, so it can't be me. Must be one of Serena's relatives. The blinds begin to close, though she doesn't see anybody inside. Now that she's seen it, who cares? She has to get back set anyway.

Thirty

Artie, 2004

The shoot wraps at sunset. Artie packs up her cameras at the crew parking lot under a shimmery pink and orange streaked sky. She's relieved that Alessandra's busy with production stuff and that Sushama has to study her lines, because she plans to call L'Heureux, and she doesn't need the pressure of their questions or advice. She has to work up the courage in her own time. Stalling, she drives south toward Marina Del Rey in slow traffic and stops at the Longs Drugs in the shopping center on Lincoln Boulevard. She buys a pack of condoms, something she's never done. She also drops off her film, which she almost never does at the drug store, because the printing is usually so poor. Alessandra's more interested in the digital images, anyway, so it's okay.

When she gets back in the car she takes a few deep breaths. She finds L'Heureux's number on her phone, and hits call.

"God bless caller I.D. Artimeza Reyes."

"Hey."

"Holy Mother of God," he says.

"What?"

"Did you *tell* me your name in New York?"

"You never asked."

"Yeah, you right. Sounds like me... Lawd. *You're* Artie. Bless your heart. Did you know who *I* was?"

"Well, you *are* kinda famous."

"I mean—c'mon shorty, y'*know* what I mean."

"I found out later."

"Wow." He sighs.

"Yeah. So, the daguerreotype… Is it authentic?"

"Huh? Oh, yeah. Sorry, I'm still trippin'…"

"It's real, right?"

"Been in my family over a hundred fifty years."

"*Your* family?" Artie laughs.

"Really. It *is* from my family."

"The woman looks just like *me*. It has to be from *Serena's* family."

"Sorry, it's *my* great, great, great grandmama."

"…Wait a minute. Aren't you white?"

"Depends who you ask, dawlin'." He chuckles. "Lotta surprises in history."

His velvet, self-assured voice makes her nether regions quiver.

"I was gonna ask you if we could get together and, um, talk," she says.

"Good, cause I's gonna ask you the same. Where y'at?"

She swallows. Her heart pounds. "Uh, you free *now*?"

"Yeah, girl, that's what I'm tryin' a tell ya. Where you at?"

She inhales and exhales, steadying her breath. "I'm in my car on Lincoln, heading toward Washington.

"Meet you on Speedway, behind the crib," he says. "Call me when you're outside."

He wants to bring Mingus in the car, but since she doesn't know how well he's trained, she doesn't want to drive. She parks in his space. His silver Beemer has a Kerry 2004 sticker on its bumper and inside it smells minty, like Altoids.

He says they're going someplace fun. He won't say where. Miles

Davis's *Kind of Blue* is on the stereo. "You cool with that?" he asks. She smirks. Like she's really gonna tell a jazz musician that she doesn't want to hear *Kind of Blue*?

Her mouth is dry. The kind of dry it gets when she's stoned, but she's not stoned. The inside of her lips stick to her teeth. Ugh. She separates them with her tongue. Wait, has she been breathing? She forgot. *Relax,* she tells herself. He looks perfectly calm, snapping his fingers to the: *Weeebop. Badoobadoobadbadoo…* Professional womanizer. Nothin' but a thing to him.

He smells of musk and vanilla in his button-down white shirt and worn-in jeans. The precision haircut, Italian leather shoes, and a Breitling on his wrist suggest status, but he rolls like a regular guy.

They listen to Trane get down as the car merges onto Pacific Coast Highway. If Kendall saw me right now, she thinks, he'd blow his horn to bits. Serves his cheating-ass right.

In the side view mirror she sees the puppy balancing on his wobbly hind legs. His front paws are on the door, little head stuck out the window, ears flapping in the ocean air. Looks like he's surfing. Reminds her of the jaunts to Coney Island with Mingus and Rico that made Serena jealous.

"What'll you tell her if she asks about my car?"

He looks at her, and then back at the road. "Folks I know come by and park there," he says, "cause we're close to the beach. She ain't gon' ask."

Artie's not so sure about that, but it's his call. Her cottonmouth is abating, thankfully. She considers peeling off her waffle T and jeans and getting right to it. But she should ask questions, right? He knows Serena better than anybody.

"Do me a favor, dawlin'. Take your hair out," he says.

She looks at him. *Huh?* The request seems to come from nowhere. She pats her braids, as if to protect them. "You serious?"

"Indulge me, dawlin'. Take it out."

She thrusts her neck back, tilts her head forward, and frowns.

"C'mon, I wanna see it the way it is in the portrait." He looks at her a moment before picking up the braid that hangs over her left shoulder. He slips the elastic off and uses his fingers to rake through it.

Does he think he owns me?

With his eyes on the road, he lifts a handful of her hair to his face and he smells it.

"You haven't changed, I see," she says. "Y'know, some people appreciate being *asked* before you just start dancing with them." There may be a chill in her voice, but watching him with her hair— breathing in its scent— the newly waxed pet (formerly known as *Chia*) is getting dewy.

"Some people *think* they wanna be asked, dawlin'," he says, "Truth be told, they like a man who knows how to do what he does." He releases her hair and smiles at her. "You're beautiful. You need to wear it out all the time."

"I don't need to do anything except what I want to do." She crosses her legs.

"Can't reach the other one, dawlin'… Ain't gon' leave it lookin' crazy like *that*, are you? Let it loose, girl."

"Will you stop ordering me around?"

He watches her as best he can while driving. She frees the other braid and combs her fingers through her the length of her hair. She pretends not to notice or enjoy the way he's looking at her. Hungry. Like she's playing with more than just her hair. She can see that it frustrates him to have to take his eyes off of her to watch the road. She sighs inside. Bits of purloined self-confidence return.

His face turns ruddy. His hips squirm. What's happening between his legs? She wants to find out. Should she? She'd like to but… *What the hell, it's what I came for.* She reaches over. He knocks her hand away.

"Uh, I, uh…" He exhales. "I'mma switch gears here 'cause— ain't tryin' to kill us if that's okay with you, dawlin'?"

"Whatever." She chuckles like she's not humiliated. His eyes hug the road.

"Story behind the daguerreotype is that there was a law that the Free Women of Color couldn't be seen in public without covering their hair. She was proud of hers and wanted a picture for posterity. It's uncommon of the time period to see the hair loose like that."

Artie knows he's turned on and she is too. Why's he avoiding it? *And why do I feel guilty? Serena started this game, not me. I left this asshole alone the first time. She should have left my asshole alone.*

"You listenin'?" he asks.

"Strange law," she says. "Is that true?"

"Yup. Quadroon women were beautiful 'kept' mistresses to European dudes who were usually married with families. Pissed off the white women in New Orleans, hence the petty law."

Artie is skeptical. "I'll Google it later."

"The woman in the portrait is my daddy's great-grandmama, Marie Rillieux. Her son, my father's granddaddy left the city for a long time. Moved to up to North Carolina for a while and passed for white. Knew he might never see her again after he left, so he took the daguerreotype to remember her face. It was hidden in his attic 'til after he died. He left a diary explaining that he loved her, but his choices were limited as a man of color and he wanted the privileges that came with being white. Said she cried like he'd never seen the day he left, and he never forgave himself."

"If he felt that guilty, he should have gone home to his mama," Artie says. "I have no sympathy for people like that. I never met my own grandmother for the same damn reason."

L'Heureux looks at her then back at the road. "If you say so. He *did* go back. He moved back to N'awlins, but it was years later. When he went to see her she pretended not to know him. Said she had no son."

Artie holds her tongue for a moment. "Does your thing with my mother have something to do with all this?" she asks.

He stops a red light and looks at her sideways. "What?"

"Trying to connect with your roots?"

He laughs. "Dawlin' I been with a lotta different types of women for more reasons than I could explain. She gets me. That's all there is to our *thing*." He runs a hand over his face. "No one else'd put up with me. Best friend I ever had."

Artie bristles.

"Well, maybe I'm lyin' a little, though, 'cause I always did think she looked like Marie, and there's something about Marie's face that feels like home."

"I look more like the portrait than she does."

He smiles, but doesn't agree or disagree as he pulls into a strip-mall parking lot. Music from a live jazz band comes from a bar boasting the name 'Cholly's,' on a blue neon sign above the door. He parks.

"'Coording to his diary, my father's granddaddy's parents met at a Quadroon Ball. You familiar with those?"

She shakes her head.

"Mixed race girls went to these formal dances where white dudes were invited to meet them. Henri L'Heureux had been set up to meet another young lady there, but he saw Marie, had a dance with her, and that was it. Said he knew from her eyes that their love was eternal. One dance." He looks at Artie. The puppy whines. "Most European men kept their Quadroon women on the side," he continues. "Wasn't legal to marry 'em, but he never bothered with anyone else. He only loved her."

"Wow," Artie says.

"I've seen pictures and I look like Henri," he says, caressing Artie's face with his palm. He turns off the engine and takes Mingus out to let him pee in the parking lot.

Artie sits in the car. The picture, the story, it's all intriguing... It's also confusing, and distracting her from what she's there to do.

L'Heureux opens the door and puts Mingus back inside.

"Come on out here, girl. Get on your feet."

"Jesus, do you order everyone around?"

"You talk too damn much. Quit fussin'," he smiles.

"Quit *bossing*." She wonders how Serena puts up with this.

The music in the parking lot is loud. Lots of bass and percussion. No one's outside, except a guy running a hot dog stand at the edge of the lot. L'Heureux takes her hand.

"Dance with me."

"Out here?"

"Sure," he says, "Why not?"

"You drove all the way up here to hang out in the parking lot? *This* is the fun place you wanted to take me?"

He points to the hot dog stand.

"Came for *those*. Best dogs in L.A. But they taste better when you work up an appetite. So come on." His voice is warm.

She's afraid it won't be the way it was at Nell's. "What if I step on your feet?"

He pulls her hand and draws her body to his. She can see the guy in the hot dog stand looking at them. She feels ridiculous.

"I'll lead you, dawlin'," he says.

And he does. He spins and pushes and pulls her and she's dancing. It's magical. She doesn't understand it. It's like she was meant to move with him.

"Look at me." He stops spinning her, lifts one of her hands to his lips, and wraps his other around her waist, holding her close. He looks into her eyes—that intense staring thing he does.

She laughs. "Why do you do that?" she asks. "You did it when we met."

"I'm tryin' to see."

"See *what*?"

"Shh," he whispers. "One dance... Look at me."

She does. While he tries to bare his soul and see hers, she finds that his eyes are wiser than she noticed before. She wonders what it is they know. Artie hadn't planned on this. It wasn't supposed to be deep. But she looks into his eyes, and he looks into hers, and something stirs inside her. What *is* it? Recognition? Desire? Love? She thinks he sees it and feels it, too; this energy, expanding in her heart and swirling all around them. She's not sure she wants to feel it, but there it is. The urge to laugh is gone. That longing she once had— to be connected to him— is back. She could sink into it and have a hard time getting out. But she *can't.* It waned because she was with Kendall and he was with Serena. And he's still with her. *She gets him.* So what are they doing here? Revisiting this is futile. And she hadn't intended to feel anything. She wanted to use him.

"I—I don't think I can do this," she says.

He stares at her, his heart still palpable. He nods. "A'ight, then."

And just like that, it's gone.

"Want a hot dog?" he asks. He walks toward the stand without waiting for her answer.

Artie blinks. She doesn't move for a moment. She breathes, steadying herself. Mingus, the picture, the story, the dancing, the soul gazing— it's dizzying. Finally, she follows, her feet less sure than they were. He hands her a hot dog with sauerkraut and mustard and he pays the guy.

"How'd you know how I like my hot dogs?" she asks, unnerved.

"You're from New York." He sighs. "Relax." He walks over to the nearby picnic table.

She follows again, embarrassed, and thinks she has little reason to be. It *has* been a bizarre evening. She sits down close to him.

"So, what do you think this all means?" she asks.

He speaks with his mouth full. "Not a damn thing, I guess." He leans closer to her. "In New York, there was *somethin'*… Thought you felt it, too. But then I never heard from you." He leans back.

"Well, isn't it obvious *why*?" she asks, licking some mustard off her lips.

"Not really. I'm still that guy. You know who I am, and here you are."

Artie doesn't say anything. If he hasn't figured out exactly what she's up to, he will.

He takes another bite and looks away while he chews and swallows. "I had this idea that there was this *one* soul I was supposed to find, and because of the picture and the way we vibed that night..." He turns back to her. "I dunno. Guess we make up things in our heads that we wanna believe, y'know? But you live long enough, you realize, shit don't matter unless you make it matter." He stands up. "Let's go. You can finish that in the car." He walks away.

They drive without talking. Mingus sticks his face out the window. A thrum ripples in the background on the Miles Davis composition. *"All Blues."* Artie finds it tense right now. Stressful. She worries that she may be missing an opportunity she's supposed to take. What if this was all predestined? What if I'm messing it up?

"So... what is it you think, or you thought?" she asks. "That we're reincarnated? Soul mates?"

"Look, just drop it, dawlin'. I'mma get you back to your car and then we don't need to have shit to do with each other. You're not interested, right? I shouldn't've wasted your time."

"You didn't. I *did* feel something in New York. And I wanted to know about the picture. She does look like me. And... I wanted to spend time with you."

"Why's that?"

He watches the road. She's quiet, waiting for his attention. Finally he looks at her. She tells him, with her eyes, that she wants him.

"Oh yeah?" He turns to the road again. "Well dawlin' I'd do the hell outta you if you were someone else, but ya *ain't* and a lotta women wanna *spend time with me*, so I don't need to mess with a lil' girl who'd try to diddle with her mama's man."

"Wait. What?" Artie says. "*You* were just trying to seduce *me*."

"No. I was tryin' to see if we had what I thought we had. If I was tryin' to seduce you, baby, we'd be fuckin' right now."

She stares at him, her mouth agape.

"I know what pussy feels like. That was *all* I wanted, you'd be my last choice."

"You crazy mind-fucking asshole. You and that bitch deserve each other."

"Yo, don't call her that."

"Don't scold me. You disrespect her more than I ever have."

"That's not true. She's my woman and I take care of her."

"By cheating on her?"

"We have an open relationship."

Artie scoffs. "Whose idea was *that?*"

He doesn't answer.

"If you have no boundaries that messes with other people's lives, you idiot," she shouts.

Mingus whines. He climbs into the front, into her lap, and licks her face. Artie begins to cry. L'Heureux sighs and pulls over along Pacific Coast Highway. It's dark, but she can see the ocean, lit by the moon.

"Why are you stopping?" She rubs Mingus's little head with one hand. With the other she wipes her face. "I wanna go home."

He takes off his seat belt, lifts Mingus, and returns him to the back. He leans close and kisses her temple. She doesn't move. She's listening to cars whizzing by and the ocean roaring when he kisses her on the mouth. His lips are soft. And curious. His tongue finds hers. She's never kissed anyone but Kendall like this. It's gentle and it lasts long enough to mean something. He puts his fingers in her hair and she hears him inhale deeply as if he's filling himself with her. And then he stops. Their eyes meet. And she glimpses that thing again as she sees inside him; that thing she could lose herself in.

"I was afraid of that," he says.

"Why?" Her courage is back. She unbuttons her pants.

He stops her, grabs her hand and kisses the back of it. He sucks the tip of her index finger. She feels wet. Her nipples itch. He caresses her hand and finds her wedding band. He spins it on her finger. She tries to pull her hand away. He holds on.

"Listen..." he says, "I care about her. I do what I do, but we've been together a long time."

Artie yanks her hand from him. "Why are you telling me this *now*?"

"I'm not denying—what this is," he gestures from himself to her. "But I think if it was gonna happen, it shoulda happened years ago."

"Why did you just kiss me?" She stares at him while hoisting her hips up and pulling her pants down over her butt.

"Stop. You—were upset and—that's what I *do*— with women."

"—Oh, fuck you. Finish what you started."

She wriggles completely out of her pants as he watches without moving. He eyes her, his expression inscrutable. He doesn't stop her as she reaches over to unzip his fly. He's poking, stiffly, though his underwear. She hesitates a moment, then wraps her hand around him.

"Stop," he says weakly.

She can hardly believe it's happening. She's touching a man who isn't Kendall.

He grabs her wrist. "I said stop, Artie." He squeezes and twists her arm.

"Ow!" She lets go.

He gently pushes her back in her seat. "I have a bad feeling," he whispers. "Even though we *feel...* something, we wouldn't be able to make this work."

"What are you talking about? Make *what* work? No one said we have to have a *relationship*." She leans toward him again.

"Artie." He holds her back with one arm. "*Be for real.* You and I start doin' it, we're *gonna* have a relationship. And what would it be, but a mess? It would ruin any chance for y'all to make your peace."

"Peace?" Artie laughs. "There's no chance for us to make peace."

"I don't believe that," he says.

"We hate each other."

"Not true."

"Uh, yeah, it is," she says.

He shakes his head. No. "I know she hurt you." He looks at the steering wheel, avoiding her eyes. "I know why you think you need to do this." He looks at her.

She shrivels. She wants to cave inside herself.

He nods. "I know."

"Okay," she says. "Then you understand. I didn't start it, she did."

"You don't have to do anything to her. She tortures herself. She wishes she could undo it."

"Well why *did* she do it?"

He scratches his cheek, and shrugs. He doesn't know.

"Yeah, of course."

"But I don't think she meant to."

Artie laughs. "Right."

"Well, we believe what we want to."

"I can't believe what doesn't make sense." She pulls her pants back on.

"I understand. And you deserve an explanation."

"Tell me something," she says, zipping up. "What makes me such a turnoff? Why do I keep getting dissed for a certain has-been singer?"

"She's not a has-been. And you're not a turnoff." He eyes her kindly. "Look at my lap. But you can't manipulate me, dawlin'. I'm a grown-ass man."

"*You've* been playing with *me* all night."

He scratches his bottom lip with his top teeth and shrugs apologetically. "Got my weaknesses."

She exhales heavily.

"Y'all need to talk," he says. "It's time."

"I don't see that happening. So if there's something I should know, enlighten me. And take me back to my car."

"No, I'm serious. I'll set it up."

She tries to imagine what that would be like. She can't. "Can we just go, please?"

"Yup. Gimme a minute." He points down at his business, then looks out the window.

Artie looks out the other window. She watches the moonlight walking on the black waves. Mingus-2 snores softly behind her.

They don't speak on the ride back. Artie thought she was *supposed* to pursue this. She has no other plan. She's no closer to being settled in her spirit. She can't meet with her mother. Not after this. *What kind of mojo does the woman put on these motherfuckers?* Serena is a super-bad-ass bitch that Artie has to concede she's just no match for.

Thirty-one

Serena, 2004

After months of agonizing, working, re-working and tweaking, Serena feels done. Done! Finally. Boppin to Mingus' "Reincarnation of a Lovebird," she puts on dangly silver earrings, and slips on a pair of nude Jimmy Choos. She's buzzing to get downstairs to show Jamie the finished compositions. She can hardly wait for the look on his face when he sees that she learned Sibelius 3 and made the lead sheets on her iBook without his help. He loves to tease and call her "old millennium," 'cause he thinks she's still writing music by hand like some little ol' white-haired relic. She may be an old dog, but she definitely *has* learned a new trick.

As it turns out, ol' bitches can go into heat, too. She's been taking maca root powder from Peru to balance her hormones. *Praise de Uniwerse, it works.* Hal-le-bloody-lu-jer. The cream-colored halter dress she steps into has matching crotch-less knickers that drive Jamie crazy. She's zipping the back when she hears his car start up behind the building. *Whaat?* He didn't tell me he was goin' anywhere. She flies across the room reaching the window just in time to see him pulling out. "Shit."

Serena blinks at the Turquoise Thunderbird Convertible parked in the space below—a fist in her gut. Months earlier, Serena stared at this car while time froze.

The bye stood in the driveway on the passenger side of his Escalade and tried to console his hysterical woman. Serena grabbed her Burberry satchel and climbed over to the driver's side. She stumbled, drunk, wet, and reeking of vomit, out of the monstrous vehicle. She crept 'round and hid behind the back bumper. In a haze and horrified by what she'd found herself in the middle of, she crouched between the two cars, too craven to face Artie. She listened to her screaming. It was clear the garrl assumed the worst—that this mess had been pre-meditated.

"YOU'RE WOFFLESS!" Artie shrieked. "YOU FUCKING WOFFLESS FUCK! GET OFF ME!"

She sounded deranged. Serena knew, of course, that what she was shouting was intended for her. She regretted subjecting Artie to that word. There wasn't a way to explain that "woffless" was what she'd felt about *herself*. How could she explain without seeming as if she was justifying it? She wasn't. Serena knew she'd wounded Artie. The guilt had been relentless for years. And now this. *Could it get any worse?* It was a quagmire so awful Serena wondered if anything short of death could bring relief. And then, as if these thoughts had manifested, Artie broke free from the young man and landed behind the wheel of her car. She threw on the engine, then the lights, and then looked directly at Serena, a frozen target, in front of the car. Serena closed her eyes and braced herself. She prayed it would be quick.

But aside from the sound of the running engine there was only silence. Even the young man was quiet. When Serena finally dared to look, Artie's eyes were burning back at her with an indescribable hatred. She made certain she had Serena's full attention before slowly and purposefully mouthing: "Woffless bitch." Then she backed the car from the driveway and ripped off, leaving the squeal of the tires hanging in the air.

The bye fell to the driveway in his undershorts. He hugged his knees to his chest and moaned. Serena knew she could be of no comfort. She started walking. No matter that her feet felt tortured and that she desperately needed to use the loo. She didn't care that she stank of vomit, or that she wasn't wearing knickers, or that she was wet and freezing from the delightful hot flash earlier. She didn't worry that she could've been raped, mugged or killed walking alone in the middle of the night. If anyone cared to get close to the wretched disaster she was that night Serena felt they could have had at it.

It was a challenge, but she eventually found Abbot Kinney Boulevard. The Mini Cooper was still parked 'round the corner from Hal's. And though she was both inebriated and traumatized she somehow made it back to the flat without killing herself or anyone else.

For a long time after, she wondered why she'd survived. If Artie had driven into her that night, she would have understood. Anyone would have. Artie once told her that she believed people lived until they had "made their effect" on the world. She was in the fifth grade and they were riding the subway, coming from a funeral in the Bronx. Serena thought maybe she'd heard it somewhere, but she'd said it after a long silence. Serena was quietly missing her deceased friend, and it seemed to have occurred to Artie on her own, her way of offering comfort. It was a sophisticated idea for a ten-year-old garrl. Serena was still wondering what her "effect" would be. She hoped it was her music. It tried to tell her story, warts and all. And it tried to heal what she had wounded.

Serena had seen the young women from the movie production sniffing 'round the portrait earlier, so she's not completely blindsided by the car in the driveway. Artie looks more like that ghoulish picture now and if she and Jamie met, *of course* he'd be drawn to her.

When she saw the garrls peering into the window at first she thought they were tourists. Loads of people look in the windows of the flats along the boardwalk. Wasn't until they left, and she watched where they went, that she saw they were part of the production she'd been seeing from her balcony. Then she became concerned, 'cause just that morning when she finished her swim she noticed a pretty garrl with long braids and a camera, milling amongst the crew. Serena was too far away to be certain that it was Artie, but looked like her. She knew that if it *was* something was likely to happen, though she hadn't expected that *something* so soon.

Serena was intent on finishing her work that day. She refused to let anything impede the goal. Forging on seemed a better option than letting her mind run worst-case scenarios. As it turns out, the Universe has done that for her, and parked the worst-case scenario in her driveway. Brilliant. Still, she resists the urge to panic. She takes a deep breath and tells herself she'll accept whatever happens. She's been journaling, praying and meditating. She's in a good place. A voice in Serena's head assures her: *it's all for the good, baby*. She breathes again and blows out her worries. They come right back. Another voice urges: *call his cell phone*. The first voice says: *Be still, baby*. Serena breathes. She tries to be still, but her mind is spinning and the voice of *fucking do something* (!) screams louder than the voice of peace. She dials. Straight to voicemail. Peace says: *Told you to be still, baby*.

She paces. She can't simply sit still and wait for him to come home. "Be still" is figurative, not literal, she reasons, so she'll pass the time productively. She can go up to Jamie's studio and record the songs. There's no one to engineer a mix, but it'll be good practice. And she likes the idea of playing piano and singing on one track, like a live performance.

After brewing a cup of chamomile tea, she connects the microphone for herself and for the piano, and she sets the levels. Before playing, she closes her eyes and thanks Spirit for getting her this far. She asks it to be with her. Serena knows she can give a technically fine performance with her skill alone. She wants to transcend that. She wants magic.

Once she begins, she plays straight through, as if for a live audience. At one point she looks up and sees Annie and Mingus sitting at a table, sipping champagne. They listen as she sings of great mistakes and big loves; of triumphs and failures, gratitude and regrets and of impossible dreams that have been a privilege to reach for even when unattained. The pride brimming in their eyes means everything to her.

She goes for forty-five minutes, breaking only for sips of tea. She doesn't check levels, listen back, or re-take anything. After the struggle it took to give birth to these songs, she glides through this part, expressing them, effortlessly. Bits of her soul shine through. *This* is what she came to do. This is "making her effect." This is her heaven.

Annie and Mingus applaud when she's done. Their love wraps around her like a baby's blanket. Should no one else appreciate this recording, at least Serena has delighted her angels.

It's after midnight when she finishes burning a CD and shutting down the studio. She returns to her flat and sees through the back window that Jamie's still not home. Artie's car is gone, but so is his. She assumes they've gone somewhere together. For a moment this stings. But as she thinks about it, she realizes, that it actually brings a sense of relief. If revenge is what Artie needs, Serena wants her to have it. Maybe it'll bring peace for both of them.

She opens a special bottle of Pinot Noir, one she'd been saving to share with Jamie when she finally finished her songs. She has no problem drinking alone. She lights candles, plays some Mingus, and sits on her white sofa with her feet up.

Annie and Mingus appear sitting on the loveseat opposite her. His thick hand holds an elegant champagne flute. "To your accomplishment, baby."

Serena smiles, raises her glass of wine. "To my life."

Annie winks without taking a sip. "You're done, darling. How does it feel?"

"Feels like de tide of my career is pullin' back in. But my thing wif Jamie is driftin' on out." She looks at Annie and Mingus.

Their eyes twinkle.

"Guess it was inevitable," Serena says, sniffling. She takes a gulp of wine. "I'm not de one for J, am I? Never have been. He stayed with me only 'cause nothin' better came along. Maybe Artie's what he's been waiting for?" She wipes tears. "Whatever's happenin' betveen de two tonight, it clears my debt to both of them. I'm free."

"Yes, darling," Annie says. "You are."

"I can go back east and not worry 'bout it, right? My tenant's lease is almost up. I wanna do clubs again. New York's where I need to be for that. It's not too late. I'm not too old, right?"

Annie shoots a quick look at Mingus. They smile warmly.

"My voice is still strong," Serena says. "Material's good. A new CD'll be the ticket back to my new life... Won't it?" She doesn't see them anymore.

Mingus's "Moanin'" pervades the room at full volume making the walls hum. It's an apt soundtrack for the polytonal way she feels—sad, with a whisper of regret and a crescendo of fortitude. I'm gettin' on wif it. I'll be okay, she tells herself. Whew! Life's a monster of a journey, innit? It'll make you lie down and despair at times. But you pick yourself back up and you keep pressin' on.

Thirty-two

Artie, 2004

L'Heureux has barely pulled into the driveway and Artie's got her seatbelt off and the door open. She doesn't bother with goodnight. He tries to tell her something, as she jumps out of his car, into her own. She backs the Thunderbird up so fast she nearly smashes into him as he hurries out of her way.

The quiet inside her car offers no respite. Her thoughts are blaring like a souped up sound system in her head. *I kissed another man. Touched him. Serena's man. I'm cheater... Okay, a half-assed, couldn't even close the deal, cheater.*

She knows she should take her ass home. Call time is at the crack of dawn. *I kissed someone that wasn't Kendall.* Her mind is too amped to go straight home.

She ends up at the Longs Drugs where she dropped her film earlier. She pulls the envelope with her name on it from the bin and she pays. *But they deserved it. Didn't they?*

Back in her Thunderbird, her is mind spinning. She needs to talk to someone...

She hops on the 10 Freeway and exits on Crenshaw Boulevard. When she pulls onto Degnan and finds a parking space down the block from The World Stage, she hears the jam session bellowing into the street. Folks with afros and dreadlocks are standing outside, chatting, smoking, grooving to the music.

As she approaches she sees Rico onstage through the bay window. This is his favorite spot on Thursday nights when he's in town.

It's like a theater inside with the stage down front and a few rows of seats facing it. She waves at Rico up on the platform. He blows her a kiss, before blowing his trumpet. The pianist, bass player, drummer, and saxophonist playing with him listen and respond as if they're having a conversation. Artie's grown up with this language. It's as familiar as the chatter at a family dinner. It usually soothes her, but not tonight. *Even if they did deserve it, I knew right from wrong.*

The seats are packed. The small space thrums like a hive of creative energy. She stands in the back taking deep, steady breaths. The pianist's light touch makes the keys tinkle like bells. Rico answers in high staccato notes. Together, they're a whimsical contrast to the earthy bass. It's a happy tune, yet she can't let herself enjoy it. She doesn't deserve to.

After the set, Artie waits in the back for Rico to pack up. She thumbs though her photos, relieved to see that she captured the chemistry between Sushama and her co-star. Alessandra will be pleased.

Rico startles her with a kiss on the cheek. "Mija. Thanks for coming out," he says, gravelly voiced. He hugs her. "I'm happy to see you."

"You sounded great. Bendición, Papi." She clings too long. His guayabera is sweaty, but his musky sandalwood smell feels like home.

"Que Dios te bendiga." He leans back, to get a look at her. "Dime. What's wrong?"

Artie eyes the people milling around. "Not here, okay?"

"Is it something in these pictures?" He winks. "Lemme see..." He takes the photos, looks through them. "Ay, mira tu amigas. Alessandra y Sushama. And Troy... directing." He beams at Artie. "You kids grew up and created your dreams together." He caresses her head. "That's nice, mija. Something to be proud of." He comes to the photo that L'Heureux took of her. He smiles and holds it up, showing her. "Who's got good genes, huh?" He laughs.

Artie takes the picture. She stares at it.

"I'm on the Redeye to New York tonight," Rico says. "Was gonna call a cab, but if you gimme a ride to the airport we can talk."

"Do you see something wrong there?" She shows him the photo.

"What?"

A couple of fans approach, distracting Rico. Artie holds the picture closer. It's not what she sees; it's what she *doesn't* see. She gets the loop from her camera bag and examines the image magnified. Wow. Nikki doesn't mess around.

"Talk to me, mija. Still rough going with you and that mufucka I'm not speakin' to?"

Artie drives past the trees out of Leimert Park and heads south toward the airport.

"Do I look different, Papi?"

Rico eyes her. "Just tell me what's on your mind, please."

"Look at me," she says.

"I'm lookin', mija. What?"

"My light. My radiance is gone. See my eyes? They're dull."

He tilts his head and laughs. "You're as radiant as ever, angel."

"No. I'm no angel. More like a devil. That's why it's gone." She stops at a light and turns to him. "I tried to do to Serena what she did to me, Papi."

"Mija."

"I know. But I had to get back at her. And at Kendall. I couldn't help myself."

"What happened? Wait, no, no, no—don't tell me. I don't wanna know."

"I *had* to hurt them. It was burning in me, like evil, like my soul was in hell." She starts to cry. "I'm a bad person."

"No. It's okay, Artie."

"It is?"

"You're human," he says, nodding. "What you did may not be *good*, but it's human. I wanted to smack the shit out of her, myself."

Artie almost smiles. "Oh, thank God it's not just me."

"Nope. And I don't feel bad about it."

"What is wrong with us, Papi? Why are we so vengeful? Rayana's not like that."

"Well… She's special," he says, chuckling.

"Yeah."

Rico exhales and rubs his chin. "Look, I know you're upset with her."

Artie stares through the windshield at the traffic. "What airline are you flying?"

Rico puts a hand on top of hers on the steering wheel. "She's sorry, mija. She made a mistake."

Artie doesn't say anything.

"Con la lluvia crece el césped," he says.

She glances at him. "*What?*"

"The rain is good for growing the grass," he says.

"Um, okay."

"We get hurt. We hurt others. We hurt ourselves—that's the rain. We apologize, we forgive, we love—that's the sun. Without the rain, we wouldn't know how good the sun is. Without the rain, we wouldn't grow. We need both."

Artie looks at his hand on hers, then back at the traffic. "Good God, Papi," she says. You sound like Rayana, but worse."

He touches her cheek. "She did wrong, mija, but it was in the past. How has she treated you since that time? She's loved and supported you. If she was consistently dishonest, I'd say, *fine*, hold a grudge. But when someone does something wrong, and it's not who they are—but a time they were going through, then don't dwell on it. Judge people by who they've shown you they are. Not who they *were*."

"But it affected a big piece of my life."

Artie looks at her father and sees something deep behind his earnest eyes. This is not just about Rayana. It's about him, too.

"Please, mija. We can't change what's behind us. We can only be better to each other now."

After dropping Rico at LAX, she drives back toward Venice. Rayana insists happiness is a choice. Wouldn't that mean sadness is a choice, too? Artie's been reluctant to believe that. Sadness is something that just *is*. It's there when things upset you. *But what if I've been wrong?* She's never tried to "choose happiness." That seems too simple. It couldn't possibly work. And again she wonders, *what if I'm wrong?* What if I were to decide I don't want to be hurt or angry anymore? What if I just stop, and commit to focusing on happiness? It really does seem too easy. Doesn't matter, though. She doesn't have a better idea.

I choose happiness she says, silently. It feels corny. She says it out loud, "I choose happiness." She feels silly, not happy. But what if this choice is like anything one has to practice in order to get results? What if it's something that can be developed over time, with effort, like learning to play an instrument?

Artie decides she can practice a commitment to happiness. She can find things that make her happy—friends and interests—and she can think about them, rather than what hurts her. "I CHOOSE HAPPINESS!" she shouts. She doesn't really feel any happier. She decides to act as if she does. What would I do? Smile, right? That's a start. She forces a smile as she drives and begins to run through a list in her head of things to be happy about. Soon she begins to feel better. It's actually not that simple. It's going to be a challenge, in fact. But she has to believe that it'll be worth it. She decides to make "I choose happiness" a mantra she'll say over and over and over until she makes it true.

Headed up Lincoln Boulevard toward home, past the shops, restaurants, and strip malls she turns on the radio. 94.7 *The Wave* is a guilty pleasure. Kendall can't stand *smooth* jazz, but Artie likes The Wave because it's not so serious. It makes her happy. As if clairvoyant, the DJ makes an introduction and those eight familiar notes begin... Ba da na na na da na na... "Europa." Artie sighs. Anytime she hears it, no matter which version, she's back in that hot car with Kendall, the seats sticking to her thighs, feeling him kiss her for the first time.

Gato Barbieri's rendition sounds like waves of sensuality. It evokes the past and sensations and desires therein. Memories of Kendall are almost all good. *Almost.* "I choose happiness, I choose happiness, I choose happiness," she says, fighting for the *good* recollections to wash over what she'd rather not remember.

She drives faster, picturing the boy who fell in love with her. Kendall still has the heart of that kid who loved her more than anyone. He's not perfect. He fucked up in a colossal way. But that's what people do, because they're human and this is not heaven. It's life.

His truck in the driveway, but there's no sign of him when she enters the house. She goes down the spiral steps to his studio. From outside the door she hears booty shaking hip hop. And not only that, she hears a woman's heavy breathing and moaning. *What the fuck?* He's moaning, too! Artie feels like she might pass out. Her first thought is to kill him. *I choose happiness. I choose happiness. I choose happiness.* Do not flip out. What can you expect? *You're* not giving him any. *I choose happiness. I choose happiness.* Dizzy with rage, she holds the wall to keep from falling down. It doesn't matter that she kissed someone else earlier and that she was damn near scandalous. Kendall isn't allowed any more than he's already had. The happiness affirmation isn't working one fucking bit. She throws the door open prepared to kick his ass. Kendall shrieks and spins around in his swivel chair. He's alone, watching porn on his desktop computer. An open jar of petroleum jelly sits beside the keyboard. His pants are down around his ankles. Artie gapes at him a moment, then collapses into a puddle of laughter. Kendall doesn't find it so funny.

When she finally catches her breath she moves over to him, takes his hand and tugs him off his butt. He pulls up his pants. She leads him out of his studio and up the stairs, through the living room and down the hall to their bedroom.

She opens herself to Kendall for the first time in a long time. She won't completely forgive him tonight. It may take a hundred nights. It's a process, not an event. But she's recommitting herself to the path of light. And she feels certain that that's the path where Kendall is beside her.

Thirty-three

Serena, 2004

Serena wakes at dawn. The wine glass is tipped over in her lap. There's a red stain on her cream-colored dress. She sucks her teeth. After going to the bathroom, she steps into the bedroom to look out the back window. Jamie's car is still gone. Bastard. I'm *not* fallin' apart, she thinks. Somethin' good's on my horizon and I'm not lettin' him, Artie, or anybody else cloud it.

She goes back to the front room, pulls the ruined dress over her head, and steps barefoot onto the balcony in her bra and daft crotchless knickers. It's cold, but so what? She breathes deeply and takes in the ocean. The misty marine layer is heavy. It feels moist and it smells like seaweed. The waves smacking the beach sound like good music. A morning swim is calling her. She pulls on her wet suit, grabs her fins and heads out.

Soon she's swimming away from shore. Being in the water is energizing and soothing at the same time. With stroke after stroke she becomes more and more relaxed. The repetitive movement, the solitude, and the vastness of the sea help to lull her into a meditative state.

Her mind drifts to her journal and the time she received the message to bring a deep love for Artie into her heart.

I followed those instructions. I meditated several times, picturin' myself sending love to Artie, waving and blowin' kisses like Johnny Barnes in Bermy. I felt the love deeper each time. Noffin' happened.

Artie's anger was supposed to have "spontaneously disappeared." That communication felt so profound and true, and Serena trusted that it was, but maybe she made it all up. Maybe there is no greater power advising her. What if she's just floating through life alone? *I'm inadequate, unworthy and unwanted.* She knows she should stop these thoughts, but they gush forth with such force that something in her heart implodes. *I'll never set things right. There'll never be peace. This life'll never be what I want!* Soon she's wracked with sobs. She's done all she knew how to do and still she's failed.

The crying makes it hard to breathe properly. She treads water and blows out to clear her nasal passages. She sees that she's farther out than she realized. She begins to go back, but she must be too tired. She's swimming and yet she doesn't seem to be getting anywhere. She's spent. Her body shuts down. It stops. She goes limp, and floats on her back, letting the waves take her where they will. Her head dips under. The body follows. She drifts farther out. Deeper and farther. She tries to feel nothing. Nothing. She surrenders.

The words, **"Spirit is never late,"** reverberate in her mind. Almost seems as if she hears them out loud. The voice is distinct from hers. **"*Spirit is never late*,"** It says again.

What does that mean? Artie's anger *will* disappear?

"Keep looking up, baby. Have faith and trust. All is well."

Who's communicating with her? An angel? The father she never knew? Her muse, Mingus? She doesn't receive an answer. Probably just my mind again, she thinks. But she feels better. Maybe there *is* something, or someone there. Maybe she's *not* alone.

She glides through the waves, weightless, yet supported and surrounded by something... What is this magical sensation? It's different. Like bein' embraced by peace. It seems to confirm that all *is* well.

Things are changing. She's feeling the flow again. Ready to pack up this L.A. life and head into a new one. It's good. It's somethin' to celebrate. There is no defeat.

Though Jamie finding a lover in Artie is a fear manifested, and the life she has with him is ending, it's not all sad because it's freedom. It's shedding an old self and welcoming a new one. In this liminal space, Serena begins to feel giddy about her next incarnation. She knows that even though she's made mistakes and things haven't turned out as she might have hoped, once again she's headed toward new experiences and new chances. Maybe she'll do better next time. Maybe she won't. One thing she *is* certain of— life does, indeed, go on and on again, and she's grateful and glad.

Thirty-four

Artie, 2004

Artie arrives for work early the next morning as the sky begins to lighten. She parks in the crew lot and walks like a zombie up the boardwalk toward set. The waves are loud, slapping the shore. It's windy. She yawns and sees her breath in the air. Having barely slept, she'd rather not to talk to anyone. Sushama marches straight for her.

"Van's been bragging that *she* slept with L'Heureux last night." She folds her arms across her chest and eyes Artie over her dark glasses.

"Okay. Mazel tov," Artie says, sniffling from the cold. She picks up a paper cup and fills it with steaming French roast.

Sushama glares at her.

"Did she say how it was?" Artie asks.

"What happened? Thought you were gonna call dude?"

Artie adds milk to her cup. "Let me have my caffeine before you get in my face."

"You chickened out, didn't you?" Sush pouts. "How do you think you're ever gonna experience anything in life if you're afraid to go for it?"

Artie laughs. "Why are you all up my ass? Go study your lines."

Sushama's face turns crimson. She turns away and pours herself some coffee.

"Okay, I'm sorry," Artie sighs. "It's just too early..."

Sushama shrugs. "I was only trying to help."

"I know." Artie kisses her cheek. "Just ease up on me, okay? I'll work it out." She takes a gulp of coffee. When Sushama faces her again, Artie sees that her eyes are glistening with tears behind her glasses.

"I'm sorry. Please don't cry."

"Both you and Ally have been so short with me lately," Sush says. She looks over at Ally and Troy near the camera, discussing the set up. "I think something's going on with her and Troy, but she won't tell me anything. Has she told *you*?"

"Sush, why do you worry about what everybody else is doing? You have your own life."

"It's not *everybody else*. It's you guys. Wouldn't *you* feel you had a right to know if I got freaky with Ben last night?"

"No."

"Well I *did*," she says loud enough for a P.A. and a couple of grips standing nearby to hear.

"Thought you had to study your lines last night."

"Oh, we studied, 'em. We explored the subtext, baby. Every inch of it."

They look up as, Van, the cute P.A., saunters past them heading toward the wardrobe trailer. She looks back and gives Artie a sultry smirk. There's a glow about her. L'Heureux *was* good, apparently.

"That should've been you," Sushama says, shaking her head.

The morning moves along. Troy directs an argument scene between Sushama and Ben that crackles with heat. Her character tells his about the kind of man his father was and he resists the idea that there was more to his dad than being an asshole. Their attraction, despite the disagreement, is palpable. Even during the camera rehearsal, Artie gets some of her most intense shots so far.

"You were amazing," she says to Sush, climbing into the wardrobe trailer behind her.

"Really?" Sushama's eyes light up. "I was okay?" She sits on a stool in front of a clothing rack with her costumes and Ben's. She removes her waitress uniform shoes.

"I'm proud of you," Artie says. "And I know Alessandra is, too. Even if you do have stinky feet."

Sushama snorts. She stands and hugs Artie. Then she looks at her and squints. "There's something..." She tilts her head. "Why do I have the feeling you got some nooky?"

Artie smiles.

Sush gasps. "And you didn't tell me?"

"Looks like I didn't have to."

"Not Kendall," she whines.

Artie gives her a stern look.

"What am I gonna do with you?" Sushama asks. "Is that why you're not disappointed about Jazzy and Van? Um um um." She shakes her head and sits back on the stool.

"Sush," Artie says, yawning, "That guy's an ass." She sits on the floor and leans against the wall facing Sushama. "What he does to Serena is messed up. Wish I could ask her why she puts up with it. Lotta things I want to ask her."

"What do you care? She's an ass, too."

"I'm curious. He wants to set up a meeting between us."

"Wait a minute? Does that mean you *did* call him?"

Artie nods.

"Well?"

She shakes her heard. "Let's just say Van got farther than I did. Wasn't into the idea of talking to her, but I'm re-thinking that."

Sush sighs. "I don't know why. But can I come? If she gets out of hand, I can beat her ass for you."

Artie smiles. "Honestly, I don't feel like being angry anymore. She did what she did. But I'm still here. Still have my marriage. What does she have?"

"What if she doesn't apologize? What if she's just crazy?"

Artie shrugs. "Crazy people don't scare me, Sush." She smiles.

She hears her name being called outside. "Artie?" Alessandra opens the door.

"Artie, Kendall's here." Her voice is gentle in a way it never is on set.

"Why?" Artie asks, getting up.

"Damn, it was that good, huh?" Sushama says. "He can't wait till you get home?"

"Um, there's an emergency," Alessandra says.

Artie looks through the trailer door and sees Kendall standing there with a uniformed police officer.

The officer says, "Artimeza Reyes? Serena Ward's next of kin?"

Artie looks at Kendall. His face is somber, his eyes bewildered. She begins to cry.

Thirty-five

Artie, 2004

It's almost midnight. Rayana, Sushama, Alessandra and Troy are draped on the sofas with Kendall and Artie in their living room. The big screen TV is on mute, playing music videos. Bottle number four from a case of Two-Buck-Chuck, sits nearly empty on the coffee table. Rayana, the most alert, moves to kneel beside Artie.

"I can't do it. Please," Rayana pleads, touching Artie's arm.

Artie's eyes are barely open. "I, I just..." Her voice is hoarse. "Can I do it tomorrow?"

"Give me the phone," Kendall says. "I'll do it."

Rayana hands it to him and steps back as if she might catch something being so close. He presses the keypad.

"Rico, It's Kendall... Oh, very sorry, sir. Forgot about the time change." He eyes Ray as she moves father away, hugging herself. "Listen, um, got some bad news... No, Artie's fine. It's her mother... Yeah." Kendall clears his throat. "Drowned."

"Aaaaaaaay!"

Rico's not on speaker, but the wail is loud enough for everyone to hear. Rayana covers her ears. Artie rests her head in Kendall's lap.

"I'm really sorry," Kendall says as Rico sobs. Kendall looks at Rayana. She shakes her head. "All right then," Kendall says. "Sorry." He hangs up.

The grief hangs in the room. No one speaks. Rayana grabs up her purse and jean jacket. She waves without looking at anyone, and hurries down the stairs to the front door.

Artie's tears make wet marks on the thighs of Kendall's slacks. He strokes her head. Choosing happiness doesn't always work.

Sushama sits alone on the loveseat. She scratches her cheek. "Am I like, emotionally deficient or something? I don't get it. Wasn't she a horrible person?"

"You don't have to understand everything, Sushi," Alessandra says. Troy has his arm around her on the sofa.

"But I thought—"

"—Shh, Sush," Kendall says. "Just be here. That's all you have to do."

Artie worries that it's her fault. She hasn't told them what she did, or that she wished Serena harm. And she certainly hasn't admitted that she wished her dead.

"Okay," Sush says, looking at Alessandra and Troy. "Can we talk about you two? And why y'all kept that a secret?"

Troy and Alessandra smile.

"What's so damn funny?" Sushama asks.

While her friends laugh, Artie imagines Serena seeing her car in the driveway and how it must have made her feel. She wishes she could go back and undo that.

೨അ

"I don't understand why I'm the one going," Artie said, stunned, on the ride in the squad car. From the backseat she looked through the wire screen that separated the front seat from the back. "L'Heureux, he was closer to her than I was," she said. She could see through the holes to the front window as they rode down a trash-blown street.

"Mr. L'Heureux made the call," the officer said. "Report says he saw her go out for a swim. When she didn't come back after an hour, and he didn't see her, he called 911. Couple of surfers found the body and called it in before he did. We did go to his place first. He said you were next of kin."

Kendall squeezed her hand. The officer was quiet for the rest of the ride. The only voice she heard was the dispatch operator crackling in and out on the radio.

In the lobby of the morgue, a family tried to console a middle-aged white woman in a Chanel suit sobbing on her knees in the corner. Broken. Artie turned away. She wished people didn't have to feel that kind of pain. Rainy days may help the grass grow, but hurricanes can destroy it. She and Kendall were led down a hallway and as Artie passed a water fountain she felt thirsty. She wouldn't drink in this place, though, for fear she'd ingest the energy of the dead.

She held Kendall's hand while they followed a morgue technician into the autopsy room. Artie held her breath and zipped her jacket all the way up against the chill. Serena was laid out, under a sheet, her head and feet exposed. Kendall let out a sigh that was like a whimper. Artie clenched his hand. It all felt fuzzy, peculiar, like a dream. She hoped it *was* a dream. She began noting details to remember them: the bluish-gray floor, the shiny white tiles on the wall. But she wasn't dreaming, she realized, because she had to take a breath. Serena's second toe was longer than the first. Her toenails had been painted with French-tips. There was a long hose above her head on the silver slab. Kendall's palm was clammy. He whispered in her ear, "I got you. You're okay."

Artie heard voices in the hall. And laughter. This annoyed her. It felt disrespectful.

When she finally focused on her mother's face, she thought they'd make a mistake. Serena was sleeping. There was still a bit of white foam in her nostrils and on her lips. Artie stared at her chest to see if it moved. She waited. They could have been wrong.

Despite her condition, Serena was beautiful. Artie had always thought so; her beautiful Mami who looked like a movie star. She wanted to shake her awake. She wanted Serena to open her eyes and to be glad to see her. She wanted her to say that it had all been a mistake. The lifetime of things that kept them apart was only a big misunderstanding.

∽∾

"Shh, baby, shh," Kendall says, kissing Artie's head.

Artie is back in her house, crying loudly.

Alessandra comes toward her with a roll of paper towels. Artie sits up from Kendall's lap. She tries to smile, takes a paper towel and blows her nose.

"You okay?" Troy asks as Alessandra sits beside him again on the sofa. Artie doesn't know how to answer. What does he mean by "okay?" She leans against Kendall. He kisses her temple.

"I wanted to ask her why she did certain things," Artie says.

Troy nods. No one knows what to say. Sushama and Kendall sip their wine.

"You *can* ask her things if you want to," Alessandra says. She leans toward Artie. "She's in the spirit world. Spirits can communicate with us."

Kendall's head drops back into the sofa cushion. "*Please* don't conjure up that Condomble stuff, Ally," he says. "Let the spirits stay where they are, okay?"

Alessandra's well-groomed brows converge brazenly. "What are you so scared of?" she asks. "They help us. Don't you feel them when you play music, or when you come up with an amazing composition and you have no idea how?"

Kendall shrugs, neither confirming nor denying it. Artie flicks her eyes at him.

"Yes, he's experienced that," she says.

"Sometimes they guide us," Alessandra says. "My Brazilian grandma would say Serena's with the Orisha Yemanja."

Kendall scoffs, smiles. "The who?"

"The Water Goddess. She rules the sea. They celebrate her on the first of the year all over the country. People dress in white and wade into the ocean at dusk."

Artie imagines the thrill of photographing that.

"She's not *gone*," Alessandra says. "She's in the other world. Think of something you want to ask, and be open to her answer. Sometimes they respond in dreams, but in other ways too. You'll know it when it happens."

"When I was in kindergarten my teacher read a story about mommy animals," Artie says. "All the mommy animals loved their babies more than anything in the world. The teacher told the class that *our* mommies loved us best too. I asked Mrs. Carmen if she was sure about that. She was emphatic. '*All* mommies love their babies more than anything.' But I wasn't convinced. So I asked mine, 'Who do you love most in the world, Mami?'" Artie smiles. Her eyes, pooling up, drift to the ceiling. "Didn't even make her list... I know she didn't love me, but I was five-years-old..."

"People are mean when they feel bad about *themselves*," Troy says. "Maybe *she* didn't make somebody's list, either?"

Artie nods, brushing a tear from her cheek. "Her mother gave her away and kept her other two kids. Of course she felt unwanted. But I wish she tried to break the pattern. Wish she thought I was worth *trying*, at least."

Kendall plants a firm kiss on her forehead. "*I* love you most."

Sushama comes and cuddles around Artie, making a sandwich of her with Kendall. Alessandra gets up and kisses her on the nose. Troy tickles her feet. She smiles wanly.

"Thank you, guys," she says. "Glad you're here."

At 6:00 a.m. Kendall, Sush, Troy and Ally are knocked out on the oversized sofas in the TV room. Artie is wide-awake and suddenly worried about what's going to happen to the body. She wraps herself in a sofa throw and tip-toes with her cell phone outside onto the deck. L'Heureux's number is still in her outgoing log. The call goes straight to voice mail. She realizes it's too early and hangs up without leaving a message. He rings back immediately.

"I'm here, Artimeza Reyes. Where y'at?" He sounds hoarse.

"Hey. Sorry for calling so early. Just wanted to make sure you, y'know, made arrangements."

He exhales. He's quiet for a long moment. "She wanted to be cremated. Gotta call the Neptune Society... I'mma take care of it." He lets out a sob.

"Okay." She listens to him cry. She doesn't acknowledge it, or offer a kind word. It feels ungenerous and it is. She's jealous. He's more entitled to grieve than she is. Serena belonged to him.

"Sorry 'bout the morgue," he says. "I just couldn't—"

She tries to tune out his crying. "No problem. I *am* the next of kin."

"I was hoping it wasn't her," he says. "If I didn't see for myself..."

"Yeah," she says. "Are you planning on having a service?"

"Don't know yet... Listen, there's some stuff I need to give you." He clears his throat and sniffles. "Can you come get it?"

"What is it?"

"*Does it matter?*" he snaps. "She wanted you to have it."

"I need to know if it'll fit in my car." Her voice is terse.

"Oh. I dunno. Maybe not."

"No problem. I can borrow my husband's Escalade."

"Yeah, you do that, dawlin'."

Is that a smirk in his voice?

"Come by in an hour. Second level unit."

Artie steps out of the shower, aghast at the dark circles she sees in the mirror. Sushama knocks on the bathroom door while she's applying concealer.

From the toilet Sush asks, "Who're you getting pretty for, Chica?"

"Pretty? I look like a Panda. L'Heureux's giving me some of her things."

"Now?"

"Yeah, why?" She meets Sush's eyes in the mirror.

"You're going over there? Alone?"

"Yeah. Why?"

"You still gonna try to sleep with him?" Her voice goes up an octave.

Artie turns to her. "What is wrong with you?" She turns back to the mirror.

"Thank God. I mean, Christ, the woman's not even laid to rest yet."

"*You're* lecturing me on decorum?" Artie says, eyeing her in the mirror. Sushama ignores that. She pats herself dry.

"I hung out with him already. Didn't happen. And it's not going to happen." Artie curls her eyelashes.

"What *did* happen? What was up with that picture?" Sushama flushes and then joins her at the sink.

"Too weird to explain. But it's some drama I'm not tryin' to get into. Especially now." Artie applies mascara.

"O-kay," Sush says, rinsing her hands. "Then why are you putting on makeup?"

Artie doesn't answer.

She puts on a long, slim skirt, a white tank top and sandals. She does want to look good, but not seductive. She pulls her damp hair into a loose ponytail.

Kendall is asleep as she's leaving. Alessandra and Sushama are out on the back deck having coffee. She asks them to tell him she's taking his car and she'll be back in an hour.

"Artie let us come with you," Alessandra says, standing up. "You don't know what these 'things' are or how you're going to feel. You shouldn't go alone."

"She's right, Artie." Sushama stands, too.

"Thank you, but I can't roll up at his house with a posse—especially not with *you two*. What if he remembers you?"

"Who cares?" Sushama says.

Alessandra blushes. *She* cares. "Keep your cell phone on you." She kisses Artie's cheek. "Ciao."

"Make sure it's charged," Sush says.

The back door to the second floor unit is slightly ajar. Artie knocks anyway. She recognizes the music coming from inside. It's Charles Mingus's "Reincarnation of a Lovebird." She taps on the door again and waits a moment. No response. As she steps in, the spicy fragrance wraps around her in an unexpectedly welcoming way. Serena wore Opium as far back as Artie can remember. It's the smell of her childhood. Though it wasn't good, she has an odd appreciation for it. It belongs to her.

She moves slowly down the entrance hallway, which is adorned with Serena's awards, framed reviews, posters and pictures. Artie wants to see *everything*, to soak in every drop of her mother that she's never seen. Mingus barks. With ears flopping, he comes running toward her out of nowhere.

"Hola perrito. Donde está tu papi?" She rubs his little head as he jumps on her and licks her chin. He runs off again and she notices the view of the ocean. The whole west side of the room is windows from floor to ceiling. Serena must have been happy here.

"Hey."

She turns to see that L'Heureux isn't wearing a shirt. Oh boy.

"Hi," Artie says, doing her best to focus on his face. The red capillaries in his eyes seem to dance with pain.

He opens his arms for a hug. She hesitates. Nothing good can come of this, but to refuse feels awkward. She sighs inside, stepping closer. He squeezes her tight and rubs her back as if to console her.

"You're the only one I got to share this with," he says. "No close family since Buddy passed and her friends are back east."

He starts to rock her in his arms a little. When he begins to massage her neck she pushes away.

"Look, I'm sorry, but I really can't stay. Is the stuff you want to give me ready?"

"You okay?' he asks. "You seem tense."

"I'm as good as can be expected. Just wanna get the stuff and get back. I have friends waiting for me."

He bites his bottom lip, and nods. "This way."

She follows him to the bedroom. He disappears into the walk-in closet. The room is spacious with ecru-colored walls and an antique, mahogany bedroom set. There's a painting of Charles Mingus playing the bass, a collection of vintage beaded bags on the wall, and a signed Roy DeCarava photograph of John Coltrane with Elvin Jones in the background. Artie nearly gasps. It's breathtaking, photographed with available light and expertly printed. There's a glow around Jones in the background, a halo, and the composition tells a story of his angelic presence inspiring Coltrane. Spectacular. Artie has seen this photograph before, at an exhibit, and in DeCarava's book, which she's owned for nearly a decade. He's her favorite photographer.

"Is this DeCarava print yours or hers?"

"Everything's hers," he says from the closet, his voice cracking. "My stuff's downstairs."

That strikes her as odd, but she doesn't ask questions.

"I love this photograph," Artie says. "His work is inspired."

L'Heureux's face appears in the closet doorway.

"You sound just like her."

Artie blinks. "I do?"

"She was crazy 'bout the way he shot musicians."

"Me too!"

He chuckles sadly. "She woulda loved that." He disappears back into the closet.

Artie stares at the photo. She imagines what it might have been like to share this passion with Serena. Whoever said "you can't miss what you never had" was wrong.

"You comin'?" L'Heureux calls from inside.

The closet is huge, big as a room, and comfortable enough to hang out in. There's an island with drawers in the center and clothing hanging around three quarters of the periphery. Mingus is in the corner atop several pairs of shoes, chewing on a pig's ear. Artie smiles, knowing he wouldn't be allowed to do that under different circumstances. L'Heureux sits in front of a safe that's about the size of a small chest of drawers. It's open, and inside are stacks of unusually adorned notebooks. Journals. He carefully takes out one at a time and flips through before placing each one gently into a large green shopping bag from Harrods. Artie kneels beside him.

"We went to London when I was nine," she says. "She loved Harrods."

"Yea, you right. She loved anything English," he says, shaking his head. "Even the food, which makes no damn sense." He holds one of the journals close to Artie. "She hand decorated these. Covered some with fabric, she painted on some, or glued pictures on 'em. My baby was hella creative."

"Why'd she keep them in a safe?" Artie asks.

"Well," he says, wiping tears off his cheeks, "she was a kook. She worried about them gettin' lost in a fire. Kept 'em in the freezer 'til I got her this. A copy of her will's in here too. You can have it. The original's in our safety deposit box." He picks up a black leather book from the pile. "And this was Annie's Bible."

"Really? May I have it?" she asks.

He nods. She puts it in her purse.

"You're her only heir, so you get pretty much everything. I'm executor of her will and she left me some stuff, but it's mostly yours." He breathes in and exhales heavily. "These I definitely want you to take *today*." He's talking about the journals. "Anything else you want, too. Whatever you can fit. Guess you'll have to get a mover if you want the furniture. I'll give you a key. You can get it when you want. She didn't own this apartment, though, if you were wonderin'. But there *is* one in New York. Paid off, too. Well, there's maintenance, but still. And so's Annie's house. Both have tenants in 'em now."

Artie sits still and watches as he continues loading the journals into the bag. She can't quite believe all this. Serena's death was unexpected enough. She certainly never expected an inheritance.

He finishes bagging the journals and puts an arm around her. He stares into her face. She leans back, loosening his hold on her. His eyes change, darkening. Something's not right. She wants to get up. She wants to leave, but she's afraid to move.

"I see her in you," he says, nodding. "Almost like she's still here." He sounds like a little boy. Artie's been around enough mentally ill people to recognize when something's amiss and something *is*.

"Well, I *will* take these today," she says, attempting a smile. "And I'll see what I can do about getting some help with the other stuff. Call you later, okay?"

He doesn't answer. He keeps staring at her like he has more to say. His eyes narrow. His jaw tightens. He breathes heavily like an angry bull preparing to charge.

"I really need to hurry and get back," she says, rising to her feet.

He grabs her wrist. "There's more to see."

"I'm so sorry, but I really can't." She yanks her hand away. Her heart beats rapidly. He stands up beside her.

"I don't know what I'm gonna do," he wails, running both hands over his head, through his hair. She was..." He starts to circle her. "I don't fuckin' have anybody else."

The Mingus CD that was playing in the other room ends. The silence makes this even more uncomfortable.

"What about your friends?" Artie asks. "Can you have some friends stay with you for a few days?" She looks back as he moves behind and around her. She keeps her voice steady.

"That's not the same. People have their own lives," he continues circling. "She was *my* life. What am I supposed to do now?" he yells. He stops in front of her.

"You're grieving," she says softly. "You'll need counseling." She takes a step back. "Look, I'll come visit you another day, but I have my husband's car. He's waiting. I need to get back."

"What about the other night?"

"What?"

He gestures from her back to himself. "This can work now."

"Work?"

"We have a connection. You felt it."

"It can't," she says.

"Of course it can," he shouts. "I saw it in your eyes."

She shakes her head and backs up toward the closet door.

"I need to hold you," he says, stepping closer. "If you dance with me again, you'll feel it."

She dodges him and starts out of the closet.

He plants himself in front of her.

"Oh, you don't wanna touch me now?" He speaks through gritted teeth. "You's grabbing on my shit the other night, though, weren't you?"

Mingus looks up from his pig's ear and starts to whine.

"Think she didn't know 'bout that?" He looks her in the eye. "Huh? Think that didn't break her heart, make her wanna swim out so far she couldn't get back?" Tears leak down his face. "Answer me. Think she didn't know what you did?"

His words sear her insides, guilt smoldering in her chest. She needs to get out, to breathe, but he's blocking the way. Will he kill her?

"It's your fault, y'know," he yells. "She's gone, and you get all her shit? How's it feel?"

It *was* her fault. Artie feels this in her gut. And that's bad enough.

Now this.

"She tried to make things right with you years ago. You fuckin' blew her off. *You're* the bitch. You don't know what she went through. I was there. I was the one she cried to when your ass didn't write back," he shouts.

"Artie! You ready to go?" The voice belongs to Sushama.

Oh, thank you, God. She exhales. "Yes! Back here!"

L'Heureux glances in the direction of the voice with a glimmer of fear in his eyes. Then resignation. He wipes his face. Mingus stands and barks. Sushama and Alessandra appear at the closet doorway.

"She has to go now," Alessandra says while the puppy barks.

"Come on, Artie." Sushama reaches for her hand.

L'Heureux turns away. He sits on the closet floor, cross-legged, with his face in his hands. Mingus licks at his knuckles, and whimpers.

Artie stares down at him. She wants to say she's sorry for his pain, but the words don't come out. Sushama takes her arm and gently tugs her from the closet.

Her friends lead her outside, down the stairs.

"Get in the car," Alessandra says. "I'll drive the Escalade. Sushi'll follow us."

Artie slouches in the passenger seat and reclines it all the way back. The last time she saw the seat in this position was the last time she saw Serena alive.

"We weren't coming," Alessandra says. "You told us not to. But a voice inside me said: *You better go get your girl.* And just as I heard it, Sushi said something was telling her the same thing. Weird, huh?"

Artie leans over and rests her head against Ally's hand on the armrest. She stays like that for the rest of the ride home.

Thirty-six

Artie, 2004

Kendall has left a note. He and Troy have gone to breakfast with Kendall's band mates. Ally and Sushama just left, after admonishing Artie to rest.

She kicks off her sandals and climbs onto the king size bed where she sinks into the down comforter. The curtains are closed on all four windows, yet it's still too bright. Crows chatter in the trees outside, but that's not what keeps her from resting. The guilt is unrelenting. *It WAS my fault. He's right.* She closes her eyes and sees Serena, in the ocean. She *is* Serena in the ocean. Devastated. Alone. Stroke after stroke, she doesn't realize how far out she's going. When she finally stops and treads water to get her bearings, she can see the shore and that she's farther from it than she's ever been. She starts to swim back, but she finds herself being carried in the opposite direction. The current is unkind, grabbing at her. She struggles until she knows that it's no use. All she can do is let go.

Artie sits up, breathing rapidly. Her chest aches. She's not equipped to deal with what she's done. The anxiety will get worse. She's had these symptoms before and they increased until she found herself locked in a mansion with people who wept and shrieked, and couldn't trim their own toenails.

Now she gets why they told her to stay on that medication and find another doctor. "Choose happiness?" Yeah. That only works when you're not crazy. Artie breathes as deeply as she can. *What do I do?* All she can think of is Dr. Ligon. She's probably been released from the hospital by now.

She calls the acute care facility and as expected she's told that Ligon no longer works there.

"I know," she tells the receptionist. "I'd just like a number for her, please."

"It's against our policy to give out that information."

Artie hangs up. "*What was her first name?*" she asks out loud, still trying to catch her breath. *Think, think...* "Clara? Cora? No, that was her baby. Think... Dr... blank Ligon... Dr... Phoebe. I think that was it. Dr. Phoebe Ligon."

She goes online. A couple of zabasearch entries seem promising, based on Ligon's age. She calls. One number is disconnected and the other turns out to be a housewife with kids, not a doctor, according to the woman who answers. When Artie clicks off, it occurs to her: *Roxy.* She'll know how to find her. Artie has her number in her phone. She calls, and finds that it's out of service. *Damn.* She rings the acute care facility again, but the receptionist says she can't put Roxy on the phone. That's against their policy, too. They can only take a message. Artie leaves one, but having been a patient there, she knows it can take days to receive a message. When she gets off the phone her heart is thumping in her chest like someone's trapped inside her ribs banging to get out. Thoughts barrel through her mind, making her dizzy.

She has to do something.

Though she knows she shouldn't drive during an anxiety attack, she does. The Thunderbird zips up PCH toward Malibu. Top down, the sun is beaming and the ocean glistening, but the beauty of the day doesn't calm her. Her heartbeat pounds in her ears—inside her brain. *I killed my mother.* No. *I didn't drown her. I* didn't tell her to swim out too far. *You kissed her boyfriend. You would have screwed him if he'd let you. You left your car in her driveway. You fucked with her.*

When she drives up to the gate, it won't open. A voice on the intercom says that all visitors must schedule appointments in advance. She isn't on the list. She backs up.

There has to be a way to get in. Kendall used to do it. Can't be that hard. She parks on a hilly street lined with dangling branched trees, and walks back down to the entrance. Her breathing is still anxious. The gate is high, too high to jump and the fence on either side is covered with privacy hedges, skinny Christmas trees that are taller than the gate. As she looks closer she sees that the fence itself is only a few feet high. She can climb it and push through the shrubs.

She has to roll her clingy skirt up above her knees and put her purse strap around her neck, but she's able to climb up. Did Kendall go through this every time he came out here? And with a big-ass saxophone, too? Jesus. She pushes through the bushes and jumps down, getting scratches on her arms.

The sting is nothing compared to the pounding in her head and heart. The courtyard is around the back. She walks her way inside like Kendall used to, only instead of playing the sax she yells, "Roxy!" She can't see into the windows, because it's light outside and dark inside. She yells again, "ROXY!" There's no way to tell if the girl is even around, but Artie knows the place well enough to trust that someone'll tell her she's out there. If she can make sure Roxy gets her cell phone number, she knows they'll connect.

She decides to write it down and hold it in front of the window, rather than shouting it. There's a better chance of someone seeing it and passing it on, even if Roxy isn't looking out right now. The only thing she can find to write on in her bag is Annie's Bible. She flips through it. Not one of the pages is blank or light enough to write on, but something falls out. Looks like a photograph. The back is white, however, too small to use as a sign. Think fast. You're gonna get kicked out any second. As she shoves the stuff back into her bag she realizes that her tank top is light. That'll work. She digs back into her bag for a pen. Best she can find is an eyeliner pencil. Still breathing heavily, her heart threatening to bust through her chest, she writes her cell phone number across her chest backwards from her right side to the left, the last four digits underneath. She hopes she's drawn the backwards numbers correctly and large enough to be legible. She realizes she's just made her number available to a bunch of crazy people, but if it helps her reach Dr. Ligon it'll be worth it.

When she's done she yells, "Please call me, Roxy!" The security guard is coming, but she holds her ground in front of the window making the number visible for as long as she can. The guy is overweight and his gait is slow. His forehead perspires as he lumbers toward her, his belly shimmying like jello.

"I 'member you," he mumbles, sweat rolling down one cheek. "What—you tryin' a move back in?"

Good Lord. His breath is decimating. She winces as it hits her in the face. He's the morning guard, not the one who squeezed Roxy's implants. Artie doesn't speak. She holds her breath, and let's him grab her scratched up arm and lead her out through the gate.

Roxy calls before she reaches her car.

"Whaddup, nut-cake?" she says, when Artie answers. "How's life on the outside?"

"Oh, Roxy," she cries. "Thank you. My life's a bitch right now. How's yours?" She huffs and puffs, walking uphill.

"Well, they tell me I'm still mad, Artie Fartie, but I can't complain. Must be getting better, cause they let me go home one weekend a month now."

Roxy seems to talk a lot faster than Artie remembers.

"Cool beans. How do you like the home visits?"

"Only two so far. Meh. Not so great. Mom's busy blowin' up. Important movie business and what not." She cackles.

"I'm sorry." Artie reaches the car. The top is down.

"Tried to tell her the picture's gonna tank," Roxy says. "She wouldn't listen."

"I know you wish she were different." Artie gets into the car. She pulls a sweater on, covering cover the tank top and the writing on her breasts.

"I know you do... So what about you? Sexin' that hot horn player again, huh?"

Artie swallows. She doesn't answer. *How does she know that?*

"I knew it," Roxy squeals.

"How?"

"It's in your voice, Artie Fartie. What're you gonna name the baby?"

"What? What baby?"

"Oops. Never mind."

"What did you say?" Artie asks.

"Heard you were working on a movie. Mazel tov. Does somebody die in it? Somebody dies, right?"

"How did you hear that, Roxy?"

"What *don't* I hear, girlfriend?" She laughs. "Has a happy ending, though, right?"

"...Right." Artie blows air through her lips, reminding herself that Roxy really *is* nuts. "How *are* you really, though, Roxy? Getting better?"

"I'm good. Doc Baldy says I have to accept who she is and I *do*. She likes spending money to keep me here and I like it here, so we're cool."

"But don't you wanna get well—get out—go to college?"

"You, kidding? I *rule* this castle, cupcake. My life is awesome. But *you* don't sound so great."

"Yeah. Less than awesome, that's for sure."

"It's what you make it, muffin. Life is but a dream. What's goin' on?"

She hesitates. Telling Roxy something is telling everyone. "I can't even get into it, Rox. I'm sorry. It's too raw."

"K. Don't take it so hard, though. Row your boat *gently* down the stream. Know what I mean? How can I help?"

"I need Dr. Ligon's number."

"That's all? Piece a easy-bake cake. She's out of the hospital. The mister bounced, but she's getting' the house. She'll be okay. Gimme a minute to shoot you the digits."

"Okay, thanks. But before you go— anything I can do for *you*. Need anything?"

Roxy chuckles. "Of all my roommates you were the sweetest. Stay that way. I'll be listening." She blows kisses into the receiver and she's gone. Minutes later a text appears with Dr. Ligon's number.

When Phoebe Ligon answers Artie hears a cacophony of children yelling in the background.

"Dr. Ligon?"

"Yes?"

"It's Artie Reyes. Got your number from Roxanne, Roxy, at the hospital."

"She's still got the 411, I see."

"Sorry to disturb you, but I'm having an emergency. I really need a session. I'll pay you, of course."

Dr. Ligon is quiet for a moment. "Artie, honey, I'm not practicing psychiatry anymore."

"But I know you can help me. Please. "

Dr. Ligon sighs. "I'm at a group home in Watts right now. We're getting ready to take some young kids to the beach. They've never seen the ocean. Would you like to come help us out?

"Uh, not really. I'm in no state to help anyone."

"It'll be good for you. We can talk after. We'll be on the beach where Washington Blvd. ends. There's a pier there. Are you familiar?

"I am."

"Right around there, thirty minutes."

Great, Artie thinks. She hopes she doesn't see L'Heureux. That's practically in front of his place.

When Artie arrives she stands back watching for several minutes. Ligon looks happy. She's playing with five small, brown children, all dressed in white shorts and matching T-shirts. There's a young black woman helping her arrange the kids in a line, between them, all holding hands. Without shoes, they step toward the water. The little ones look tense, shoulders up around ears. When a wave comes in and wets the kids' feet they shriek with horror, but glee as well. They let go of each other's hands and run back to the dry sand jumping up and down. Despite their fear they're fascinated, and soon they're creeping toward the water again. Again they scream as the water rushes over their toes. This activity entertains them for several minutes.

Artie finds herself smiling, watching them. The panic is abating.

Dr. Ligon spots Artie. The other woman plays with the kids while she walks to Artie and hugs her. She steps back. "Well, you look fine to me," she says. "Still shining."

"Really?" Artie asks. "I haven't slept and I'm freaking out. But *you* look well," she says. "How long have you been out of the hospital?" She glances at the terry cloth wristbands that cover the injuries.

"Not very." Ligon's eyes twinkle. "I guess being unemployed, unmarried and…" she sighs her sadness shining through. "I was going to say losing everything agrees with me, but that's not really true." Her eyes water as she smiles.

"I'm sorry," Artie says.

Dr. Ligon shakes her head. "I'm okay. Figuring it out."

"Whose kids?" Artie asks.

"Uh…God's?" she says, glancing over at them. "They're in foster care.

I was lucky they let me volunteer. Got turned away from a few places. History of mental illness is not a plus on a background check."

Artie nods.

"It's not going to be helpful for adopting either. You were right, though, when you told me to mother someone. Being around kids is saving me. Thank you."

"You're an inspiring person," Artie says. "I feel bad taking up your time with my stuff."

Ligon touches Artie's shoulder as one of the little girls comes over. The child wraps her arms around her leg.

"Play with me," she begs. Her hair is messy, frizzing out of braids that appear to have been done a while ago.

Ligon scoops her up and cuddles her. They rub noses.

"You my favorite lady," the little girl says.

Ligon kisses her forehead, then looks at Artie.

"Come splash around with us," she says running toward the water hand in hand with the little girl. Artie watches for a moment, before catching up to them. She takes the child's other hand and they move into the water, getting their feet wet.

Later, the kids play in the sand with the other woman. Artie sits on a towel with Dr. Ligon. After telling her about Serena and the episode with L'Heureux, she asks Artie what it brought up for her.

"Like I said, I'm freaking out," she says. "It *was* my fault."

"Breathe deeply." Ligon touches Artie's back. "You really believe that?"

Artie nods, sniffling. They both watch the waves roaring in.

"Why?" Ligon asks.

"I *meant* to hurt her." She wipes her eyes.

"Well, that's unfortunate, but does it really make you responsible for what she did?"

Artie stares at the water.

"Have you considered *his* guilt? Or that blaming you may be his coping mechanism?"

"It doesn't matter, Dr. Ligon, 'cause *I* blame me. What I did was wrong."

"Okay. Even so, didn't Serena have agency? What about *her* responsibility?" Ligon holds up her wrists. "Who's responsible for this? A baby that died? A husband who blamed me?"

"That's not fair. What happened to you was more painful than most people could take."

"Maybe. But *I* made my choice. I could have chosen differently." She inhales deeply and blows it out. "It's *hard* being human. *Too* hard, sometimes. If we want to keep at it, we have to learn to ride out the rough times."

Artie looks at her. She nods. "You got me through one."

Ligon takes Artie's hand. "You got me through one, too. And things are still hard. Relentless." She squeezes her hand. "But we can do this, because if we choose to ride it out, we can."

"I don't know *how*," Artie says. "That's why I looked you up."

Ligon laughs. "You think I have all the answers?" She shakes her head. "All I can tell you is that there are some tools I think you'll need— a desire to heal. You have to want to. No one can do it for you. And you have to take responsibility for yourself. Just yourself. That's empowering. But blaming yourself, or anyone else isn't."

Artie tries to make sense of this. She exhales. "Probably gonna take a while before I can stop blaming myself, *and* her. I was already struggling with forgiving *her*. Now there's me, too."

Ligon smiles warmly. The clingy little girl comes back and wraps her arms around her neck. She tickles the child's tummy then pulls her into her lap.

"I made a house in the sand," the girl says, giggling. "You could live in it with me. Wanna see?"

"Yes, in a little while. First, I have to finish my conversation with my friend. You'll let me do that, won't you?"

The girl frowns. "Okay." She begins to wiggle away.

"You can stay if you sit quietly."

"'kay."

Dr. Ligon touches Artie's leg. "What's the best you can hope for with her? What would it look like?"

Artie's eyes drift to the sky. "Peace, I guess. I want peace between us."

"Speak to her from your heart, and tell her. She'll hear you."

"How do you know?"

"… I speak to Cora." Ligon's eyes shine with tears as she looks into Artie's. The little girl fidgets in her lap.

"Oh," Artie says.

"I know it sounds strange." Ligon smiles. "But try it. Find a way to connect with her in your mind. You can mediate, picture her, or you can write to her. Communicate in the way that feels best to you. Can you do that?"

Artie isn't sure, but she nods.

"Good. Because if you do, your relationship can continue, and it can improve."

A couple of the other kids approach and begin pulling on Dr. Ligon. They want her to play. The other woman working with the kids stands a few feet away, breathless from handling them on her own. She shoots an impatient look at Ligon. The little girl wriggles out of her lap and pulls on her, too.

Artie smiles. "Guess my time is up, huh?"

"You have my number," Ligon says, climbing to her feet. "We'll talk again."

"Thank you, Dr. Ligon."

"Call me Phoebe." As the kids lead her toward the water, she blows a kiss.

Artie stands and watches them play. After a while she looks past them and stares at the sunlight waltzing on the waves, making them glitter like something magical, sacred. Somewhere out there Serena drew her last breath. Artie feels indelibly connected to this ocean. It belongs to her, and she belongs to it. And no matter the quality of their relationship, Serena *was* her mother. They were each part of the other's journey. Maybe they still are. Artie hopes that what Phoebe said is true. She doesn't want to leave things as they ended. From her heart, she asks Serena if she would be willing for their relationship to continue and improve.

Kendall is still out when Artie gets home and collapses on their bed. She drops her purse beside her and the picture that was in Annie's Bible spills out. She hadn't looked at the photograph earlier, but now she sees that it's a baby picture of her. One she's never seen. A pair of golden brown arms cradle her.

Artie's story has been that Serena *never* held her. Her story has been that she was wounded and that she *became* the wound. But what if the story isn't over?

❦

Sometime later, Artie wakes to find Kendall's arms around her.

"It's okay, baby. You're okay," he whispers in her ear.

"I was dreaming."

"You were crying in your sleep."

She wipes the tears on her face. "I'm fine."

"That bag was on the front porch when I got home." He gestures toward the floor.

It's the green Harrods bag L'Heureux tried to give her.

"It's full of notebooks and there's a CD taped to the top. It says,

'Serena's last recording.' Should we play it?" he asks.

Artie nods. "The dream was good," she says, smiling. "It was amazing."

"Okay." Kendall sounds unconvinced.

"I was in the middle of the ocean and there was a ladder stretching down from the sky. It went up so far I couldn't see the top. It was too bright. But I reached up, grabbed onto it and started climbing. I kept climbing and climbing until I was tired. And I got pretty high, but at some point I knew I wasn't supposed to go any further so I stopped. My mother appeared above me, way up the ladder. She was radiant. Gold beams of light shined out of her. Her eyes were so kind. She smiled. Then she waved at me. She waved and she reached out like she wanted to touch me, but she couldn't. She began blowing kisses. She blew me so many kisses. She was like an angel sending me love."

Acknowledgements

This story has been with me for decades in different forms. Many generous friends have provided feedback on the drafts. Thanks to Kate Maruyama, Eriq La Salle, and Dan Charnas for kindly reading multiple drafts. Thanks to Alma Luz Villanueva, Dana Johnson, Frank Gaspar, Brad Kessler, Susan Taylor Chehak, Tara Ison, and Steve Heller my mentors at Antioch University who each provided something that helped me complete the book. Thanks especially to Leonard Chang who hugged me and endured the drama when his notes left me weeping for hours.

The following are friends and colleagues to whom I'm grateful for reading early drafts and providing feedback: Avi Hoffer, Michael X. Ferraro, DeeDee Gordon, Dena Crowder, Claudette Groenendaal, Linda Davis, Ann Marsh, Lisa Richardson, Pat Kaufman, William L. Johnson, Vera P. Johnson, Mary Ellen Arrington, Montae Russell, Billy Person, Ben Tobias, Konrad Kirlew, Brian Bacchus, Richard Torres, Maureen Regan, Meri Danquah, Leslie Conliffe, E. Jeffrey Smith, Sarah Wright, Charles Tolbert, Angela Cheng, Darryl Taja, Robin McKee, Nicole Sconiers, Susan Turley, Marie Brown, Lisa Ruiz, Jeff Stetson, Jesse Rhines, Adrienne Crew, Bill Contardi, Claudia Menza, Johnny Temple, Jessica Ableson, Pamela Mshana, Bruce Cook, Karin Wilkinson, Valerie Smith, Janine Monroe, Sonia Seigler, Sandra Lucchesi, Amy Schiffman, Larry Kennar, Michael LaPolla and Debralyn Press. To Nathan Gonzalez of Nortia Press thank you so much for all your hard work and for believing in the story.